ALMOST
THE TRUTH

By the same author:
SUMMER FLIGHT
PRAY LOVE REMEMBER
CHRISTOPHER
DECEIVING MIRROR
THE CHINA DOLL
ONCE A STRANGER
THE BIRTHDAY
FULL CIRCLE
NO FURY
THE APRICOT BED
THE LIMBO LADIES
NO MEDALS FOR THE MAJOR
THE SMALL HOURS OF THE MORNING
THE COST OF SILENCE
THE POINT OF MURDER
DEATH ON ACCOUNT
THE SCENT OF FEAR
THE HAND OF DEATH
DEVIL'S WORK
FIND ME A VILLAIN
THE SMOOTH FACE OF EVIL
INTIMATE KILL
SAFELY TO THE GRAVE
EVIDENCE TO DESTROY
SPEAK FOR THE DEAD
CRIME IN QUESTION
ADMIT TO MURDER
A SMALL DECEIT
CRIMINAL DAMAGE
DANGEROUS TO KNOW

Patrick Grant novels:
DEAD IN THE MORNING
SILENT WITNESS
GRAVE MATTERS
MORTAL REMAINS
CAST FOR DEATH

Collected short stories:
PIECES OF JUSTICE

MARGARET YORKE

ALMOST
THE TRUTH

THE MYSTERIOUS PRESS

Published by Warner Books

A Time Warner Company

Copyright © 1994 by Margaret Yorke
All rights reserved.

 Mysterious Press books are published by Warner Books, Inc., 1271 Avenue of the Americas, New York, NY 10020.

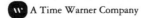 A Time Warner Company

The Mysterious Press name and logo are registered trademarks of Warner Books, Inc.

Printed in the United States of America

First published in Great Britain in 1994 by Little, Brown & Company

First U.S. printing: March 1995

10 9 8 7 6 5 4 3 2 1

Library of Congress Cataloging-in-Publication Data

Yorke, Margaret.
    Almost the truth / Margaret Yorke.
      p.   cm.
    ISBN 0-89296-582-7
    I. Title.
  PR6075.O7A66   1995
  823'.914—dc20   94-36601
                                                         CIP

To Paul Sidey

PART ONE

Then

1.

When the man entered the house, Derek heard nothing. There was no sound of breaking glass nor of a door being forced. He was reading a company report, half listening to the television news, when the drawing-room door was thrown open and a masked figure stood on the threshold, gun in hand.

"One sound out of you and you're dead," the intruder warned, advancing towards Derek, whose heart seemed to stop as he stared at the figure of a stocky man in a black leather jacket and blue jeans, a black woollen helmet with holes for his eyes, nose and mouth over his head.

For a moment Derek felt as if he were watching a scene in which he had no real part; then his heart began to pound and his papers fell to the floor as he started to get to his feet.

"Stay where you are," ordered the man, brandishing his revolver. He stepped up to Derek and struck him on the face with the weapon, pushing him back into the chair. "Is there anyone else in the house?" he demanded.

"No," said Derek instantly, though he knew that Hannah was upstairs in her room. She was working on an essay which was to be handed in when she returned to college at the weekend. She could not have heard anything unusual or she would have called out or come downstairs, but she often worked with music on as a background.

Was there any way in which he could warn her? If he turned the television off, then managed to knock over a table or chair, she might hear, and realize something odd was happening. He picked up the remote control but the man knocked it out of his hand with the revolver. The blow hurt more than the one on his face and Derek just managed to repress a cry of pain.

"Leave it on," said the intruder.

And then the second man came in.

The two men's selected target for that night's operation had been a larger house on the fringe of Bicklebury, a village with some three hundred inhabitants, a church and a pub, but no shop or school. Morris Black had marked it down on an earlier visit to the area, leaving the motorway ten miles away and searching out isolated or secluded houses of some size, which could be approached from the shelter of surrounding trees. His pattern was to break in at the rear of the house while the occupants were either out, or in one room watching television. If the house were large enough, the upstairs rooms could be raided without discovery; he had outlets for getting rid of jewelry and was always satisfied to leave undetected, imagining the occupants' dismay when later they discovered their loss. However, with a gun, it was easy to deal with anyone who attempted to resist.

He used to work alone, but since a recent spell in prison had formed a partnership with Barry Carter, whom he had met inside. Barry was a practiced car thief and together they had carried out several successful raids.

Approaching Bicklebury Manor, their chosen target, in a

Vauxhall Astra which Barry had stolen that morning, the two men had parked in a lane outside the boundary wall over which Morris's plan was that they should climb when night came and it was time to carry out their raid. Beyond the wall was a belt of trees, bare now because it was winter, but still offering cover. They had brought a chain-link ladder, sold as a fire escape, with which they could scale most protective fences. Barry saw a spot where he could pull the car up on to the grass verge. He was impatient, wanting action, grumbling when, after their reconnaissance, they had to wait for darkness. They had driven off to Norlington and sat in the car in a side street, eating chicken and chips. Barry wanted to carry out a smaller scam to occupy the interval.

But Morris would not agree.

"There'll be jewelry in that place," he said. "Silver, too, and money and credit cards, for sure. Worth much more than we'd get in some casual job. We'll wait." He liked to work things out in advance, whereas Barry was more of an opportunist.

At last Morris agreed that they could return to Bicklebury. He went over the wall first, and Barry followed, hooking the ladder to the far side for their escape and to prevent it being seen by someone passing. They crept through the sheltering trees towards the house, which was built of stone with a tiled roof; it had two small wings on either side. There might be an alarm but that was no deterrent to Morris. People only set them when they left the house, and if they sounded there was time to get in and out before anyone responded.

But their scheme had to be aborted, making Barry angry. Five cars were parked outside the Manor, exterior lights were on, most of the windows were lit up and a party was in progress.

"Now what?" said Barry. "You said you'd sussed it out."

"Didn't know they'd sent out invitations for tonight, did

I?" Morris, also frustrated, answered. Now his authority was in question and he must reassert it. "Let's go," he said.

They made their way back to the wall, blundering through the long wet grass, heaving themselves over it and hurrying back to the car. Barry started the engine, ground it into gear, and drove fast up the road towards the village.

"Slow up, you git," said Morris. "You'll have us in the ditch." He had been thinking quickly and now added, "I've got another plan. Turn left here."

They had reached a fork in the road. Opposite them stood The Grapes, a square building with a plastered frontage painted pink. Several cars were drawn up on some cobbled paving outside it.

"I could do with a pint," said Barry.

"Thought you were keen to do a job," said Morris. "There's another house down here that's likely. Watch it, can't you?" he added, as a small van approaching them narrowly missed being pushed off the road when Barry accelerated. "Slow up, can't you?" he repeated. "It's along here somewhere."

By now they had passed a row of terraced cottages, three bungalows, and several scattered houses, until they reached the last one in the lane. "There it is. Stop," said Morris.

Barry braked sharply, nearly pitching Morris, who had not fastened his seat belt, onto the windscreen. They were at the entrance to a short drive where two stone pillars supported wrought-iron gates, both open. On one of the gateposts were etched the words The Elms. Beyond was the dark bulk of a square Edwardian villa.

"Front door's round at the side," said Morris.

"Not a front door, then, is it?" said Barry, and laughed harshly.

"Makes it easier to get round the back without being seen," said Morris. "I'll go first. You stash the car up the road a bit, where it won't notice. I'll have a look around. If I'm not back at the gate by the time you are, you follow."

"Glad we don't need no ladder here," said Barry, who had not enjoyed scrambling over the wall.

He'd got soft inside, thought Morris, who kept fit by exercising. Still, Barry could tickle up a car, and drive well when he had to, but he was impetuous, wanting quick results, and he had a temper. Each time they'd done a job together, he'd wanted a change of plan, and he'd lost his cool when once a window wouldn't open, smashing it and breaking up the place when they did get in, so that the householder woke up and had to be silenced with several blows to the head. Another time, an old lady had had some sort of fit when they took her silver photograph frames. She'd wanted the pictures out of them, and Morris would have let her have them—she wasn't posing much of a threat, wailing in her dressing gown—but Barry took them out and burned them before her eyes. Morris thought he'd find a new partner next time he went thieving, someone with a longer fuse.

For his part, Barry liked working with Morris, because he had good methods of disposal of the loot, and because he took a gun. Morris had already been inside twice for armed robbery, though he'd never fired in anger. It frightened folk; made the snatch easier. Barry carried a knife and was not afraid to use it, but it didn't have the same effect a gun did at a distance. You had to get up close to hold a knife at someone's throat. It worked a treat with girls, though; you didn't need to cut them up, or not a lot. He liked frightening them.

He drove a short way up the road and pulled the car onto the grass verge under overhanging trees, taking the key—he had a bunch of them to fit many cars, and several other useful gadgets—but not locking it as they might need to leave in a hurry. When they began working together, Morris had wanted Barry to stay in the car, ready for a quick getaway, but Barry was having none of that; if he did the job alone, Morris might keep the best of the stuff for himself, in his pockets.

Meeting Morris in prison had been a bonus for Barry. Morris was respected by other inmates because he had carried out some major scams, and Barry, as his partner, saw that he could get into the big time, but he hadn't reckoned on being ordered about and treated as though he had no brains. He'd show Morris, when he got the chance.

He padded back to The Elms, his white trainers twinkling in the darkness, and ran softly up the drive, which was level, with no potholes. He did not stumble. Near the house, he switched on his torch and turned to go round to the left, as Morris had instructed. There was a garage block, formerly the stables though Barry did not realize that, across the yard and he could see that one set of doors was open, the garage empty. He tried the back door of the house and found it unlocked. Morris must have left it for him, but before entering, Barry went round to the front of the building, where there was a small gravel area bordering a lawn marked off with several stone ornamental tubs. Light showed behind curtains drawn across a bay window beside the front door, and in an upstairs room. Pausing, Barry could hear the sound of a television set broadcasting some news item about strife in a distant land: boring stuff, he thought. Silently, he returned to the back door and slipped inside.

A passage led through to a square hall, with a staircase rising on the left; on the right was the open doorway of the room from which the sound was coming.

Barry drew his knife and entered.

Upstairs, working on her essay, Hannah had heard nothing. She wanted to finish making notes tonight, because tomorrow Peter was coming and they were going to London, hoping to pick up some cheap tickets at the National Theatre. They had met through an interest in amateur dramatics; Peter was doing media studies and she was reading English.

She would have to decide what to do about Peter, whom she thought she loved and to whom so far she had made no commitment. He could not understand her reluctance, and she did not altogether understand it herself, except that taking the final sexual step would be a major action, one she could not reverse. The situation must be resolved, one way or the other; Peter was already talking about going backpacking together in the summer. Most people slept with their boyfriends, he had pointed out; it need not mean fidelity for life, though that might be the result.

"You know you want to," he would tell her, and at such moments she thought she did; why wasn't she certain?

Concentrating on her notes, Hannah managed to put the problem from her mind, unaware of Morris approaching the back door, over which a light was burning. He had seen the open, empty garage and understood that the light was on for the benefit of whoever was out in the car—the whole household, he hoped. He tried the back door, but it was locked.

People did silly things, Morris knew, and before breaking a window to get in, he looked around him. There was an inverted flowerpot near a water-butt; he lifted it, and beneath it was the back door key.

He entered the house without making a sound, found a light switch by the door and extinguished the rear light: no point in illuminating the scene for any neighbor. The kitchen lay to one side of the door and, ahead, was a room from which the sound of a news broadcast could be heard. On the other side of the hallway was the dining room, and Morris, peering in, saw silver candlesticks and an ornate silver tray. They might all be plate and not worth taking, but he'd check.

The hall and staircase were in darkness; Morris could not know that Derek Jarvis was fanatical about saving electricity. He chose his moment to enter the room from which the broadcast came; it might have been left on as a false indication that the house was occupied; however, he was ready to discover several people in the room when he burst in.

But there was only one man, thickset, with graying hair, in a blue pullover and half glasses, a folder and some loose papers on his knee. This would be an easy one, Morris knew, as he saw the shock on the man's face. Morris struck him sharply when he tried to rise and he fell back, dropping his papers on the floor.

When Barry came in, Morris told him to get the phone.

"Where is it?" he barked at Derek.

"In the hall." Derek saw no point in antagonizing the men by refusing information they could quickly discover for themselves. What did it matter if they stole every bit of Janet's jewelry, took all their possessions, as long as he and Hannah were left unharmed?

His own first shock abating, he wondered again if Hannah, upstairs, had heard anything. Would she come wandering down to investigate? There hadn't been time for her to find out what was happening and ring the police; the second intruder was already out in the hall cutting the line.

Barry had sliced it neatly with his knife.

"There's a light on in an upstairs room," he said, returning. "I'll go up and see who's there."

"It's been left on in error," said Derek. "My wife's out." And would be returning soon from her evening class; what if she walked in on them?

"We'll make sure," said Morris. "You'll come too. Go on,

squire." He caught Derek's arm and twisted it up behind him, pushing him forward.

They'd find Hannah. Derek, ascending the stairs behind the second man, thought of falling back against the leader, as he had decided the one with the gun must be, taking him crashing down the stairs. The noise would warn Hannah, and the other man's attention would be deflected. Of course, he might be shot if he did it; the first man still held the gun. He did nothing, apart from moving as heavily as he could; surely Hannah would notice something? He coughed loudly, but if Hannah were playing music while she worked on her essay, it would drown out other sounds.

He tried to calm himself. They were simply burglars; when they'd got what they came for, they would leave.

Barry was opening the doors on the upper landing. The bathroom and the main bedroom were in darkness, but the third door he tried was the one to Hannah's room. With Vivaldi in the background, Hannah heard nothing until Barry spoke.

"Look who we've found," he crowed, advancing towards her, waving his knife.

Hannah turned to see her father, a red mark on his face, blood on his cheek, being thrust into the room by two masked men, one carrying a gun. As in a nightmare, she could not move.

"You said there was no one in," said Morris, and he twisted Derek's imprisoned arm viciously.

"Take everything you want—I'll give you all the money I've got in the house," said Derek. "There's silver downstairs. Take my car. The keys are in the kitchen—I'll get them for you. Just leave us alone."

"Maybe later," said Morris. "You—Barry—tie the girl up."

"No!" shrieked Hannah as Barry approached, and she

lashed out at him, kicking and screaming as he caught her by her hair, pulling it hard.

"Leave her alone," cried Derek. "Hannah, do what they tell you and they won't hurt you."

"Good advice," snapped Morris.

Barry held his knife against Hannah's neck, and then he sliced off a swath of her hair, leaving a tuft by which he still held her while he cut at her sweater, ripping it under her chin. He hit her across the face and she covered it with her hands.

"That'll show you I mean business," he said, and he threw her onto her bed, then released her while he searched through her chest of drawers until he found some tights.

Hannah had shrunk away from him, but as he grabbed her again, she kicked and screamed and struggled, while Derek watched as though he was paralyzed until Morris pulled some cord from a pocket and began lashing his wrists together.

At that moment both men had laid down their weapons in order to bind their prisoners and Derek, as he later realized, running the scene through his memory, might have landed a punch, even grabbed the gun, but failure, he consoled himself, could have ended in death for both of them.

"Best not resist," he told Hannah.

Morris forced him out of the room and tied him to the towel rail in the bathroom, then secured his feet with a pair of tights. A wad of tissue was rammed into his mouth as a gag and secured with another pair of tights. By this time they had found Janet's; she had plenty of fine ones in various colors.

"Good for strangling, these are," said Barry, who had been tying up Hannah.

Her shrieks had stopped. Derek could only pray that the man called Barry had not hurt her as he bound her. Left alone in the bathroom, with the door closed, he began working his wrists, trying to loosen the cord securing them, but with no success. He could hear the men moving about now. That meant they were not mistreating Hannah. They must be raiding Janet's jewel case. He heard them both going downstairs and felt immense relief. They'd leave soon, once they'd found everything they thought worth taking.

He rested briefly. Sweat was pouring off him, yet he felt cold and clammy. He looked about for something to use to free himself but everything in sight—the lavatory brush holder, the bath cleaner in its plastic bottle—had rounded edges. His razor was in the cabinet over the basin but he could not reach it. He could just move his hands to his trouser pockets, but apart from a few coins, they were empty.

Some coins had sharp rims. He wriggled and writhed until he managed to get hold of a twopence piece and then a new, shiny tenpence coin; he was able to hold it in one hand and rub it against the cord round his wrists, but without result. Then he dropped it, and it rolled out of sight.

After a while he heard the men coming upstairs again. They were arguing, and one said, "Don't do it, Barry."

"Won't take long," said Barry.

He smelled horrible.

Hannah had been aware of it as soon as he came towards her and caught hold of her hair. A weird, stale odor came from him, a mixture of musty clothes and body smells. When he came into the room with her father and the other man, she had flinched away from him as much in distaste as simple fear.

He had tied her up with her own tights and had stuffed a pair of her briefs into her mouth to gag her, binding more tights over that. Hannah had fought hard. She had seen him put the knife aside while he pinned her on her bed and tied her hands together; she had kicked while he caught at her legs, but he was strong enough to overcome her, holding her down with his weight as he lashed her ankles together. She could not believe that her father had not tried to help her. There were two of them, and two invaders; couldn't she and her father have saved themselves? But he was telling her not to resist.

He had cast a sorrowful glance in her direction as he was dragged from the room, but she was still sobbing and struggling, not looking at him.

Then her Vivaldi tape ran out.

Left alone while the men robbed the house, Hannah had listened to their movements. After a time she heard them going downstairs and began to breathe more evenly. She was alive and unhurt, and so was her father, apart from the bruise on his face. The men would leave, once they'd found whatever they thought was worth taking.

Now she could hear nothing except, from downstairs, the dull echo of the television. The house was so solidly built that noise did not carry far. Perhaps the men had already gone. She twisted and turned, trying to free her hands, but her bonds seemed only to tighten.

Then the man who smelled so dreadful, Barry, came back.

He stood looking down at her, running his gloved hand along the edge of his knife, then savagely cut off another hank of her hair, pulling it taut before slashing it.

She was wearing a gold chain round her neck, with a pendant on it, garnets in a gold setting. Her parents had given it to her for her eighteenth birthday.

"Pretty," he said, and seemed about to tug it from her neck when he had second thoughts. "Pity to break the chain," he added, and took off his gloves to unfasten it, pulling at it so that he could see the catch, breathing heavily, the smell from him stronger than ever. After removing it, he put it in his pocket and then looked down at her; all she could see of his masked face were his eyes, which stared like black pebbles.

Then he untied her legs.

She kicked again, trying to shout, but her screams were muffled by her gag. She felt as if she would choke and she tried to roll away from him, but he hit her on the face and cursed her, and the smell grew even worse.

The other man came into the room, saw the struggle and protested at what Barry was doing to her, but his words had no effect and he left them to it, banging the door and going back downstairs.

2.

Driving home from her German class, Janet Jarvis was running over phrases in her mind. This was her first term, and she could now supply her name and ask others for theirs, count to ten, and utter a few words connected with travel. By repeating what she had learned, she might remember it, she thought; she was determined to succeed and go on one of the holidays organized by the adult education center.

Turning in at the gate to The Elms, she told herself, *"Ich heisse Janet Jarvis. Ich wohne in Bicklebury,"* and then wondered if it should be *aus.* I'll never learn those difficult constructions, she thought, driving her VW Polo into the open garage. Getting out, locking the door, she found herself in darkness. The bulb over the back door must have gone; what a nuisance, but there would be a spare in the kitchen cupboard.

She felt about for the flowerpot under which the key should be, and could not find it. That was odd. Perhaps it had been knocked to one side by a passing cat. She had her front door key and could go in that way, but before doing so, she tried the back door and found it unlocked. Surprised, she did not notice that the key was missing; Morris had pocketed it; such things were useful.

It was a few moments before she realized that anything was wrong. The hall light was on, the drawing-room door was ajar, and she could hear the television—all normal, except that the volume was rather loud and she would expect the door to be closed, but Derek might be in the cloakroom.

Still in her outdoor coat, Janet went into the drawing room and saw chaos. A lamp had been knocked over and the bulb had broken; Derek's papers were scattered on the floor. The desk drawers had been pulled out, their contents tipped onto the carpet and the drawers flung down.

Burglars. But where was Derek?

"Derek?" she called out, throwing down her bag and textbooks, and hurried from the room. "Derek, where are you? Hannah?"

She glanced into the dining room and saw at once that all the silver from the sideboard, and the candlesticks that had been a legacy from her godmother, had gone. Passing the telephone, she paused, but perhaps Derek had already rung the police. She had to find him and Hannah first. Panic bit into her, catching her in the throat as she ran upstairs.

It occurred to her that the thieves might still be in the house, and she paused on the landing. Then she heard a whimper, and opened Hannah's door.

It seemed to take so long to get help.

Hannah's legs were not tied, but her hands were still lashed together and the gag was in her mouth. She was curled up on her bed, naked knees against her chest, uttering little moans from behind the fabric stuffed into her mouth. Her face was blotched with tears and she was shaking as if she had a fever.

"Oh, my God! Hannah!"

Janet looked wildly round for something to use to cut her daughter free, but in the turmoil of the room could see nothing.

"I'll get some scissors," she said, and dashed across the landing to her own room, where drawers had been pulled out and emptied but there was less disorder. She found a pair of nail scissors and soon released Hannah, then held her close, hugging her and crooning over her as if she were an infant. She was her baby. "Who did this?" she asked, and, "Are you hurt?" But of course she was, and maybe mortally, although no wounds were visible.

Hannah's mouth, the gag removed, was dry and she could hardly speak. She needed a drink, but she needed comfort more. Help must be summoned, but not yet.

"There were two of them," Hannah croaked at last. "They haven't been gone long. Daddy—" her voice broke. She had been trying to find the strength to get to her feet and leave the room to search for him.

"Where is he?"

"They tied him up, too," Hannah said, in what was little more than a whisper.

"Will you be all right while I look for him? And I must ring the police." And the doctor, Janet thought. "Get into bed and try to keep warm." Some blood had seeped from between Hannah's legs. A hot water bottle, Janet thought, and towels, and a warm drink laced with brandy, while they waited until help arrived. But she must look for Derek first.

Out on the landing, she heard a noise. Derek, still bound and gagged, was making grunting sounds and thumping with his legs to attract her attention. The bathroom door was not locked. Janet opened it and saw his desperate eyes looking at her above the gag.

Janet freed his arms and he pulled the gag down as she released his legs.

"Hannah?" he asked hoarsely.

"She's been raped," she told him. "Can you stand?" He'd better be able to; there was no time to deal with him. "I'm going to phone the police."

"They cut the phone," said Derek. "It's useless."

"Well, I must fetch help, then," said Janet. "Unless you can do it." She would be quicker, but Hannah needed her.

Derek had struggled up. He made an effort.

"I'm all right. I'll go next door," he said, swaying where he stood.

Janet had seen the mark on his face; the small scratch had already crusted over. He was fit to go. She made the decision coldly while an icy rage succeeded the terror she had felt at first. How dare anyone do this to her daughter? In that moment, if she had seen the culprit, Janet could have killed him. Why hadn't Derek done that?

He seemed to read her mind.

"They had a gun and a knife," he said. "They cut Hannah's hair."

"I know," snapped Janet. "Can you go now? Hurry."

"Does she need an ambulance?"

Perhaps she did. She might be injured internally, and Janet knew, with sickening certainty, that there would be swabs to be taken and other grim procedures to be followed.

"Not immediately," she said. "Get on, Derek. Don't waste time."

She left him, and Derek, who had wanted to rush to comfort Hannah, heard the bedroom door close. He lumbered heavily downstairs.

"Daddy's all right," Janet told Hannah. "He's gone to call the police. Are you bleeding badly?"

"I don't think so," Hannah said. "But I hurt."

"I'll get you a towel. You mustn't wash. Not yet. I know you want to, but—evidence," said Janet.

Hannah nodded mutely.

Thank goodness she understood, thought Janet. Girls were informed, these days. She hurried off, and filled a hot water bottle for Hannah which she brought her with a big fluffy towel.

"I don't think you'd better take your clothes off till the police come," she said. "When they get the man, there may be something on them they can use."

Derek was not gone long as their nearest neighbor, at a bungalow just down the road, sent him straight back, saying he would ring the police himself. He'd got the message clearly: two masked men, one armed with a gun, the other with a knife, and there had been a sexual assault. The neighbor was uncertain as to whether Janet or the daughter was the victim; perhaps both had been attacked, he told the police.

When Derek returned, he burst into Hannah's room where she was now sitting up in bed clutching a hot water bottle and sipping coffee laced with brandy.

"Hannah! Thank God they didn't hurt you," he gasped, hurrying to her, arms outstretched, ready to hug his precious daughter. "Your poor hair will soon grow. They didn't mark your face."

"Don't touch me," Hannah said, almost hissing, drawing back from him, holding the duvet to her. He saw that she was sitting on a towel.

"They didn't kill you," Derek said, almost pleading.

"They've hurt her dreadfully," said Janet. "Face it, Derek. And yes, her hair will grow." She gave Hannah a hug as Derek stepped back from them, looking at them both in horror: they had suddenly turned into two strange, hostile women instead of his familiar wife and most beloved daughter. "I'll bathe your face now," Janet said. "You'll be all right for a few minutes, Hannah. Daddy has been badly shaken."

She took Derek into the bathroom and bathed his cuts with cotton wool soaked in disinfectant, which stung. He began talking feverishly then, telling her what had happened, how the men had been so threatening and he had thought it important not to antagonize them.

"Don't talk," said Janet. "I want to deal with this cut by your chin. It's not bad. It'll heal up in a day or two."

She took him downstairs and made him a cup of coffee, laced, like Hannah's, with a slug of brandy.

When the police arrived, all three were in the drawing room, Hannah wrapped in a clean duvet from the spare bedroom. Hannah and her mother were sitting on the sofa, and Derek was across the room from them in the chair in which he had been seated before the raid. No one spoke. Hannah's trembling had eased a little, but she began to shake again as soon as the two uniformed officers appeared.

Later, the police took her away with them because she had to be medically examined.

They let her go home when they had finished their examinations. The police had said their surgeon would do what was necessary, and her clothes were collected as she shed them, standing on a sheet. Later, she told her mother that the doctor had hurt her more than her attacker, and his investigations had lasted longer than the rape, which was quickly over because Morris had been impatient for them to leave.

Each man had used the other's name, and this was helpful, said the police. Hannah had scratched Barry and there were wool fragments from his mask beneath her nails. While they were scraped, she was told that there might be other tissues, even skin, under them. Best of all, there was a clear finger-print on the heavy buckle of her belt, which Barry, his gloves off, had undone.

Only one of the men had attacked her, and the other, Morris, had tried to stop him, saying that was not what they had come for. In the end he had gone downstairs to wait, meanwhile finding more plunder. They had left only about ten minutes before Janet returned, Derek estimated. They had taken his watch, but he could time their arrival by the television news which had just resumed after the commercial break. Usually Janet was back from her class before eleven.

So the ordeal had lasted less than an hour.

"If only I'd been here," Janet said.

"You couldn't have stopped him. He'd have done you, too, or his mate would have, to pass the time," said Hannah, and gave a sobbing laugh.

Her mother had run her a deep bath, adding scented foam. She had had a shower at the police station, and had come home in a bathrobe, wrapped in blankets, but she thought she would never be clean again. The sour smell of her attacker lingered in her nostrils. She had said that she did not know how his partner had endured being with him.

"Perhaps he's lost his sense of smell," said the police-woman who was present when she made this comment.

That was not the sort of information likely to appear on details of past offenders, but it might help identify a suspect.

They had taken away the chunks of Hannah's hair, which Barry had left lying on her bedroom floor. It was probable that strands of it had attached themselves to him.

"Once we get a lead, we've got plenty of evidence," said Detective Inspector Brooks.

They were kind to Hannah, and kind to Janet, too. The woman officer lamented that they had no proper rape suite at

Norlington Police Station. "It helps," she said. "Maybe we'll get one in time." Some of the more modern police stations were equipped with them, and there were officers who were skilled in counseling victims. Hannah would be helped to overcome her dreadful experience.

Wearing one of her mother's nightdresses, Hannah went to bed in the spare room for what remained of the night, and Janet occupied the other bed. Sedated, Hannah slept at last, but Janet lay wakeful till the dawn.

Hannah had made a full statement to the police, quoting every word she could remember hearing the men utter. She was glad her mother had not had to hear her recount how, when the taller man, Morris, had tried to stop Barry from attacking her, the answer had been, "It's too good a chance to miss. She needs a lesson, this one. Besides, she likes a bit of the rough. Lashed out like an alley cat, didn't she?"

They wrote it all down and she read and signed it. Meanwhile, other officers were examining the house, dusting it for prints, looking round outside and alerting colleagues to be on the watch for two fleeing villains.

"But you don't know what sort of car they're driving," Janet said.

"That's true, but it may be stolen, and anyone looking the least bit suspicious—speeding, say—will be stopped. If they've got masks, a gun and a knife with them, that'll need some explaining," said Detective Inspector Brooks.

But by now the men were long gone, and would probably be at their base, counting up their gains.

3.

Peter arrived the day after the raid, wearing his usual confident smile and expecting the welcome he always received from Hannah's parents. He lived in Leeds and he liked spending a night or two in Bicklebury on the way to or from college. Hannah's home was more comfortable than his own; his mother was an ornithologist, never happier than when out in wild weather on some lonely rock or moor, and his father, who worked in television as a cameraman, was often away. Meals were hit and miss in their household, and washing piled up. At the Jarvises', everything ran like clockwork.

So it was a shock when he found The Elms in a state of siege, with newspaper reporters and photographers at the closed gates, and a police car parked by the front door.

In the aftermath of the robbery, no one had thought of telling him not to come. He opened the gate and drove through, fending off the reporters' questions but aware of cameras flashing as he drove through. *Victim's boyfriend calls,* the next day's papers proclaimed, captioning shots of him and his well-polished Mini.

Derek heard his car and came out of the house to greet him.

"I'm sorry, Peter. We should have put you off," he said. "We forgot."

"What's happened? You've been hurt?" Peter could see for himself the marks on Derek's face.

"We had a robbery last night," said Derek. "Hannah got hurt, too."

It took Peter a few moments to understand what Derek was telling him, and then he went quite white.

"Come in. Janet will want to see you," Derek said.

They both liked Peter, who seemed a steady young man. Apart from local youths whom Hannah had known for years, he was the only one to visit the house, and Hannah had stayed with his parents in Leeds, finding their careers more interesting than Derek's in commerce and her mother's charity endeavors.

Sitting at a table in the kitchen, Peter heard a sanitized account of the night's ordeal. Janet could not bring herself to go into any details, but the facts spoke for themselves. Hannah was still asleep, she said.

While they were talking, Hannah, in her dressing gown, came into the room. She looked very pale, and her hair hung jaggedly around her head. There was a bruise on her cheek.

"Your hair!" Peter exclaimed.

"He cut it. That man last night," said Hannah flatly. "It'll grow, as everyone keeps telling me, so don't you."

"I—" Peter stopped. He did not know what to say. "It's dreadful. I'm so sorry," he tried.

"Well, I'm not dead. Everyone seems pleased about that," said Hannah.

"Of course they are," said Peter, bewildered by her tone.

Hannah shrugged.

"I fought him," she said. "I did my best."

She thought she would never forget a single detail of the

night: the smell, the weight and strength of her attacker, and the horror.

"Well, yes," said Peter, and moved towards her. If he hugged her—gently, of course, after what she'd been through—she might feel comforted. That was what she needed.

But Hannah jumped back as if he had scorched her. She put the table between them and stood with her hands on the back of a chair. He retreated, feeling badly snubbed.

"You won't want to go to London," Peter stated.

"Why not?" said Hannah. "I wasn't killed, or even slashed with a knife, as everyone keeps pointing out. I'll get dressed."

"Hannah, I don't think you ought to go so far," said Janet. "The police may want to see you again."

"It's too soon to find out if I'm pregnant, or if I've caught some disease," Hannah said.

Janet had never seen Hannah in such a mood of truculent defiance, or not since she was a small girl determined not to eat the Brussels sprouts her mother had decreed were good for her. She caught Peter's eye and mouthed at him, "No."

"Let's go another time," said Peter quickly. He couldn't take her off for the rest of the day and a late night after such an experience; the responsibility alone was too much. "Luckily we haven't already got tickets," he added.

"There'll be no waste, you mean," she said, and then she suddenly burst into a torrent of tears.

At this, some of Peter's panic dissolved, and again he put his arms out to her. She allowed him to hold her while she sobbed. Janet went quietly out of the room; let Peter handle this as best he could, she thought. Instinct might guide him. Given time, Hannah would, to some extent, heal, but there would be lifelong scarring. How well she would adjust could not be foretold; perhaps Peter would be her best help.

But ten minutes later she heard him start his car up and drive off.

"Peter's gone, then," she said, returning to the kitchen.

Hannah had dried her eyes, and had made another cup of coffee.

"Yes. There was no point in him hanging about here," she said. "I was mad to think I could go to London. I hurt too much."

Janet knew she was not referring only to her physical injuries. At least she was admitting it, which was something.

"Some of that will mend quite quickly. The rest will take longer," she said. "Perhaps you'd better postpone going back to college."

"If I do, I'll never go," she said.

"We'll see how you feel in a day or two," her mother said.

It might be best for her to stick to her routine, go back to the house she shared with two other girls and two young men. Perhaps she would confide in one or both of the girls. Young company might be what she needed, once the first shock had worn away. She would be distanced from the media attention likely as a consequence of the raid. Janet knew that the identity of rape victims was protected, but not always with success, and there were reporters at the gates.

"I'll go back to bed now," said Hannah, getting up. "I'm suddenly completely shattered."

The police had already matched up the fingerprint found on Hannah's belt buckle with that of Barry Carter, recently released from prison for a series of car thefts but so far not accused of rape, when a jeweler reported that a man had tried to sell him her pendant.

Details of the articles stolen had been circulated. Derek, meticulous in business matters, had photographs of most of them, and some were reproduced in the press. Barry Carter had not been at the address of the woman he had been living with when last arrested, where the police expected to find him when they called, and the woman herself said she did not know where he was living. They had had a row and he had left a week or so before, she said; for all she knew, he was living rough. They had failed to find him at the flat where his mother had lived with her second husband, and they were trying to trace his real father when the call came from the jeweler who, with Barry still in the shop, had taken the pendant to the rear office on the pretext of examining it more thoroughly, while he telephoned. Stolen goods had passed through the shopkeeper's hands before: you did not demand the provenance of minor items, after all, but he would not knowingly aid a rapist and it was quite clear from the media reports that those responsible for the robbery had committed a worse crime than theft.

Two officers arrived while he and Barry were discussing prices for the pendant.

It took longer to trace Morris, who had left no clues as to his identity at the scene. The pendant was the only item Barry had taken from the raid, and Morris had not known about it. The credit cards and checkbooks stolen from the house had been sold later that night, and the other articles had been passed on to a fence with whom Morris had dealt before; Barry had received his cut and was planning to buy some presents for Sandra, his girlfriend, in the hope that she would take him in again.

He had no chance to do so. He was taken away from the shop and charged, and finally, in an attempt to win concessions from the police, he declared that Morris had planned and organized the robbery and that he had merely been the driver. It was almost the truth.

There was plenty of scientific proof to link Barry with the attack on Hannah.

"You can really prove it?" Derek asked, when Detective Inspector Brooks came to tell them that two men had been arrested. "Hannah won't have to identify that—that fiend?"

"How could she? He wore his mask throughout," said Brooks. There was the smell, though; she had mentioned it, and the man stank when he was brought in to the cells. Still, he'd had a shower now, while in custody, and had been given a change of clothing as his was needed for examination. He'd spent the time since his row with Sandra sleeping in a dumped van in a scrap yard, confident that after the robbery he would be in funds and so, eventually, back in her favor.

Brooks did not tell Derek that Hannah would have to give evidence; there was time enough for that when Carter came to trial.

A key found in Morris's possession proved to be the missing back door key from The Elms: proof enough to send him down.

Hannah returned to college a week late. By then she knew that she was not pregnant, but it would be months before she could be certain that she had not contracted a disease. She would need various tests at intervals.

She had complained of pains in her chest which at first were thought to be due to bruising and were eventually found to be caused by a cracked rib, but there was no treatment for this; time would cure it.

"At least I fought," she told her mother. "I tried to save myself."

"I know," said Janet. "You did well."

Hannah had had fits of weeping after Peter's visit, and had been sleeping badly. She had received counseling from two experienced policewomen who attempted to help restore her self-respect but made no foolish assurances that she would soon forget the incident. In time the memories would fade, they said, and explained that rape was a crime of violence, not a sexual offense, except technically.

"It's all about domination," said one of them. "And punishment. Those men hate women."

Hannah knew that there were more brutal rapes: attacks where dreadful damage, needing surgery, resulted, and where the woman's—or child's—body could be affected for life. She kept thinking that she should be thankful for her escape from worse injuries, not dwelling on what had happened to her, but it was difficult.

Back at college, she was very quiet. The others in the house suspected what had happened to her because of the slanted reporting of the robbery, and the photographs of Peter and of her father with his bruised features in the papers. There is always someone who recognizes something, and identities which should be protected are revealed.

The two girls in the house she shared gave her hugs and were ready to offer sympathy, but Hannah said she did not want to talk about what had happened. The men were wary of her, treating her with embarrassed thoughtfulness, not getting close to her.

As if I'm a leper, she thought, and, indeed, she felt infected.

She went to lectures and the library and tried to work, though her concentration span had diminished, but she never went out at night, even in a group, and gave up the amateur dramatics through which she had met Peter. As the weeks went by, she made an effort to be less reclusive and she and Peter went on seeing one another.

He thought a good sexual relationship would put her right, efface bad memories and superimpose good ones.

He discussed this with Emma, one of the girls who lived in Hannah's house.

"In time," said Emma. "She may not be ready yet."

Hannah and Peter still kissed; they still held hands when unencumbered with bags and books; and sometimes Hannah seemed to respond, especially if they had had some wine.

He reopened the subject of their summer trip, but she would not commit herself. In the Easter vacation, she went to stay with him and his mother in the Lake District, where his mother was on a bird-watching foray in a rented cottage.

While his mother was out, off early to some spot where she hoped to see buzzards and, if she was lucky, a merlin, Peter came into Hannah's room with a cup of tea for her.

She was grateful, and sat up in bed in her long T-shirt with a Snoopy motif on the front. Why not now, he thought, and sat down on the edge of the bed, leaning forward to kiss her, smoothing her hair away from her face. It had grown a little and reached her ears, neatly trimmed in a bob.

At first she seemed to welcome his careful, tentative approach, but then, as he grew more persistent, she pushed him away.

"No," she said.

"But why not? I thought you loved me," Peter said.

"I did—I do," said Hannah.

But did she?

"I understood before. The first time—all that," Peter said. "But it's different now."

She was leaning forward, pushing against the pillow behind her, but her instant anger swiftly turned to tears.

"So that's what you think," she wept. "Because of what happened, I'm a tramp."

"No, of course not. But things have changed, you must admit," he said. However, he drew back. "Perhaps you need a bit more time," he conceded, and gave her a friendly pat. "Drink your tea."

Later, they went for a long and silent walk. This is impossible, Peter thought, striding along in waxed jacket and waterproof trousers. Hannah was similarly clad as she followed him over stiles, across paths, and through copses. A fine rain was falling, but the air was soft and mild, and the exercise was good. Starting out late, they did not stop for lunch, and when they returned to the cottage they were hungry. Peter's mother had not come back from her expedition; Hannah had talked to her about the birds she found so interesting and was rather drawn to the idea of spending hours alone, miles from anywhere, with just a pair of binoculars and nature for company. Peter lit the fire and Hannah found them bread and cheese to last them until supper.

Both had been thinking things over while they walked and Peter, whilst deciding that matters could not go on in the same way indefinitely, had decided to apologize for pushing her.

"I'm sorry," he said. "I shouldn't have been so impatient."

"It's not fair to you, though," Hannah said.

"Someone else might be better for you—turn you on more," Peter said, a little bitterly. But he used to be able to do that, up to a point.

"The thing that really bugs me is Dad," Hannah finally burst out. "He didn't try to help me. I can't stop thinking about it. He came into my room with those two men and said we shouldn't resist them."

"But that was when he thought they were just burglars," Peter said.

"I know, but I was there. It happens," Hannah answered. "I fought," she added. "When he tied me up, and later."

"Maybe that was why he decided to go for you," Peter said. "If you hadn't struggled, maybe he'd have left you alone."

That could be true, but Hannah wouldn't have it.

"You can't just let such people get away with everything," she said.

"At least they didn't scar you," Peter said. "You're not marked forever."

"You don't understand, do you?" she said. "Perhaps no man can." Certainly her father didn't. "But at least Dad hasn't said that he forgives them. The vicar came to see us and said we'd both feel better if we could."

"That's going a bit far," Peter said. "Why did he think you should?"

"Oh, forgive your enemies. All that pious stuff," said Hannah.

Her mother's comment had been What about righteous wrath? She said that she would never forgive Hannah's attacker.

"Perhaps you ought to forgive your father," Peter said.

But Hannah couldn't.

When they returned to college, she and Peter stopped going out together, and in the vacation he went backpacking with a girl called Marie, while Hannah and her parents went by car to Italy, staying in a villa with a pool, and gently sightseeing.

That was after Morris and Barry went on trial. It was a big ordeal for Hannah, who gave evidence and who had to endure hearing Barry's counsel allege that she had offered him intercourse.

Anger had come to her rescue then.

"Why should I do that?" she demanded, from the witness box.

"In exchange for a promise not to hurt you," came the answer.

"He did hurt me," Hannah said. "He raped me, and he hit my face and cracked one of my ribs. And he cut my hair."

This line of questioning did not get very far, but it made Hannah understand the degradation felt by rape victims when that was the only offense of which their assailants were accused. Barry had stolen property, which was proved. He received a seven-year sentence, but with remission would serve only about five; Morris, because he had been the brains behind the robbery, had carried a gun and had disposed of the goods—apart from a few items which were still in his flat when he was arrested—was given eleven years.

PART TWO

Now and Then

1.

Derek Jarvis came back to his empty house. He and Janet had separated three years after the robbery and now he lived alone.

He turned the key in the lock and walked into the hall. A pile of letters and circulars lay on the utilitarian beige carpet which, like the curtains, he had acquired with the house. He stooped to pick up the clutch of mail and glanced through it: bills and circulars, mostly; there was never a note from Hannah except on his birthday and at Christmas. He walked through to the living room, turning on the light. It was a drab room, furnished with the leather-covered chairs which had been in his study at The Elms; they would last for ever. Beige carpet matching that in the hall covered the floor. There were a few books on some shelves beside the fireplace, in which there was a coal-effect gas fire: paperback novels by Frederick Forsyth, Dick Francis, Len Deighton, and *The Oxford Book of English Verse* which had been given to him by an aunt. There was a television set with a video recorder, and a portable radio, but no music center; Derek had no ear for music.

Hannah had not finished her degree. After parting from Peter, she had struggled on for two more terms and then, the next Easter, while she was back at The Elms but now occupying a different bedroom, freshly decorated and furnished, she had tried to take her own life.

Janet had woken early that morning, thinking she had heard a sound somewhere in the house. She had not been sleeping well since the attack, and when Hannah was at home—she had been back for term-time weekends—often heard her walking about at night, for Hannah, understandably enough, was still a poor sleeper. Sometimes Janet would get up and seek her out, suggest tea and a chat, but she sensed that Hannah wanted to be alone. Now, Janet waited for a while until, propelled by some gut instinct that there was reason for unease, she swung herself out of bed, put on her dressing gown and slippers and went onto the landing.

Hannah's bedroom door was closed, which was unusual if she was on the prowl; she would leave it ajar so that she could return silently to her room. Hesitating, Janet looked about, then went downstairs into the kitchen. It was empty, and Hannah was not in any of the other ground-floor rooms. Janet thought she must have imagined the original noise and returned to bed, but she could not sleep; she still felt that something was wrong, and after a while she got up again and looked in Hannah's room.

The bed was empty, the duvet drawn neatly up to the pillow.

Real fear clutched Janet by the throat and she went downstairs again and tested the doors. The French window in the drawing room was closed but unlocked. It was always double-locked now; after the robbery extra strong locks had been fixed to all the doors and security lights fitted outside, and Derek checked everything punctiliously before going to bed. When Hannah was at home, he checked twice.

Janet opened the window and went out onto the paved terrace. Beyond lay the gravel sweep and the lawn, with its large stone tubs placed at intervals round its edge. As she ran towards it, the security lights came on, and she could see the daffodils and tulips which Derek had planted in the autumn now flowering bravely in their containers. To the east, the sky was getting lighter as the new day began to dawn, and she started to run over the grass, her thin pink satin slippers sodden with dew. The ground fell away, past a willow and some apple trees which had replaced the elms after which the house was named, and which had succumbed to the disease that had proved fatal to so many of them. At the bottom of the slope, where the setting sun reached it while much of the garden was in shadow, was a summerhouse. Deck chairs were stacked inside, and the croquet set which in summer was used on the level patch next to the boundary fence.

Janet had seen the trail of Hannah's footsteps in the dew. She opened the summerhouse door, knowing already what she would see.

Hannah had swallowed a quantity of paracetamol tablets, and drunk half a glassful of gin. Because she was found so soon after she lost consciousness, she escaped the terrible liver damage that would have killed her even if the pills had failed, but she was ill for some time, and when she was physically better, she went into a psychiatric nursing home where she stayed for some weeks.

After she came home, she was able to tell her parents that she felt dirty and worthless as a result of what had happened to her, and that life had nothing to offer her because she was so tarnished, but while in the nursing home she had understood that her action was punishing her parents, while providing herself only with an escape. They would have grieved and blamed themselves for the rest of their lives, if the suicide attempt had succeeded, and the rapist would have beaten her.

"You don't want that to happen, Hannah, do you?" the

gray-haired woman doctor had asked her. "It wasn't their fault, and it wasn't yours."

"My father might have saved me," Hannah had said. "He thought it was best not to risk being killed."

"And you being killed, too. That was in his mind," said the doctor. "Not his own safety."

In a later talk, the doctor advised Hannah to imagine that she had been injured in an accident, something that was not her fault at all, a matter of being in the wrong place at the wrong time.

"Think of the rape as an artificial leg. It has to be accepted, and you have to adjust, but it needn't stop you walking—even dancing and playing tennis, though you may limp a little from time to time," she suggested.

When Hannah went home, the doctor told her mother that she thought the girl had been as badly damaged by the fact that her father had made no attempt to save her as by the rape itself.

"She knows she struggled. Even if he'd been badly hurt, perhaps killed, and the rape had gone ahead, she would have had the consolation of knowing he had tried to protect her," said the doctor. "She idolized him until then, didn't she?"

"They were very close," Janet agreed.

"Our first major disillusionment is always a bitter experience," said the doctor. "And it's hard if it comes through a parent."

In the autumn, her parents took Hannah on a Mediterranean cruise. They had thought about a holiday in Greece, but came to the conclusion that, as in Italy the year before, she would lack young company if they rented a villa, but on board ship, even if the passengers were older, there would be the crew.

She shared a cabin with her mother; her father had one to himself on a lower deck. Hannah did not know quite how this arrangement came about but she was glad she was not alone in a narrow cell in a long, anonymous corridor. Perhaps the psychiatrist had suggested it; anyway, she was grateful.

They all, if only superficially, enjoyed the trip. The ports at which they called were interesting: they had a lovely day on Mykonos, and another in Venice; these were the high points of the voyage. Janet and Hannah became skilled at deck quoits and Derek went to bridge classes. There were films and cabaret entertainment, and two swimming pools.

Derek, alone on the lowest deck, had a brief affair with a girl who worked in one of the bars, where he took to drinking in the evenings after Janet and Hannah had gone to bed.

"Drowning your sorrows?" she had asked him, a banal comment on a banal situation.

One thing had led to another. Derek felt rejuvenated, and consoled for the hostility where once there had been real love emanating from Hannah. The girl herself, who was recovering from a divorce, found their brief romance therapeutic.

Janet and Hannah did not suspect a thing.

When they returned, Hannah started a secretarial course, and Derek bought her a secondhand Metro, tried and tested by the garage he had dealt with for years, so that she was independent.

She worked hard, spending her evenings on revision and practice, and never went out. Janet tried to encourage her to take up a leisure activity and after a while persuaded her to join a badminton club which met once a week at the Sports Centre in Norlington. She went off to their sessions but was always home promptly, and no other social life seemed to evolve from this.

"It's as if she's dead inside," said Janet, one night when Hannah had returned from such an evening and had gone straight upstairs to bed.

"She ought to have snapped out of it by now," said Derek, who read daily reproach in the expression on his daughter's face, and could barely live with it.

"It's not going to happen suddenly," said Janet. She longed to help Hannah but felt powerless. "Perhaps some nice young man—" her voice trailed off. The answer to problems caused by one man was not necessarily another.

"She'll never attract one, at this rate," said Derek impatiently.

"She can live a fulfilled and happy life without marrying," said Janet, though like most mothers, she hoped Hannah would one day be settled and content, with children. Her dreadful experience could have been so much worse: since it happened, Janet had read up on the subject and knew of sadistic attacks and frightful physical damage that some victims suffered. Hannah knew this, too, and it made her feel that she was being weak, but there were other things in life than sex and having what people called relationships, though most of the girls on the secretarial course had boyfriends and thought that having any man was better than no man at all.

In an attempt to accept that dictum and conform to the pattern she knew her parents wished for her, Hannah began going out with Tom Villars, who was a chemist working in a pharmaceutical works in Norlington and a member of the badminton club. They had partnered each other in several matches; he was a quiet, studious young man who wore glasses and who did not join in the light, loaded badinage which passed for conversation among some of the players. She went to a concert with him, and the cinema, and he took her to an Italian restaurant and, one Saturday, a riverside hotel for a dinner-dance.

Tom needed a girlfriend. He found the girls he worked with brisk and alarming, but Hannah was quiet and un-threatening. She seemed very reserved, but she had enjoyed the concert and knew about orchestras and their composition. She discussed the film they saw with intelligence.

Like Peter before him, he enjoyed going to The Elms. Knowing it would please her parents, Hannah invited him to lunch there one Sunday. After the dinner-dance, when he had brought her home, he had kissed her and she had managed not to jump back from him in terror though she had kept her lips clamped firmly together. At her own house, in the daytime, she could control how they proceeded, she decided. It was safe, and Tom would appreciate her mother's excellent cooking.

He did. He lived in a one-roomed flat, and for him it was luxury indeed. After lunch, he and Hannah went for a walk over fields at the back of Bicklebury Manor and stood on a small bridge watching the Bickle stream flowing beneath them. He held her gloved hand in his, and she let it rest there. She was not afraid of Tom, but she was convinced that she would never feel totally secure again.

As the weeks went on, Tom kissed her with more fervor and she tried to respond, but the best that she could do was to rest her arms around his neck and let him do the kissing.

Perhaps if she got a little drunk, she thought, she might feel aroused, as she had with Peter; sometimes she had wanted, with him, to let go, but it seemed such a step to take, the first time. Well, as he had pointed out, choice had been removed from her over that. People enjoyed sex; they thought life revolved around it; and for the continuation of the race, so it did. She might get to like it, if she tried it under favorable circumstances.

So when Tom suggested going up to London for a theater and a weekend break, she agreed. She knew what her consent implied, and she meant to fulfill her part of the undeclared deal.

They enjoyed the play they saw, a comedy, and Tom took her to a small intimate restaurant for dinner, where she surprised him by the amount of wine she drank; she had always been rather abstemious, before. Back at the hotel, in their large, comfortable room—Tom had been extravagant with their bargain booking—she seemed more supple in his arms and she moved her mouth against his, giving him the illusion of response. She let him take her clothes off, helping with her tights, and he was very gentle with her, sensing she was nervous. So was he: a first encounter, though exciting, can be fraught with hazard, and while Tom did not lack experience, he was no Lothario.

I like him, Hannah was telling herself. I don't love him, but I like him. He won't hurt me. Perhaps I'll get to love him. She let him touch her body, but she could not bring herself to caress him; suddenly, he disgusted her and she sprang away from him, flinging herself out of the bed and rushing across to the corner of the room where she crouched in a naked bundle, knees to her chin, and began shuddering, as she had that dreadful night.

Tom was bewildered.

"What is it? Did I hurt you?"

He came over to her where she squatted, now weeping and shivering, and she hid her face from him, her fair hair, long again, falling forward over her clasped knees.

"No—it's me. I'm so sorry, Tom. I can't," she said, and waited for his wrath.

It did not come. Tom returned to the bed, pulled off a

blanket and wrapped it round her. Her reluctance proved a most effective turn-off; he felt no urge to make her change her mind.

"Don't worry—it doesn't matter," he said. "Would you like a cup of tea?"

Suggesting this was the best thing he could have done.

"Yes, please," she mumbled, and he put on his boxer shorts and the hotel's towelling robe, then filled up the kettle thoughtfully provided by the management.

Hannah wrapped the blanket round her and went into the bathroom where she stayed for some time, emerging with a scrubbed face and brushed hair. By then Tom had made the tea and had placed a pillow down the center of the big double bed.

Sitting up, propped against pillows, in her dressing gown, Hannah drank her tea. Then she told Tom what had happened to her more than a year before. She owed him that explanation.

"I thought it might be all right. You're so kind," she said. "I thought maybe I'd get over it, with you."

And so she might have done, if she had loved him, thought Tom, who did not love Hannah, either, though she intrigued him and he found her attractive in her restrained way. He had seen her as an eventual appropriate marriage prospect, if they could grow fonder of each other, bring some romance into their lives.

"I can understand why you feel like that," he said, and he did. Forcing a woman was an awful thing to do; gentle Tom was horrified.

Her revelation had made any vestiges of desire he might still feel for Hannah vanish. Eventually he went to sleep, but Hannah lay awake for most of the night. She understood that he had been extremely kind and sympathetic; another man might have got very angry, called her a tease and a cheat. In the morning, when their breakfast, ordered the night before, arrived, she told him so.

"What would be the good of that?" he asked her. "It wasn't your fault." Perhaps it was his, for want of a more beguiling technique. "Not all men are beasts, you know."

"Yes."

"Someone else will spark you off, one day," he said, to encourage her, but he thought it unlikely. "Friends?"

"Yes—friends," she agreed.

They went on meeting for a while after the weekend, but then he began taking out another girl, a newcomer at the pharmaceutical works.

Janet dared to ask her what had happened, and, after some doubt, Hannah told her.

"I behaved very badly," she said. "But I meant to go through with it."

"Tom is very dull," said Janet. "Very nice, but very dull. Easy to admire, but difficult to view romantically." Like Derek, she thought.

"I think he knows that," said Hannah. "Sad, isn't it? Of course, he didn't love me. I was just available, or so he thought."

"Poor Tom," said Janet. "Never mind. No serious damage done."

"Not even to his self-esteem?"

"It seems to have recovered," said her mother.

"You've been great about all this," said Hannah. "It would have been much worse if you hadn't understood."

"A friend of mine was date-raped once," said Janet. "That's what it's called now, I think. She was one of the girls in a flat where I lived when I was doing a secretarial course. She went to a party with this man and, innocently, asked him in for coffee when he brought her home. They were alone. He probably thought he was seducing her but he wouldn't stop. It upset her dreadfully."

"I bet," said Hannah. "Poor girl. You stood by her, though."

"Yes," said Janet.

"Good old Mum," said Hannah, then added, "I think I'd like to get right away. Make a real break. I thought I might go in for birds, like Peter's mother. She said it was quiet and peaceful and that was why she took it up."

"How do you mean, go in for them?" asked Janet. "Do you mean study ornithology?"

"Sort of—but on the job. There are nature reserves where you can go and work," said Hannah. "I've asked about it. Not much pay, but you get your keep, and there's not a lot to spend your money on. I thought I might find out more. Would you mind?"

"Not if it's what you really want to do," said Janet.

At last Hannah had expressed a genuine wish.

"You've been marvelous, Mum. I don't know how girls cope who haven't got mothers like you, when they've had this sort of thing happen. And worse than what happened to me. I feel such a wimp."

"You're not a wimp. It was dreadful."

"I wish the world didn't go round in pairs," said Hannah. "You feel a freak if you don't have a special chap."

"You won't among the birds," said Janet. "I'll miss you."

"You can come and stay and get up at dawn to look for grebes," said Hannah.

"Do grebes get up at dawn?" asked Janet.

"I'll soon find out," said Hannah. "I've got a lot to learn."

Two months later she went to Scotland to live in a wildlife conservation area, where in winter it was cold and bleak and, in summer, often wet. She was still there when Barry Carter was released from prison.

2.

After Hannah left home, Janet and Derek's façade of marriage crumbled. His working day had always been long and now it became still more extended. His company had bought another and were off-loading sections that did not interest them. Derek was much involved with the restructuring process and often went to Sheffield, where the new acquisition was.

He began to spend nights away from home, and, having given it no thought for months, remembered his brief affair during the cruise.

He could have another, before it was too late, and most conveniently he found an available partner in Barbara Wright, a woman made redundant by the takeover. She had been the production manager's assistant, but he had gone, too, replaced by someone from the original company. She had three children ranging in age from eight to thirteen and lived in a pleasant small house outside the city, with views towards the moors.

Derek, on his journeys north, soon became an accepted overnight visitor, but he said nothing to Barbara about the breakup of his marriage. The separation had been amicable; Janet, if she suspected there might be someone else, never mentioned it, and their divorce was arranged by mutual consent with no bitter arguments about money. Derek knew that he did not want to become a second father to Barbara's children, who demanded her attention for their homework and who squabbled among themselves at intervals. The youngest, a boy, clearly resented his visits, although Derek brought small electronic games and other gifts when he arrived, and tried to get along with all three of them. But he had come to see Barbara, and to go to bed with her. He was anxious about her, too, because she was finding it difficult to get another job. However, finally she succeeded and now her evenings were crammed with chores that must be fitted in, mundane tasks such as ironing.

She ended it, putting into words what both were feeling: that it wasn't worth the hassle.

"I need my time and energy," she said flatly.

He sent her an enormous bunch of flowers as a farewell gesture, and set about planning his new life. He had been living in a rented flat, and with the divorce settlement concluded, he moved to Petty Linton, nearer his Slough office. The Elms, bought years before property prices soared, was sold; the mortgage, which by now was negligible, was repaid; and he and Janet divided what was left. He made an additional capital settlement on her instead of maintenance, cashing in an insurance policy to do it, and Janet opened a fashion shop in Norlington. She rented premises in a new cloistered development that linked the High Street to a row of shops fronting another road.

Derek soon settled to his new routine. He saw few of their old friends. There had not been many, when he thought about it. There had been acquaintances, people he worked with on village committees, and the Fords at the Manor, with whom Janet and Hannah had been on closer terms than he, though he found them amiable enough.

Janet had always filled her time with voluntary work and exercising at a leisure center with a swimming pool; she had fitted in classes of varying kinds in other slots and had made a feature of her housekeeping. Now her life was altered totally. Women she knew, coming to the shop, expected discounts, and others lost interest in her because they no longer shared the same activities, but she still saw the Fords. Veronica Ford had worked with her at the Citizens' Advice Bureau in Norlington, and Janet had been one of four women who had played tennis regularly on the Fords' hard court, meeting once a week during their children's school terms. The Fords had two daughters, both younger than Hannah, who, as she grew older, had sometimes babysat for them between au pairs. Veronica encouraged Janet to open the shop and was sure it would be successful, for Janet had always been interested in clothes, dressed well herself, and was an efficient, energetic woman.

Before opening the shop, she took a temporary job helping in Madge's, a dress shop in Enworth, ten miles beyond Norlington, where she had bought a small modern house in a new development near the cricket ground. She needed her capital to equip and stock the shop and wanted to commit as little as possible in other areas, so the house was among some bought mainly by first-time buyers. Norlington had scope for a high-class dress shop, she knew. While she waited for appropriate premises to fall vacant, she learned all she could about the trade and, in the evenings, did a bookkeeping course. Nothing must be left to chance; she meant to succeed in her new life.

She was so busy that she spent no time thinking about the breakup with Derek. They had divided the furniture between them, and had sent a small vanload to Scotland where Hannah was now renting a small cottage near her bird sanctuary. Before she moved, her parents had been to see her, together, to explain about their parting, fearing her reaction, but she had taken their news calmly and was interested in her mother's plans, encouraging her, sure that the shop would be a success.

She was looking well and had put on weight. She introduced them to the warden and his wife, who were friendly and straightforward. No one else worked with them on a full-time basis, but volunteers came at intervals to cut bracken and carry out the labor needed to maintain the many acres of wild countryside and, when necessary, protect the birds.

"I hope she's not going to spend the rest of her days up here," said Derek, in the hotel room where they were staying, in the nearest town.

Janet knew that Hannah had run away from life. Whether she would ever run back again could not be foretold.

"She seems content," she said.

Soon after this, their separation took effect and Janet's new routine was established. She was stimulated by the need to be well-organized, smart, and apparently confident, and once her shop was open, she began trying to instill confidence in others, suggesting, when they tried on garments, appropriate accessories—gloves and costume jewelry, and makeup, even keeping a small stock of blusher and various lipsticks to augment her advice. The younger women did not need this sort of encouragement; the older ones could often be persuaded, and she was delighted when she sent them out remodeled, ready to face the big occasion—wedding or anniversary celebration, or whatever it might be—with earrings that went with their outfits and hurrying off to the beauty counter at Fawcett's, the large chemist's near the Market Square.

Occasionally a customer rebelled, saying that she knew what suited her and it was not large dangling earrings or bright lipstick, but most took Janet's suggestions in good part, and some were grateful. At first she did not urge her own preferences upon them beyond a certain point, but after a while she began to alienate some of her customers because she was too persuasive, or when she had not got what they were looking for, tried too hard to get them to buy some other type of garment.

She was very busy, but that had always been the pattern of her adult life. If you kept on the go, you had no time to brood or repine. It was difficult for her to sit idle, even to enjoy a book, and she felt guilty watching television for there was always some outstanding task or duty she should be performing.

Getting the business under way and keeping the books up to date occupied her fully in the first year after she opened Clarice. She could not explain how she had thought of the name: it just came to her, and seemed appropriate. Months later she remembered an old doll she had once cherished, a pigtailed one which her older brother, in a fit of malice, had dismembered and cremated. Her name had been Clarice. Janet, six at the time, had never forgiven her brother, and she never saw him now. It was his wife who sent the Christmas and birthday cards to which, grudgingly, Janet responded in kind.

The shopfitting was done by a local builder. Janet kept it simple, to reduce costs. She provided a chair for accompanying friends of customers, and the two changing cubicles, with their maroon and gold striped curtains, were large enough for the proper inspection of what was being tried on.

Janet's markup was high; her brief apprenticeship at the

other shop had taught her that good profits could be cleared. When she held her first sale, she made spectacular reductions and sold nearly all her surplus stock. Her early debts were paid and she could meet commitments. At home, her tiny house, brand new, needed no maintenance. She adapted curtains from The Elms, and sold some of the larger pieces of furniture she had taken in the share-out in order to buy smaller items. The garden had been leveled and a patio laid. Veronica Ford, a keen and knowledgeable gardener, advised lashing out on turf for the small lawn to get a quick result, and gave her some rose trees because they would yield the best reward for the least effort. A New Dawn was planted along the fence separating her from her neighbor on one side.

"That will soon give you a wonderful show and be a screen," said Veronica. "It'll need some support. We'll put in a frame for it."

She supplied and planted lavender, and several small shrubs which would look neat and fill the gaps.

"You can go in for tubs of geraniums and so on if you have the time," she said. "They need watering and you may not want to do it. On the other hand, it could unwind you after your day's toil."

Janet, in her years at The Elms, had never shown much interest in the garden, and Derek's endeavors had been unimaginative, concentrating more on tidiness and well-mown lawns rather than anything creative, though he had grown vegetables and had liked his tubs of bedding plants. Veronica thought it unlikely that Janet would suddenly become a passionate horticulturist, but you could never tell. She admired her friend's resourcefulness in setting up the shop; Norlington was a prosperous town and she would undoubtedly succeed.

Janet's lease had two years to run; at the end of that time the rent could be revised, but if it were to be increased, her anticipated rising profits should cover the extra outlay. The mortgage on the house was catered for; Janet paid bills on time and planned ahead; and her customers did not run accounts, as in some other shops where unpaid bills caused problems.

She had almost no social life. There wasn't time.

She did not miss Derek at all, and seldom thought about him. Only when she went to Bicklebury Manor on a Sunday, as she sometimes did, and found the Fords—the parents and the daughters—all relaxed, with in-jokes among themselves and what Janet defined as a team spirit operating, did she sometimes think it would be nice to live like that.

Derek, meanwhile, had settled to routine in Petty Linton. His work had always occupied the major part of his time and most of his energy. It gave him a perfect excuse for avoiding other obligations, although in Bicklebury he had audited the church and village hall accounts—soon done, for he was a qualified accountant and they were simple. That was the limit of his voluntary work. He had regarded tidying the garden as a necessary chore, but had liked seeing the neat striped swathes of mown lawn appearing behind the machine, and trimming hedges. Now, in his small, square house, he undertook domestic tasks in the same resigned way, vacuuming and dusting regularly on Saturdays until he found a contract cleaner, Dazzle-U, who came once a month to give the place a thorough going-over. Then, when a flier came through the door offering an ironing service, he followed it up and discovered Angela Battersby.

"I take it away and return it the next day, or another time by appointment," she had explained on the telephone.

"You don't work in the client's house?"

"No."

They had fixed a meeting, and she had arrived in a small blue Fiat van. She was about thirty, he thought, thin and pale with straight brown hair cut in a fringe and a long bob, and she wore jeans and a checked shirt.

"The next day, or by arrangement, would be all right for me," said Derek, who had thought that they could have some scheme whereby he left his damp, washed shirts in some agreed place and she delivered the ironed ones in the same manner. He might even give her a key; Dazzle-U had had to have one. "Why do you do this work?" he found himself asking.

"Most people hate ironing, but I enjoy it, and it's something I can do at home. I can't be out too long," she said. "Family commitments."

She wore no wedding ring, but that meant nothing these days. She was probably a single mother, he decided, though if so, how did she manage evening deliveries and why couldn't she work in school hours? Or did she cart a baby round in her van?

She gave him her price list, which rivaled laundry prices.

"It works well for me. I don't do the actual washing, you see," she said, with a smile.

It altered her long, plain face, and he saw that her eyes were a deep blue, like gentians.

It was agreed that she would collect his bundle, which he must keep damp in a polythene bag, on Tuesday evenings at eight or later, at the same time returning the previous week's work. He had plenty of shirts, enough to last a week. If for any reason he had to be out, he would leave the bag of washing in the garage, which had a pedestrian door at the side. They arranged a spot beneath a stone where he would put the key on those Tuesdays.

Angela said that if this didn't work, they'd try another

plan, and Derek said he would leave the check in an envelope under the bag with the shirts.

Angela did not linger. She made a note in a small black book with an alphabet index. She seemed organized and capable; oddly, he was reminded of Janet, always so practical and contained, yet the two were not remotely similar in appearance. Angela herself, driving away, was pleased to have collected another customer; the fliers, and an advertisement in the local paper, had produced a lot of response and she hoped to acquire enough clients to bring in a reasonable return. There would not be much outlay, just her petrol and the electricity, and she need never be out for long. She had had to find something she could do at home, and in this area there were plenty of couples who both went out to work and were glad to have a time-consuming burden lifted.

There was no need to explain to any of them why she was so tied; that was her business.

She forgot about Derek Jarvis as soon as she drove off.

3.

Two years after she opened Clarice, Janet's rent was increased far more than she had anticipated, and she had to pay high business rates. Her outgoings began to eat away at her profits, and at the same time her customers were finding things difficult, too. Expensive clothes were a luxury that could be reduced or eliminated.

Businesswomen still came to the shop. They bought straight black skirts and smart jackets which she had introduced when she found the secretaries and personal assistants, the accountants and solicitors, wanted those sort of garments.

She enjoyed encouraging them to make choices.

"Try this," she said to a pale thin woman who was returning to work now that her children were in their teens and needed, Janet knew, to garb herself with a disguise of confidence which, once adopted, would become the real thing. This had been her own experience: dressing for the part.

She showed the woman a short charcoal skirt.

"I'd never wear that," the woman said. "It's much too short."

"It's chic," said Janet, whose own legs were too sturdy to be so exposed.

"It'd be very uncomfortable," said the woman, who was

going to work in an estate agent's office. But she had to look smart in her job; at her interview, that had been implied.

Under Janet's pressure, she was persuaded to try on the skirt, and allowed Janet to clip big gilt earrings to her lobes and fasten a gilt necklace round her neck. She was wearing a white round-necked blouse, and Janet planned to sell her a cerise shirt in a synthetic fabric which could be washed and drip-dried overnight.

"You could wear a range of jackets with that skirt," said Janet, producing one that matched the cerise shirt.

The customer agreed, wavering, and went so far as to try all this on. Then common sense came to her rescue.

"I'd like it, but I can't afford it," she said. "I can't blow my first month's salary on clothes. Just the skirt, thank you."

She left the shop and resolved to avoid it in the future. The woman who ran it was too forceful. Her suggestions were good and the clothes appropriate, but as she looked at herself in the mirror, she had seen a new creation and was not sure she liked what she saw. The skirt was a success, however; her husband approved, and when she wore it to the office, she noticed it was like one worn by a senior negotiator, so she felt there had been some point to the remodeling efforts of Clarice.

Janet, however, was disappointed at selling her only one item. She knew she pushed too hard. She had tried it with Veronica, who had wanted an evening dress for a dinner in the City to which she was going with Roger, who was a member of one of the guilds.

"It's appropriate, but it isn't me," Veronica had said, twirling round in the décolletée purple taffeta. She was really only comfortable in tweeds or trousers, or soft summer dresses. "I must have a higher neck and sleeves, but the fabric can be special."

"It suits you," Janet had said, surveying her slim friend.

Veronica's collarbones stood out and her upper arms were as thin as a child's, although they were quite muscular with all the gardening she did. "Earrings, a necklace, your hair done in a topknot to show off your long neck—you'd look wonderful."

"Janet, I'm not a film star up for an Oscar. I'm a skinny, middle-aged countrywoman with scraggy bits that are better hidden. I don't have to cut a dash, as long as I look my best and feel comfortable. You know, you'll put people off if you try too hard to make a sale," said Veronica, who had heard other women comment on Janet's powerful sales pitch.

"I'm only helping my customers to make the best of themselves," said Janet. "I'm good at it."

"Yes, you are," said Veronica. "But you're casting them in roles as you see them, and that may not be how they want to see themselves. You don't always recognize the real person. And I'm not going to be able to buy my dress from you, which is a pity. I'll show you what I get, so that you understand the point I'm making."

Three days later she came back to the shop with a large shiny bag. It had not been easy to find something she liked, she said, but she showed Janet a simple dress in black velvet with long sleeves and a high boat-shaped neck which covered her boniest points but revealed the whiteness of her throat. The figure-hugging bodice flared out below the hips to give some fullness to the skirt. In it, Veronica looked ethereal and fey, and Janet could see that when her hair was done and her makeup fresh, she would seem beautiful.

"This does a lot for me, Janet, and I feel good in it," said Veronica. "And it will do duty for a good few years. Sorry to hurt you, Jan, but you'll lose customers if you push them. You must coax them, and listen to what they're telling you. Now, why don't you come to supper tonight? Roger says it's

ages since he saw you," and she smiled to soften the reproof
she had administered.

Janet accepted the invitation. She did not want to quarrel
with Veronica, although she was deeply hurt by the criticism.

Perhaps it was justified?

"Have you heard from Hannah lately?"

Roger asked the question, handing Janet a large gin and
tonic.

She looked tired, and he was not surprised. Even though it
had happened more than three years ago, he still remembered the shock of those awful days after the attack. Who
could forget it, and Hannah's drawn, peaky face in the
months that followed?

"I spoke to her on Sunday," Janet said. She laughed nervously. "It's difficult to know how often to telephone, or if
one's interrupting or being intrusive. Whenever I do, she's
almost always there. I don't think she has any social life. But
she sounds all right. She'd been ringing birds."

"It must be interesting." Veronica wondered how often
she had said this since Hannah went to Scotland. It was a
true statement, but it was difficult to proceed beyond it and
expand the conversation.

"Is she going to stay there forever?" Roger asked.

Janet shrugged.

"She's never mentioned other plans," she said.

All of them were silent, picturing Hannah standing in
waders, binoculars to her eyes, bundled in thick clothing.
There were many worse places to be, they all thought.

"She must be very fit," said Roger. "All that fresh air."

"In time, she might return to civilization," said Veronica.

"She may be best on her own," said Janet.

"Who's up there with her? Who does she see, apart from a few crofters?" asked Veronica. "I'd be happy for our girls to spend some time like that, but not their whole lives."

"Some girls go to the jungle and live among chimpanzees," said Roger.

"They're trained zoologists," said Janet. "Hannah has no training."

They all knew that she worked for a pittance, subsidized by money left to her by Derek's father, who had died soon after the robbery. He had been living in a retirement home for several years, and when he heard what had happened—reading about it first in a tabloid paper and piecing together the clues which identified his family—he had had a heart attack. He had recovered from that one, but a second, less than a year later, had been fatal. In his will he left everything to Hannah. It was the only way he could help her, he told Derek; the legacy would give her a measure of independence.

"What she's doing is worthwhile," said Veronica. "There's that, at least." Perhaps, she thought fancifully, a handsome young ornithologist will visit Hannah's sanctuary and espy her among the reeds. Such a man would probably be of a gentle disposition, so necessary if Hannah were ever to lead a normal life. By which I mean a sex life, I suppose, Veronica reflected. Her own two daughters, one at college, one doing "A" levels, were bright, confident girls, Tessa good at languages, and Carol keen on science. Promising futures lay ahead for them, she hoped.

Hannah had been down once to visit Janet in her new house, and had seen the shop. Unable to face the journey by coach or train, when she would have to jostle among strangers, she had flown. As she traveled on a Sunday, Janet had been able to meet her at the airport. Hannah admired her mother's enterprise, and Janet had had the good sense not to offer her a partnership to lure her back again, nor any clothes at a discount; she had no use for fine feathers where she lived, and warm jerseys could be bought at bargain prices in Scotland.

Hannah knew nothing about the problems Janet was having now, with increased costs and fewer customers.

"How's Derek?" asked Veronica, during dinner.

"He's been made redundant," Janet said. "Ironic, isn't it, when his company ate up those others and people lost their jobs. Now it's happened to him. He's doing some sort of consultancy work."

"You keep in touch, then?"

"Sort of. Once or twice a year," said Janet. "He went up to see Hannah, but she wasn't very pleased. She asked him not to go again."

He'd just turned up, Hannah said, appearing outside her rented cottage in his car.

"Poor Derek," said Veronica. "He doesn't understand, does he?"

"Understand what?" asked Roger.

"That she can't forgive him for not trying to protect her," said Janet.

Roger could not imagine a scenario in which either of his daughters, or his wife, was threatened without him trying to save her, even if he died in the attempt. However, he answered diplomatically.

"We all react differently to danger," he said.

"But if one of the girls was drowning, you'd dive in to rescue her without thinking of your own skin, wouldn't you?" said Janet.

"She'd end up saving me, whichever one it was," said Roger. "They're both far better swimmers than I am."

After dinner, and coffee by the fire in the drawing room—

a large, comfortable room with faded linen covers on the chairs, and Paddy, the golden Labrador, lying on the rug before the fire—Janet felt soothed and relaxed, very reluctant to leave this friendly company, and Veronica suggested she should stay the night. If she did, she would weaken, Janet knew; she must get back to her own place and her own responsibilities. She had to face the problem of the bank loan she had been forced to take out to meet her bills. Her house was her security; if she lost that, she was finished.

The Fords discussed her as they went to bed. She had developed a hard shell, they agreed, but perhaps, for her business persona, it was necessary. Veronica related what had happened about the evening dress and how she had seen Janet putting pressure on customers to buy something quite different from what they were originally seeking when they went into Clarice. Poor Janet. It wouldn't have mattered so much if the boom days had lasted, but now the whole of Europe was in recession, and businesses were closing all the time. Janet had not mentioned financial problems but she might be having them; a shop near hers which sold children's clothes had recently closed down; so had another selling gifts. In order to meet high rents, a business needed a big turnover and you had only to look in shops selling nonessentials to see that there was a lack of customers.

"Janet's got a lot of problems," Roger said. "And what about those men? The robbers? When does that bastard who attacked Hannah get out of prison?"

Veronica did not know, but they were both aware that he would not serve his full sentence; no one did, unless they were disruptive and violent in jail, and even then they seemed only to get a rap over the knuckles and a small loss of remission.

"At least Hannah won't run into him in Scotland," Roger said.

* * *

Janet's business worries increased after that evening. With every month her debt to the bank, which charged high interest, grew larger.

She had long since dismissed the assistant she had employed, part-time, when things were going well, and she had begun buying less expensive stock, but these economies were not enough. After little more than eighteen months of success and profit, she was now into serious loss and would be bankrupt if she kept on much longer.

She could accept that result. Then her debts would be wiped out while receivers dealt with her creditors. After that, if she found new backers, she could start again; such things were done all the time. But who would back her in another venture when she had failed in this one?

She struggled on for a few more months, hoping things would improve, the recession end. Then, after a painful meeting with the bank manager, she was forced to accept defeat. She ran a closing-down sale, slashing prices. Everything had to go.

"What will you do?" Veronica asked her. She was saddened by Janet's failure and understood the financial plight into which her friend had been cast. If the landlords had not been so greedy, pushing up their rents, it might not have happened. Janet was not a sole victim of the trend; well-established firms were collapsing in the town, which until now had always been quite prosperous, and houses in the area were repossessed when people could not meet their mortgage payments. At least Janet had not fallen that far behind, but how would she manage with no income?

"I don't know," said Janet. "I'll find something. You were right, Veronica. I was too pushy. It put people off."

Veronica now felt mortified at having uttered such a criticism.

"It wasn't that," she said. "It's the climate of the times."

A year ago, Roger might have found a niche for Janet in his office: nothing spectacular, just filing, and, if she could learn, word processing, or even something humbler on the production line, but not now, when he was having to cut down.

For the first time in her life, Janet saw that she might be rendered penniless, and, if she could not keep up her mortgage payments, lose her home. What good did it do, turning people out of their houses to cost the social services money for bed and breakfast accommodation, while the houses they had occupied now stood empty, waiting for a buyer who would not come? It was a mad situation. Surely some form of reduced payment or debt suspension could be arranged? And what about those like herself, encouraged to open small businesses with loans and then crippled by increased rents and taxes? She felt very bitter.

She could let a room, but that would mean sharing her house, her haven, with a stranger, someone it might be difficult to get rid of if it didn't work out, and she would lose her precious privacy.

She must find a job, but what could she do? She had had no career as a girl, marrying Derek when she was only nineteen and just out of secretarial college. What a mistake that had been. A girl should secure her own life before she threw her lot in with a man. Girls still did what she had done, or some of them: it depended on their progress at school and their home circumstances. The no-hopers leaped into early pairings and some had babies for want of anything to do. And to gain something—someone—to love, she thought. There were plenty of small prams being pushed round Norlington by mere children in a sort of game of living dolls. What about when the babies turned into demanding children, and rebellious teenagers?

Janet found the whole concept so depressing that she preferred not to think about it; anyway, she was powerless to affect the pattern. She tried to concentrate on her own problems and devise a program for the future. She was almost fifty; was she too old to embark on a training course of some kind? If not, what could she attempt?

While the last weeks of her lease ran out and she cut her prices more and more, selling up the remnants of her stock, her mind squirreled round the difficulties ahead.

"She should marry again," said Roger, who was finding Veronica's concern about her friend a bore, sympathetic though he was. "She's not bad looking, and she always ran that house well, you must admit. Derek didn't realize his luck."

Veronica looked round their untidy drawing room, where a dog lead lay on a chair, books from the library were stacked askew on a table and her gardening gloves and secateurs were on a bookcase.

"Comparisons are—" she began, and Roger caught hold of her and kissed her.

"You're much more fun," he said.

"I'm not facing penury," said Veronica, later. "I'd be pretty wretched, if I was."

"It all began with that business with Hannah," Roger said. "Look at the trail of damage those men caused. Janet and Derek would have stayed together, but for that, and Hannah would be married by now, and maybe had a baby. Janet would be a marvelous grandmother."

"Marriage isn't the remedy for everything—or everyone," said Veronica. "And I'm sure Janet wouldn't go into it again just to get a meal ticket. She's been much happier until the business all went wrong—more confident. Too confident, perhaps. But now she feels that she's a failure."

"It's not her fault. Why didn't they stick it out together? It wasn't as if either of them had found someone else. Has Derek got anyone now?" asked Roger.

"Who knows?"

"Janet hears from him. She told us so."

"Not often. He rings now and then and sends flowers on her birthday. Sort of conscience-assuagers, I think," said Veronica.

"Might they get together again?"

"I doubt it," Veronica stated, certain they would not. "I'll ask her over a good deal, to make sure she gets fed," she added.

"What if she has to give up the car?" said Roger, who did not want to be unkind but saw no joy in Janet becoming like a poor relation, recipient of patronage.

"If so, she'll have to catch the bus," she said. "But something may turn up before that happens. Not another husband, though. That's not the way to solve her problems, but it might follow one day."

Something did turn up.

While she ran the shop, Janet had become involved with Chamber of Commerce activities in the town and knew most of the other tradespeople, who saw that her business failure had been due to circumstances, not to any inadequacies of her own. Her character was beyond reproach and her appearance was good: she was well turned out and alert.

She was offered a job running the bar at The Swan, lunchtime and evening, to include weekends, with time off in lieu in the week.

She took it.

4.

Derek could not imagine Hannah's life. At Christmas and on his birthday she sent him a card, with a small impersonal gift, usually of Scottish origin—shortbread, a tweed tie, something easy to post. Meticulously, he wrote and thanked her by return, hoping she was well and happy. Beyond this, he could find nothing to say.

He knew that Janet had not been up to see her since their joint visit; she could not take enough time off from the shop; but soon after being made redundant, he had gone.

He had turned up without warning and uninvited, booking in at the hotel where he had stayed with Janet. Then he had driven over to her cottage. Hannah was out, and he had walked up and down, pacing by the loch, until he grew too cold and retreated to his car. Surely she was not away? He ran the engine to get warm, then sat listening to the radio and wondering what he hoped to achieve by coming here. After a while, tired by the long drive—he had started very early in the morning—he dozed off, and woke to find Hannah looming over the car, dressed in a black waxed jacket, a knitted cap pulled down over her ears, and holding in her hand a large and knobbly stick.

Derek had blinked himself awake and put the window down.

"Hullo," he said, and smiled.

"What are you doing here?" asked Hannah, her tone accusing.

"I came to see you," he replied.

"You didn't let me know," she said.

"No. I only decided suddenly," said Derek.

"I can't put you up." Hannah spoke abruptly.

Derek felt a little sick. There was no mistaking her hostility.

"That's all right. I've got a room at the hotel in Killiemanoch," he responded.

Wasn't she even going to ask him in? He waited.

Hannah had had a shock, seeing his car. She had not recognized it, since it was not the one he was driving when she first went to Scotland. Then, he had a Rover Montego; now he was driving a racy-looking Citroën. When she saw a strange car outside her cottage, with a man sitting in it whom she did not realize was her father, she was frightened. Now, as her fear abated, anger and sorrow filled her. Once, she would have been so happy to have seen him; instead, she felt a sort of fury: what did he mean by turning up unannounced, terrifying her and upsetting her calm, ordered existence? He was no longer the father she had loved and trusted; he was unreliable and, she realized, looking at him, shifty, for Derek wore a sheepish, hangdog expression as he smiled at her ingratiatingly, hoping she would thaw.

But she did not. She did not utter welcoming remarks, nor invite him in, and he did not dare suggest that he should enter her house.

"Will you come and have dinner with me at the hotel?" he asked, humbly, and Hannah knew she must accept. Derek offered to collect her, but she said that she would drive herself.

"In that?" he asked, looking at the old pickup in which she had arrived and which was parked in front of his Citroën.

It belonged to the reserve and as she had full use of it, she had sold her Metro.

"It's in good working order," she said. "I'll be along in time for dinner at half past seven. That's when they like you to eat at the Killiemanoch Arms."

He drove off, had a bath, and was on his third whisky in the bar when she came in, dressed in a gray flannel skirt and a green sweater. Her hair was drawn back with a green ribbon holding it in a ponytail, and her face was innocent of makeup. She looked about sixteen, he thought, but then, as they faced one another across the small table in the dining room, he saw something else in her regard that was not young at all.

He kept busily talking, ordering the meal and a bottle of burgundy to go with the roast beef. There was very little choice, but there were other diners, two farmers and an elderly lady and her son, who wore the kilt.

Hannah was hungry and ate every morsel on her plate, clearly enjoying it; when he had come up with Janet, over two years ago, she had merely picked at her food. She made an effort, asking him about his new house and his life in Petty Linton. He had not told her that he had lost his job, and did not do so now. He said he was thinking of joining a choral society and taking up golf, neither of them activities he had shown the slightest interest in before. Hannah expressed approval of these plans, which Derek had dreamed up on the spur of the moment to help the conversation and had not the least intention of implementing.

He asked her how she spent her leisure.

Well, there wasn't a lot of that, she said, as hers wasn't exactly a nine-to-five job, and she did what was required when

it was required. In winter, much of what she did was paper-
work, bringing records up to date. It was dark for so long
that she spent a lot of time indoors, and she read a great deal
then. She went skiing when there was enough snow, and in
summer there was sailing; she could use a little skiff owned
by the warden.

"Very healthy," Derek said. She certainly looked well; this
outdoor, lonely life suited her.

She left straight after dinner, saying she always got sleepy
at night because she rose so early in the morning. She kept
her distance, so that he could not kiss her, thanking him for
dinner like a polite child after a party. As she got into her old
pickup, he urged her to let him know if she needed anything—anything at all. She had only to ask, and if it lay in
his power, he would grant her request.

"There won't be anything," she said, and added, "You
think you saved my life, but you destroyed it," and he
wanted to cry out that he was not the guilty one; the blame
lay with Barry Carter, now in prison.

Hannah wept as she drove home. She had been cruel, but
his visit had upset her, reminding her of the fact that once he
had been her hero, someone she trusted more than any other
person, and it was his betrayal, as much as the attack by
Barry Carter, which had damaged her so badly. She had been
haunted by childhood memories of long walks with him, of
him making her a snowman in the year of the blizzard, of
him reading to her, playing chess with her. They had been a
pair, often, she had realized belatedly, shutting out her
mother, but it was her mother who had understood the extent of her pain, and without whom those dreadful days
would have been unendurable. She still thought about it, try
as she would to dismiss it from her mind. Others had
pointed out to her that the rape had taken only minutes of

her life, a fragment, but you could lose a limb, a life, in seconds: it was no argument.

Up here, in this wild country, she felt safe. No masked man would surprise her here, and no smooth seducer, either. She had control over her life in this place where there were few people, and those few were friendly enough but did not pry.

After she had driven off, Derek was wretched. He returned to the bar to consume more whisky. He had had most of the burgundy; Hannah only drank a glassful.

He left early the next morning. There was no point in staying any longer.

"What would Derek say if he could see Janet in the Swan bar?" said Veronica one evening, several weeks after Janet had started her new job. "He was always so determinedly upwardly mobile."

"Mobile from where?"

"His nice old father was a bookie," said Veronica. "I'm not supposed to tell anyone. Janet swore me to secrecy when I met the old boy. He used to stay at The Elms sometimes, but Derek didn't want him on display. He made a lot of money and sent Derek to public school to acquire some polish."

"Well, it worked," said Roger. "He ended up quite glossy. I wish they were still up the road. Derek could be relied on for a few supportive gestures and no interference in things he didn't understand. Not like the Poulsons."

The Poulsons were the new occupants of The Elms. They had come from London and took living in the country seriously, even complaining about the smell of silage on the wind and the braying of Mr. Micklethwaite's donkey down by the church. They walked the local footpaths and found fault with the stiles because moss grew and made them slippery, or there was mud under them where booted walkers trod. In green wellingtons, with his Alsatian dog at his heel, Mr. Poulson, an investment broker, paced the countryside while his wife was taking what she called "horse-riding" lessons at a stables in the next village.

"What else would you ride but a horse?" Roger had wanted to know, on first hearing her use this expression.

"Don't be snobbish," Veronica had rebuked him. "Who knows, we may be cantering round the fields together, when she's learned."

Veronica often rode the girls' ponies, which spent most of the year in the fields round the Manor. It had become too expensive to keep a horse of her own.

"You might take her horse at livery, when she gets one," Roger said. "Could be profitable, and give you free rides. Things have swung too far round," he added. "People who belong in the country and know that cocks crow and muck stinks have moved to the towns, and townies reared on hygiene and recycled effluent come to the country and swoon at the sight of a beetle."

"I can't argue with that opinion," said Veronica, who liked to challenge Roger's statements. "Streetlights and speed limits and No Parking signs. That's what they want. The Poulsons should be living in Norlington, in one of those lovely Georgian houses in the square."

"He's made a bomb. Good for him," said Roger. "I hope he hangs on to it, but I guess it's all paper money and he's living on tick. Derek was more soundly based."

"The bookie father took his chances," said Veronica.

"But he hedged his bets," said Roger. "I called on Derek the other day. Did I tell you?"

"You know you didn't. Well, spill it. How is he? Has he got a woman?"

"A pale girl was there," said Roger. "Something to do

with the washing, she said. A laundress." He laughed. "A nice girl. Woman. Thirtyish. Seemed quite at home. They were in the kitchen having coffee when I turned up."

"Did you warn him you were coming?"

"No. I went in on the spur of the moment, after I'd been to see a man in Staines."

"And how is he?"

"Different," Roger said. "He's lost his sheen."

Derek had been startled when Roger arrived at his house in Petty Linton. Ten minutes earlier, he and Angela would have been caught out. She had been collecting his ironing for some time now, and for several months they had been going to bed together when she made her weekly call.

It had begun when, one week, she had telephoned to say she could not return his shirts because her daughter was ill and she could not leave the house. He had volunteered to collect them, had arrived and rung the bell and been admitted by a wasted man in a wheelchair. This was Stephen Battersby, her husband, victim of a hit-and-run road accident which had left him paralyzed. The driver, Derek learned, had been caught and charged with careless driving. He was drunk, it seemed, but by the time the police traced him, it was too late for a blood test to be relevant. He had been fined three hundred pounds and had his license endorsed.

Stephen could look after their small daughter, Pippa, age six, some of the time—and she him, while Angela was out—but not for long: Pippa was too young, and her present ailment, a major stomach upset, was too difficult for him to manage. Derek had delivered Angela's ironing bundles to several other customers to help her through this awkward patch, and the next time she came round, they talked about her problems. Stephen was still waiting for compensation for his accident; with luck, when at last it was paid, they would be able to move into a properly adapted bungalow and have more of the things that would make life easier for all of them. They were being looked after by a specialist lawyer, having transferred from another one who seemed in no hurry to effect a settlement. The driver had, at least, been insured, said Angela. Stephen's injuries had made him very bad-tempered. Angela tried to bear his moods with patience, but one Tuesday, lonely and sad, she had burst into tears in Derek's kitchen and the rest had followed.

She would never leave Stephen, she insisted. She loved him—the old Stephen, who sometimes appeared; the new one, a bitter, angry man, was the result of his frustration and the drugs he was receiving. But he was impotent, too. Derek's small kindness to Angela had been enough to unstop the plug on her own misery. As the weeks went by, Derek had grown fond of her. She was much younger than he was, almost a daughter, in fact. He looked forward to her visits. They did not always go to bed; some weeks she was short of time; but there were a few minutes just to hold each other close, achieve some human contact. This hadn't happened in his own marriage, Derek realized, nor in his short affair with Barbara. He learned a lot from Angela.

The nature of their relationship had been obvious to Roger. There was a calm, relaxed atmosphere between them, an easiness which had been lacking at The Elms. Perceiving it had made Roger aware of the difference. They were comfortable together: Janet and Derek were not; it was as simple as that.

Angela had left soon after Roger arrived, and Derek had explained her circumstances.

"Poor Angela," said Veronica, when Roger told her. "It sounds as if she's got the short straw there. I hope Derek's making the world of difference to her life."

"I rather think he may be," Roger said.

"I wonder if her husband knows."

"Might suspect something. Wouldn't dare face it, I'd guess," said Roger.

"You don't think she's got something going with all her gentlemen clients? That she's not really a laundress at all?"

"Well—who can say? And does it matter?" Roger said, and both of them burst out laughing.

As long as we still laugh, we're all right, thought Veronica, who knew that she was one of the lucky ones. She didn't think Roger had ever been unfaithful to her, but if he was, she didn't want to know; it would be her fault, because she would have failed him in some way.

It was depressing to think about Derek, Janet and Hannah, once a family, now divided and each operating alone. She shivered. How quickly things could change, just on the chance of a single night's events.

5.

Angela thought Derek's house a very impersonal place. It had most modern aids to living but was furnished in a functional way. A sweep round, a spray with Pledge, and it would be cleaned in a flash, unlike her own untidy home. She wondered what his contract cleaners found to do on their visits, for he was very tidy, did not smoke, and had no dog strewing hairs around.

Stephen had a computer which he used for writing letters and he played computer games to keep his mind alert. Angela had no time to learn how to work it, but Pippa could; she and her father spent hours together playing with it. It kept them occupied while Angela ironed, listening to the radio. It grew so hot and steamy in the small room she used that she would end up wearing just her bra, too warm in a shirt or sweater.

How long would all this go on? Sometimes she grew despairing, though help came from various sources. A nurse bathed Stephen regularly; the doctor called. Handles had been fitted to walls, and other aids supplied to aid mobility and help her move him round, but when he was difficult and sulky she sometimes felt like screaming at him. She wasn't like the devoted heroines shown in television documentaries who rose nobly to the challenge of adversity and never seemed to lose their temper. She longed for the day when the insurance money would arrive and they could move to the West Country near her family, and be less alone. She seldom looked beyond that goal, for years of effort would still lie ahead.

By now she had worked up quite a clientele. Most of the ironing she did was shirts, but there was an old lady who still slept in embroidered linen sheets, much patched and darned, once part of a prewar wedding trousseau, and other customers who had elaborate tablecloths and napkins, kept for special occasions. I ought to be a laundry, do the whole thing, she thought, when consulted by a caterer who wanted her to wash the table linen used for functions. Angela had to turn her down because the work would be spasmodic and, when it came, might overwhelm her, making it difficult for her to satisfy her regular customers. She didn't want to spend the rest of her life doing this, but saw no other way of making ends meet at the moment. When the money came, everything would change. Perhaps even Stephen's temper would improve. She had meant her marriage vows, and this was a "for worse" situation. She kept reminding herself of how restricted Stephen's life was, how little he could do, and it was only natural that he should take his frustrations out on her. When they moved, things would improve. Sometimes she fantasized about living in a cottage in a village, where she would take in bed and breakfast guests. She dreamed of roses round the door, Pippa skipping down the road to the little school, Stephen in a powered chair able to propel himself around and make friends with all the locals, herself cheerfully hanging out the visitors' sheets. Then she would think of rain, mists, long winters with the wind blowing in from the sea, no guests, and herself and Stephen confined beneath a thatched roof with no respite from one another. And she imagined the guests being subjected to hostile responses from Stephen, who would not be a jolly host.

He had never been jolly. Before the accident he had been a lean, interesting man who taught science at a comprehensive school and went mountain climbing. What had drawn them to each other? She had loved him, hadn't she? He had been witty and amusing, and a tender lover. Now he was none of those things.

Derek was sturdy and calm. He was not amusing; he was not witty; and she knew he was not in love with her, as Stephen had been. But he was alone, and he had been kind to her. Perhaps he loved her, just a little, and she needed his affection. As a lover, he was not in the same league as Stephen had once been. He seemed rather out of practice, and was shy at first, and hasty, but he was improving. She began to wonder if poor technique had been a problem in his marriage.

He never talked about his former wife. There was a daughter; she had asked him once if he had any children. There were no photographs on display, but he had one of Hannah as a child of twelve in his wallet.

"She lives in Scotland now," he had said. "She's keen on birds."

He did not want to talk about her, and Angela did not want to talk about Stephen. She drew comfort from the actual bulk of Derek and the fact that he was older. Perhaps it was incestuous, she thought, like going to bed with her father. She giggled at the idea and would not, at first, tell Derek what had made her laugh. When she did, he did not find it funny, and she hoped he did not feel insulted, but Derek himself was wondering if part of her appeal for him was that he felt paternally protective towards her. He wished that he could wave a wand and make her problems vanish, restore Stephen to health and his earlier disposition or, if that was asking too much, at least remove his pain and bring him acceptance of his condition.

You could put few things right for other people. A donation to a charity could salve your conscience, and money could make hardship easier to endure, improving small things, but major calamities could not be ignored.

He knew that his affair with Angela would end one day. He thought he almost loved her, but perhaps what he felt was only grateful pity.

When he lost his job, the wise course would have been to cut down on costs. He dismissed the contract cleaner, and he should have ended his arrangement with Angela, but he could not bring himself to do so. She needed the money, and he needed the human contact. He let it ride while he did some consultancy work, but soon that ceased, too.

Meanwhile, after his visit to Scotland, he had been brooding about Barry Carter, who would be released from jail before too long, and after Roger's visit his thoughts began to crystalize.

It was Roger who told him that Clarice had failed and that Janet was working at The Swan.

"Oh," said Derek. "What a comedown." Then he added, "I thought the shop was a success."

"It was," said Roger, and explained about the climate of the times. "It's difficult for a middle-aged woman to get work," he added. "She took out a loan on the house to stave off bankruptcy and she must keep up the payments, so any job's a good one, in her situation."

"I'm glad you told me," Derek said.

"I'd have thought she would," said Roger.

Derek thought so too, and he was hurt because he had heard something so important in this manner.

"We don't communicate a lot," he said, trying to sound as if it did not matter. "After all, it's not as though Hannah was a child and we had to pass her to and fro. That keeps couples in touch, I imagine. Perhaps I'll come down sometime and take a drink off her at The Swan. How's she doing there?"

"Oh—all right, I suppose. It's very different from running her own business, though. I imagine she was offered it because she looks good and can assume command," said Roger. "People know her, in Norlington. It may lead to something else more suitable, in time. Anyone starting up a new project might think of her. Much better than some young chick with small children posing problems."

Like Angela, thought Derek.

They could have survived mere robbery. If Morris and Carter had simply taken what they wanted from the house and gone, even if they had destroyed furniture, messed the place up—he knew thieves sometimes urinated and defecated in the course of a break-in, like dogs leaving their mark—he and Janet, and Hannah too, would have recovered. The house could have been cleansed and their lives could have returned to normal. Detective Inspector Brooks had told him that sometimes, after a burglary, householders, and particularly women, felt violated and had to move, though there were counselors to help them overcome this feeling.

"It's a sort of rape," said Brooks, and sighed. "Years ago," he added, "burglars burgled and that was it. They didn't mug old ladies and rape any female in sight." Some of the violence was due to drugs, drink, or even glue-sniffing, but much of it was simply the degradation of the age, the absence of a moral lead from all the sources which had once provided such a framework. This was the grab-it-now era. He often grew depressed about the rising tide of crime and the inability of the police to stem it. Little dabs and temporary containments were effected here and there as villains were caught and taken out of circulation, but all too soon they were back on the streets again, ready to commit new offenses. In the case of rapists, even in the rare instances where they received treatment while in prison, they often struck again within days of their release.

Derek had remembered this conversation, and since his visit to Scotland, he had slowly developed the intention to do something about the particular man who had destroyed Hannah's life, and, for that action, been inadequately punished.

He had tried to banish from his mind the events of that dreadful night, but now he did his best to recall them, seeing again the first masked intruder enter the room, feeling again the blow as Morris hit him and then knocked the television remote control from his hand. This was obviously a man who meant serious business and would use force to obtain what he wanted, and Derek had tried to protect Hannah by saying that the house was empty. At first, he had even blamed Hannah for not hearing the men enter the house in time to telephone the police from upstairs. If she hadn't been listening to music, and if he had not had the television on, there could have been some audible warning. When it was discovered that the men had let themselves in by unlocking the back door, he had blamed Janet for not leaving the key inside and going out of the house through the front door, but they hardly ever did this, any of them. The men would have got in anyway, but they might have made more noise, and with less element of surprise, Derek might have grabbed the poker or thrown a chair at them, gained some advantage.

And I'd have been shot for my pains, his rational self observed. Maybe, but I'd at least have tried to protect my own, he thought. Primitive man did that: men had always fought for hearth and home: that was what wars were about. True, there was an aggressor, but there was also a defender. He thought of moats and battlements, boiling oil, all the means used through the ages to ward off attack. Turning the other cheek, the soft answer, did not work. If he had died trying to save Hannah, even though her fate might have been un-changed, she would have known he had done his best and her trust would not have been betrayed. To her, he would have been a hero.

And it was always possible that the fact of having killed him might have made the two assailants back off and leave her unharmed.

Or they might have killed her in case she could identify them, though that was scarcely likely, with their masks.

Derek went over and over it, playing different scripts with alternative endings in his mind. You could, with hindsight, select any scenario you chose, appropriate to your mood. If he had his chance again, he would play it differently. There was that moment in her room, when the men had put down the knife and the gun in order to tie up their victims; then, if he had acted, he might have saved them both. Morris had been holding him, but Derek could have tried a kick or jabbed his elbow back, hit Morris in the groin. Hannah, though, had struggled until she was overpowered.

But I'm no James Bond, thought Derek. I might have failed.

You would have tried, his other self kept repeating.

One Tuesday night he asked Angela what her father would do if, while he was held at gunpoint, someone tried to rape her. He knew her father was a journalist working for a provincial newspaper in the West Country.

Angela looked astonished at the question but she said at

once, "He'd try to help me, if he could. Perhaps he'd try to talk the rapist round."

"Say there were two men," said Derek. "One with the gun, the other the rapist."

"He'd have a go," said Angela. "I don't know how, but he wouldn't just stand there. Why do you ask?"

"He'd die in the attempt?" said Derek, not answering her question.

"Probably. He wouldn't be able to bear it."

"He wouldn't think that by not resisting, at least your life would be spared?"

"What sort of life would it be, after that?" asked Angela simply. "I'd never recover from it."

"But you wouldn't be scarred—I mean, he wouldn't mark your face—say you escaped real injury."

"But I would be scarred, invisibly," said Angela. "Wounded forever." She looked at him across the table. "It's the most terrible thing, for a woman, apart from someone hurting her child, that is." Angela drank some coffee. "Of course, in our grandmother's day—yours, not mine, perhaps—brides were raped all the time on their wedding nights. Lots of them didn't know what to expect. It still happens in marriage, though it's now a crime. My father's done some pieces on it, but it's mostly women journalists who write about that sort of thing. Why are you asking about all this?"

"Oh—I knew someone whose daughter was raped," said Derek.

"By someone she knew, or a stranger?"

"Someone who was doing a burglary," said Derek.

"And they had a gun, and the father couldn't save her?"

"Yes, that's about the size of it," said Derek.

"Oh, poor girl," said Angela.

"She tried to commit suicide," said Derek. "Luckily, she failed."

"She may come to terms with it one day," said Angela. "But she'll never forget it."

"What if it had been someone she knew? Would that have made it any better?"

"You mean a date rape? It might be a cleaner business," said Angela. "He wouldn't be a stinking drug addict who'd pounced on her in the street. But what about trust? If she let things go a certain distance and then said no, he must listen to her."

"But a woman doesn't always mean it, when she says no," Derek insisted.

"Oh yes, she does," said Angela. "You sound like one of those judges who say it wasn't a very bad rape, or, if the girl shows courage in the witness box and keeps her self-control, that she can't have been badly affected. I wonder what those judges' wives and daughters say to them, when they've made such a comment. In fact, I'd guess their wives are in sexual prisons with cold, selfish men who've as good as raped them. Consenting rape, because they've signed themselves over."

He had never seen her so animated. Her cheeks were flushed and her blue eyes shone. He wanted to make love to her all over again.

"I suppose you're right," he said weakly, instead.

"I know I am," said Angela, getting up to leave. "That girl—your friend's daughter. There are people to help her, you know. She must have been told about them. The police have counselors, and there's the Rape Crisis Centre—I think that's what it's called—it'd be in the phone book. I believe some victims work there—they'd be good at helping others. Perhaps you could suggest it to your friend."

"I will," said Derek. "Thanks."

At that moment he made his decision. He would avenge Hannah.

And Angela drove off, suspecting that Derek's daughter had been raped and that he had failed to try to save her.

PART THREE

Now

1.

Barry Carter's death was the only just retribution for what he had done to Hannah.

As soon as Derek came to this conclusion, he felt an immense sense of relief, as though a burden that had pressed on him for years had gone. He would be acting to correct the ineffective punishment the legal system had thought adequate. Violent men who attacked total strangers, raping and murdering them—sometimes both—should be locked up for life, not released to hurt and kill again.

He spent some time in the local library, reading up on procedures. Those granted parole—as happened to most offenders given a life sentence—were liable to rearrest if they committed even a small misdemeanor, but those who had served their full sentence, which was cut by at least a third of what had actually been given, were considered to have paid their debt and were not supervised in any way. What was more, if they reoffended, the jury were not allowed to know about their past record. The law had lost its way, thought Derek, more determined than before to carry out his plan.

How could he find out where Barry Carter was being held,

and when he would be freed? He must track him, pursue him, somehow contrive to do away with him.

He thought about ringing Detective Inspector Brooks, asking him straight out when Carter would be released from prison and where he would be living then, but abandoned the idea. Even if Brooks would tell him, he would remember the conversation when Carter was found dead, and might make the connection—in fact, he would be stupid not to do so, and Brooks was not a stupid man. Probably the police sat on such information in case a reception committee of disgruntled victims waited, vigilante fashion, outside the prisons to greet the malefactors.

He had not kept any of the newspaper reports about the case; they made him feel uncomfortable. Once the trial was over, he had decided that the whole business was best buried and forgotten. He wondered if Janet had filed any cuttings away; she had read the papers assiduously, shaking her head about inaccuracies and flights of journalistic fantasy. The coverage had been extensive. In court, Carter had admitted nothing, so Hannah had had to give evidence, and, in effect, was put on trial too. Another notorious case, where the victim had suffered a more physically damaging assault, had attracted the headlines at much the same time; at that trial, the men had pleaded guilty and she had not had to appear, but the same irrational form of sentence was imposed and the judge's comments drew an outraged response from women's groups and others who were shocked at such an attitude. The other case diverted some attention from Hannah's, but the tabloids had not ignored her and a meal had been made of her supposedly anonymous ordeal.

Would one of the journalists so interested then know Carter's whereabouts, and the date of his release, or the address of his family? Derek seemed to remember a mother going to court, being led away in tears after the verdict. A journalist would know about the mother; that was human interest, which they were all so keen on.

Assuming he could trace Barry Carter, how could he be killed?

Derek's first thought was to shoot him down, like a mad animal—just fell him in the street with a gun, as happened all too often to innocent victims of violent crime, and the police. It seemed the most obvious way, but there might be others. If he trailed him to a station, could he push him under a train? Or run him over? Or could he stab him with a knife?

Such ideas were too chancy, carrying great risk of being caught himself, and of failure. Derek soon dismissed them. It would have to be a gun. Guns could be legally bought. Roger Ford had a shotgun for shooting rabbits; it was licensed, and locked up securely. How did you buy a revolver? Were there rules about it? Derek thought that the vendor might have to comply with some form of registration when he made a sale. Perhaps the buyer had to have a license. He must find out. Villains seemed to have no difficulty acquiring weapons; for him it might not be so easy. He must look into the regulations, learn to shoot, and find Barry Carter: quite a program, but it had given him a goal.

Newspapers retained back numbers, piles of issues which could be consulted in their offices. Derek thought about doing this to track down Carter's mother, then wondered if he would have to sign, certify what he had read. He could use a false name, but even so, he would have left a trail which might be discovered when Barry Carter died.

He decided to visit Janet, ostensibly to ask how she was but really to find out if she had kept the cuttings. He would not warn her he was coming; she might refuse to see him. He would pretend to be passing through on business; she'd be sure to ask him in—after all, they weren't enemies—and then he'd lead the conversation round to Hannah.

He was sleeping badly. He had nightmares about the attack, and other dreams where Hannah was in danger up in Scotland, menaced by furious birds that looked like vultures, threatened by tidal waves sweeping in from the sea loch. He was sure it was because now he was consciously thinking about her traumatic experience instead of expelling it from his mind. He suspected that throughout his marriage his tactic had been to blot out anything painful or unpleasant. Accepting this, for the first time for years he remembered the severe late miscarriage which Janet had suffered; today, it would be called a premature birth. She had never seen the small body; there had been no funeral, nothing tangible to mourn.

He had grieved for the tiny son who had never drawn breath, but he had not made that clear to Janet; they had not talked about it, nor wept together, as people nowadays were encouraged to do. They had not shared that blow; nor had they shared the recent dreadful damage done to Hannah.

Thoughts like this made Derek uncomfortable. It was one thing to reflect on Hannah and the vengeance Carter deserved; quite another to dwell on personal guilt.

He rang Janet's bell at five o'clock one afternoon.

He did not know what hours she worked; The Swan might open its bar all day but the probability was that it closed during the afternoon, so he decided to call before what might be the evening shift.

His reasoning was sound, and she was at home.

When she opened the door and saw him on the step, she was astonished.

"Derek—oh!" she exclaimed, taking a step back and clutch-

90

ing her front door, rather a nice mahogany one, mass produced but in the best of taste and matching the others in the row.

Derek had rehearsed his speech, but now that it was time to make it, he felt nervous. He licked his dry lips and began.

"I was passing through and thought I'd see if you were in," he said. "Roger told me you'd given up the shop." Out of curiosity, he had been past it and saw that it was now a card shop, selling birthday and anniversary cards, toy bears and other cuddly animals.

"Yes. Well, it gave me up," said Janet. "The recession." She took a breath. "Do you want to come in?"

It was not an enthusiastic invitation, but it was the best that she could manage, taken by surprise like this.

"Thanks," said Derek.

He felt awkward as he crossed the threshold of her house. He tried not to peer round inquisitively, but experienced a pang when he saw, hanging on the wall opposite the steep flight of narrow stairs, a Peter Scott print of wild geese in flight which had hung on the landing at The Elms.

"Maybe that had an effect on Hannah—inspired this bird thing of hers," he said, with a half laugh.

He's embarrassed to be here, thought Janet, who was feeling nothing except amazement. She had not seen him for nearly two years.

"Maybe," she said, but it was the urge for flight itself which had influenced Hannah, not the birds. "Would you like some tea?" she asked. "Or coffee?" He was not overfond of tea, she remembered.

"Coffee, please," he said. "Black." She might have forgotten that he never took milk, even at breakfast.

"Come and sit down, then."

She led the way into a living room which stretched the full length of the house. At the garden end was a small round table with four chairs tucked under it. These had not been at The Elms. Janet indicated that he should sit on the sofa, which he recognized, still in its Elms covers of apricot rough silk-type fabric, and disappeared into the small kitchen which led off from the dining area.

He looked round, avidly curious, recognizing other items from The Elms, including the curtains. It was oddly unsettling to see them in this very different room.

Meeting Janet again was strange, too. She was so familiar, yet unknown. Perhaps she had always been unknown and alien; she had certainly been remote. When she returned carrying a cafetière of fresh coffee on a tray, with a cup and saucer from their Crown Derby set, he felt a pang of nostalgia. She was still a perfectionist; no instant coffee in a mug for Janet.

She had put on weight and her skin seemed darker, almost ruddy. Could she possibly be drinking? It might be an occupational hazard in her job. He pushed the thought away, replacing it with the positive acknowledgment that she was smartly dressed and her hair, rinsed a sandy shade that was lighter than her natural color, looked good. She had not dyed it before, but he supposed she was going gray and wanted to keep that hidden. She was wearing a straight black skirt and an emerald-green shirt. The color was too bright, he thought; Janet had always dressed well, but not in brilliant colors.

"I see there's another business where you ran Clarice," he said. "Cards."

"Yes. And they pay less rent than I did," Janet said. "Ridiculous, isn't it? I was forced out because of higher rents and then they were lowered. It doesn't make sense."

Janet had heard from Veronica that Roger had been to see Derek. That must be when he had learned about the collapse of Clarice.

"I'm sorry it didn't work out," he said. "I hope you're managing."

"Oh yes." Janet would not let him know that she was still struggling to break even. "I'm working at The Swan now. Did you know that?" Of course he did; Roger would have told him.

"Yes," he said. "How's it going?"

"It's a job," she said, plunging down the filter on the coffee pot. She poured him out a cup. "I'm not joining you," she added. "I've just had some tea, and I'll have to leave for work soon. How about you?"

"Oh, I've settled down quite well," said Derek. "I was made redundant, but I've been doing some consultancy work and I'm looking into the possibility of setting up on my own. I've got several ideas."

"I see." Roger had not told her this. Perhaps he did not know about it.

Derek waited anxiously in case she asked more questions about his life in Petty Linton. Had Roger mentioned Angela? But she was silent, and at last he dared to mention Hannah.

"I speak to her most weeks," Janet said. She always rang on Sundays and usually Hannah was in the cottage, but she had recently acquired an answering machine and now seemed to use that as a barrier. Janet suspected she was sometimes sitting there, listening to the caller and not responding. "She sounds all right," Janet added. "As all right as she'll ever be. I don't think she's actively unhappy anymore, and that's a big advance."

She waited for Derek to say that he had visited her. Hannah had told her that she had not been very kind to him and felt bad about it, but she couldn't help it. He'd given her a fright, appearing without warning, uninvited.

"Perhaps he thought you wouldn't want to see him, if he said that he was coming," Janet had said.

"And he'd have been right," said Hannah.

But Derek wasn't going to tell her. Perhaps he thought she didn't know: so many things unspoken lay between them, so many near-truths, incomplete communications. It was too late now to change things. There he sat, bulky and impassive, apparently emotionless, and never to be forgiven.

"That man Carter will be out of prison soon," Derek said. "Ready to go and attack some other girl."

"I suppose he will be," Janet replied. "Martin Brooks— the detective inspector, you remember—he's a superintendent now—comes into the bar sometimes." Brooks had said he still thought about the case and the wretched sentence, which had made a mockery of the police as well as being an insult to the victim. "He'll know, I expect."

"Where's Carter now? I suppose he's in some smart open prison?" Derek asked.

"No. I think he's in Wandsworth. I've got a feeling he's been there all the time, but I don't really know. Or perhaps it's Wormwood Scrubs. I'm not sure."

"What happens when he gets out? I suppose he'll have to live somewhere while he goes thieving."

"That poor mother of his will take him in, I expect," said Janet. "Mothers always do pick up the pieces."

"Did you keep any newspaper cuttings about it?" Derek said. "I remember you collected them, at the time."

"Yes. I thought Hannah might need them one day, to lay her ghosts," answered Janet.

"Would you let me look at them?" Derek made it sound as if he'd just had the idea, instead of it being the reason for his visit. "I've got a few ghosts to lay, too," he said.

After all, he thought, he had been hit quite hard, and trussed up and gagged.

"All right," said Janet, thinking quickly. She did not really want to lend them to him, but nor did she want him coming back to read them another day. "I've got to leave in a few minutes. You can read them here, then let yourself out. Would that suit you?"

"Yes," he said. "Thanks."

She found the large leather-bound album and put it on the round table.

"There you are," she said. "Please make sure the snib catches on the door when you go."

Five minutes later she was ready to leave the house, in a scarlet coat with a wool throw over her shoulder. Though it was March, and spring would soon be here, it was still cold at night.

He thought about inviting her to a meal later, but of course that wouldn't do: the bar would stay open late and then she would want to hurry home to bed.

Janet always walked to The Swan. She went past his smart Citroën; it was quite a racy car, in contrast to the Montego he had run before. She had no qualms about leaving him in the house. She did not hate him. She felt nothing at all.

After Janet had gone, Derek found it difficult to face the task that he had set himself.

He poured himself another cup of coffee—it was still warm enough—and drank it, sitting in the empty room. Nothing was out of place; there was not even a newspaper, folded neatly, on a coffee table. Perhaps Janet did not take a paper now; plenty of people didn't, relying on the radio and television for their information. He saw that the chair covers were a little worn: they had been in use at The Elms for a long time before Janet bought this house. If they had all still been together, these would have been replaced by now. The paintwork was fresh, but then the house was new; Janet was, he thought, its first owner. When he had finished his coffee, he took the tray out to the kitchen and rinsed the cup and cafetière, leaving them on the drainer. Janet must find this very small after the large kitchen at The Elms, but it was well planned and there was even a slim dishwasher installed beside the sink unit, part of the builders' package, no doubt. One spotless tea towel, scarcely creased, hung on a rail. Did Janet never fall below her own high standards? He sighed, and returned to the album on the table. How like Janet to arrange it so neatly.

Sitting there, it took him a few minutes to feel able to turn the pages, and then he saw it all: cuttings clipped from broadsheets and from tabloids, some short reports in chilling terms, others sprawled across the page with startling headlines and emotive phrases in the text. Derek's eye ran down the lines of print: it was unreal, as if he were reading fiction. Because Hannah's identity was supposed to be protected, there was no photograph of her, but there was one of Carter's mother, with Janet in the background. STORY OF TWO MOTHERS, said the caption, with a paragraph about the crime and advice that there was more to learn on an inner page.

One paper featured Mrs. Carter, who some years earlier had separated from her second husband. She had said that she would stick by Barry, who was her only child. He had served several prison sentences for theft. A doomed youth, thought Derek, maybe wicked to the core. Mrs. Carter's address was not given but her first name was Noreen, and at the time of the trial she lived near Willesden; one of the reporters had lured her into saying she hoped Barry would be sent to Wormwood Scrubs because it was not far from where she lived so visiting would be easy.

This was very useful information, always assuming that Noreen Carter still lived at the same address. He could look for her in the telephone directory, and if that failed, he could consult the voters' registers for the area. Of course, she might by now be dead, or married again, or have left the country. Carter had not been living with her when he was arrested; he had been living rough, it seemed, after splitting up with his girlfriend.

That accounted for the dreadful unwashed smell: Hannah had mentioned it, had said she could not get it out of her nostrils. There would be no bad smells in her Scottish retreat, unless bird droppings gave off a stench.

He read the paragraphs about the girlfriend. *Did her rejection of him lead to rape?* asked one paper. Her name was Sandra Mason and she was quoted as saying that he had shown no violence towards her, though he had often been moody and sometimes did not speak for days.

She might know his mother's address.

Odd that Noreen and Barry shared the same surname when he was the son of her first husband: perhaps the stepfather had adopted him, or at least given him his name. It happened sometimes.

Now Derek had two lines, however vague, to follow. How much time had he got in which to pursue them? Would Carter be released in weeks, or months?

There was no need for haste; vengeance must be carefully planned, not bungled by impatient action. Even when the man came out, Derek, assuming he could find him, would be able to choose his moment for revenge. There would be a certain satisfaction in deciding how to act, when to pounce, like a cat playing with a mouse, only this mouse would not know a cat was stalking him.

Derek began his search with the telephone directory. There were a good many Carters to choose from, but no Noreens: that would be too easy, and nowadays women living alone were advised to have themselves listed under their initials. He developed a technique, crying out brightly, "Noreen Carter?" when a woman answered, but always he drew blank. To vary things, he decided to try to trace the girlfriend, Sandra Mason: she might know where Noreen Carter lived, or had lived. There were plenty of Masons in the book, but there might not be so many Sandras. On the other hand, the one he sought might not be on the telephone, or might live where there was a pay phone shared by several tenants. The same thing might apply to Noreen Carter.

As the weeks went by, he kept ringing round, doing several calls each evening, and at the same time he joined a shooting club in order to learn how to use a weapon, and to discover the restrictions on obtaining one legitimately, which he soon found were stringent.

Then one night he struck gold.

His routine when a man answered was to ask to speak to Noreen Carter, or, if he had rung a Mason number, Sandra Mason. This worked well; in most cases the man simply replied, with varying degrees of civility, that he had got the wrong number as no one of that name lived there. Until the evening when a man said, "Who wants her?"

For a moment Derek almost forgot the story he had fabricated.

"She's won a prize," he said, his voice enthusiastic, but then he was imparting good news. "A voucher for a hundred pounds' worth of goods at Marks and Spencer's."

He had thought this out. If he hit the jackpot, he would offer bait, and who could resist a free shopping spree?

"That's great," said the voice. "You'd better tell her yourself."

Seconds later, Derek was speaking to Sandra Mason, but was she the right Sandra? He told her about her good fortune in winning a Spot-the-Difference competition, and she said she hadn't entered one; there must be some mistake.

"You are Sandra Mason of—" and Derek glibly read her address out of the directory.

"Yes."

"Well, you're one of the lucky winners. Perhaps your mother or some friend entered your name," he said smoothly, ready for this one, and now surmising that Sandra Mason was an honest person or she would have made no disclaimer.

"Well, maybe," she said. She still sounded doubtful, but she accepted his story. He would not have minded if she had not, because he had traced her, or someone with the same name.

He suggested that they meet at a hotel near Heathrow, where he would hand the voucher over, and proposed lunch in three days' time, or, if that was too difficult, dinner one evening. She said lunch would suit her better.

So she wasn't working. Derek did not think she would recognize him; she had not been in court and his photograph had not been in the press except in long shot, rather blurred. She would expect to see a stranger.

She rang off in a state of excitement, and Derek was excited too: he had put things in motion. Now he would have to trap her into revealing what she knew about Barry and his family. Always assuming she was the right Sandra Mason.

2.

She would be young: Derek knew that much, watching for Sandra Mason to come into the hotel lobby. He sat beside a potted palm, scrutinizing all the women entering the place, watching for one to look around expectantly.

Some of the papers had carried a shot of her, taken in the street. The reporters must have hung around her doorstep, Derek thought, waiting for a "human interest" opportunity, when probably she wanted to forget all about her liaison with Barry Carter. He had extracted several cuttings from Janet's album and had had them photocopied on a good machine which made the faces at least as clear as they were in the originals. Then he had posted them back to Janet, explaining that he had decided he wanted to keep some reference to the raid and apologizing for his action. He enclosed, also, a check for fifteen thousand pounds, saying that it was from his severance pay and he wanted her to have it as a cushion in her present difficulties. This left him with enough to see his plan through; he had investments he could sell, and the house, if necessary. It was conscience money, he had thought, posting off the check. It would buy her time, or help with debts.

He had made copies of the photograph of Noreen Carter,

showing Janet in the background; it was repeated in several papers, each exposure varying a little.

When Sandra arrived, he did not recognize her from the black and white print in the newspaper. She had thin, stick-like legs, and she arrived wearing black leggings and a frill of a skirt just visible below a long black sweater. She had on a maroon velvet hat with a turned-back brim beneath which emerged a blonde fringe. No other hair was visible. She was pretty, he saw, surprised. The photograph had not prepared him for that; it had shown shoulder-length straggly hair; but the thin nose was the same, and the large eyes with straight, finely plucked brows above them.

Derek was holding a green Marks and Spencer's bag as a form of identification, and the girl came towards him, some-what hesitantly.

Derek stood up.

"Miss Sandra Mason?" he said.

"Yes," she said, and went on, "I still don't understand about this. My mum didn't put an entry in, and nor did any of my friends. What paper did you say it was in?"

Derek had carefully avoided doing that. He went on glibly, "Well, the form arrived, with your name and address on it. I shouldn't query it, if I were you." How easy it was to spin a tale, once you began.

"As long as no one else comes along and says it's really theirs," she said. Then she smiled, and he warmed to her. She was a nice girl who had escaped the clutches of a pervert, and she was getting a free lunch and a present of a hundred pounds. He would not begrudge a penny of his outlay.

"Shall we go in to lunch?" he said.

He had booked a table in the name of Mr. Black, the name he had given her on the telephone—anodyne, he thought, and ordinary—and the first minutes were taken up with getting the waiter to take their photograph with a camera which Derek produced, as he handed her the envelope which contained her prize.

"It'll be in the paper, for sure," he said. He would keep the film until he had carried out his mission, in case he needed it in some way which he could not foresee now; then he would destroy it, because it could link him to the fate of Barry Carter.

He did not begin questioning her until they had started their main course, content at first with discussing the weather—dry but chilly—and her journey to the hotel. She had come by bus. She tucked in heartily to avocado with prawns, followed by roast duck, while Derek had soup and salmon. Afterwards, she ate an enormous slice of Black Forest gâteau while Derek had cheese and biscuits. Derek enjoyed watching her put it all away and hoped that it would do her good. She was so thin: the long bones in her hands were skeletal. He wondered about her circumstances and the identity of the man who had answered the telephone.

"Have you a job?" he asked her at last, and she giggled. She had drunk more than half a bottle of claret now, having had a glass of Derek's Sancerre with her avocado.

"I give massage," she said, and Derek raised his eyebrows, wondering if he had understood her.

"Really?" he responded calmly.

She nodded. Her cheeks were flushed, and her lips curved in a smile of genuine amusement.

"I'm quite choosy," she said, and now she glanced at him in a coyly flirtatious manner.

"What shall we say in the report?" he asked her.

"Oh—that I'm unemployed," said Sandra instantly.

"Have you had your picture in the paper before?" he pursued. "Perhaps you won a beautiful baby contest? I'm sure you were a beautiful baby." It was so easy to talk like this: Derek was amazed at himself.

"No, but I was in the paper once," said Sandra, and as she spoke, the animation left her face. "It was a few years ago."

"Oh? When was that? Were you married? A gorgeous bride?" tried Derek, and as she shook her head, he filled her glass.

"A boyfriend I had did a terrible crime," she told him. "When he was caught, a paper found me."

"What did he do?"

"Went on a burglary and raped a girl. He's still in prison," she said. "We'd split up by then. He got into terrible moods and I told him good-bye."

What a phrase: had she picked it up from some film?

"Just as well," said Derek. "He might have attacked you."

"Yes," said Sandra.

"Tell me about it," said Derek.

"Some people said it was because of that—us splitting up—that he attacked that girl," she said. "It made me feel bad."

"Oh, you shouldn't." Derek felt dismay. "It wasn't anything to do with you. Some men who seem to be happily married are rapists. They lead two lives," he said. "How did you get into your present line of work?" He was genuinely curious.

"You're right about the two lives," said Sandra, cheering up. "I see a bit of that, in my profession."

So that was what she called it! Well, it was the oldest one of all.

"Sometimes it's best if people don't know the truth," said Derek.

"Right!" She laughed. "I get all sorts," she said. "You'd be surprised."

She'd said that she was choosy: just as well, for her own

safety, Derek thought, partly shocked but wholly fascinated. He would have liked to learn more, and thought of Gladstone and his rescue projects, but he had other important things to find out. Even so, he asked her again how she had got into her present occupation.

"I couldn't get a job," she said. "I used to work in a factory but they laid people off, and then I met this guy who runs a massage parlor. He's quite good to me. It was him that answered the phone when you rang," she said. "I take a few private clients," she added, giving Derek a meaningful look. "At my home."

The man was her pimp. Derek swallowed hard.

"I'll remember that," he said. "You're a pretty girl, Sandra. Your clients are fortunate fellows." He patted her hand. "Now, tell me about this man who's in prison. What's his name?"

She told him. There was no mistake.

"Did he hurt the girl?" asked Derek.

"Of course he did," said Sandra, eyes flashing now. "He was vicious. He cut off her hair and cracked her ribs. And he hit her father, or his mate did. But he didn't cut her up inside, if that's what you mean. Some of them do that, you know."

"Yes," said Derek, trying to stay calm. "So where did he go when you parted? Had he parents?"

"He'd a mum. She was nice—I liked her. She was ever so sad about it all," Sandra told him.

"Do you see her now?"

"She's a waitress at a place I sometimes go to with a client," Sandra said. "I'm not sure if she recognizes me, though," she added, with another giggle.

"Where's that?" asked Derek.

She named it. "The Lunar Moon," she said, and gave him the address.

Derek was smiling as he saw Sandra off. He had put her in a taxi with ten pounds for her fare, and had watched her climb in, tiny skirt rucked up around her skinny thighs— thighs that had clasped a thousand backs, he thought fancifully. What would become of her? Might she, one day, marry a faithful client? It was possible, he supposed; that way, she might gain some security. It seemed as if she could reject men she did not like the look of, but would she be able to do so when her looks began to go? There was a charming air of knowing innocence about her; becoming one of her clients might be quite rewarding.

Now he knew the route to Barry's mother, but if he had a meal in The Lunar Moon, she might recognize him. It was too chancy. He would have to watch for her outside, hope to catch sight of her when she left for home and then follow her. Once he managed to track her down, he need not make direct contact; he need only watch her and, eventually, he would see Barry. The man must, surely, meet his mother after his release.

It could take months. He still did not know when Barry's time inside would end and he saw no way of finding out, not unless he openly revealed his interest and that would be remembered afterwards. Besides, the police or other authorities such as the prison staff probably would not tell him.

Derek spent a great many nights outside The Lunar Moon in the next weeks. Sometimes he found a parking space beside the single yellow line and waited in the car, but he did not want to become conspicuous, so on other nights he parked some streets away and walked about, late, when the pubs and restaurants were closing.

He maintained his routine in Petty Linton but now time was taken up with his shooting practice and his observation tactics. He still did consultancy work for his old contacts; this brought him in an income, and did not take up every minute of the day.

At last, after almost seven weeks of spasmodic vigilance and increasing desperation, he saw Noreen Carter leave The Lunar Moon.

He was standing on the far side of the street, dressed in an old raincoat and with a hat pulled low over his eyes, like Humphrey Bogart in his role as Philip Marlowe, when she emerged, soon after midnight. He had given up on some other nights, when the place seemed dead, and had begun to wonder if there was a staff entrance at the rear. Once or twice two or three women had left the restaurant but he had not been able to get a good enough look at their faces to recognize them. This time, seeing her, he walked towards her, passing her near a lamppost and was certain: one close look at the thin, haggard face was enough.

She hurried to a car parked beside the kerb and he turned to see her enter it. He could not follow: the Citroën was in a side street; but he memorized the number of the other car, a blue Ford Sierra with a G registration. If it collected her again, he could be ready.

The next night, he was waiting in his car when she came out with another woman. He realized he must have seen her several times before, but had not been close enough to recognize her. She and the other woman walked along the road to a bus stop. He followed behind the bus they caught and saw the two alight, watching the direction they took, but he did not dare drive slowly after them for fear of being accused of curb crawling, which was exactly what he would have been doing.

Two nights later, he waited near the stop where Noreen

Carter had got off the bus, but did not see her. After that, he let several nights elapse; he did not want to become familiar to other users of the street, or to any police in unmarked cars who might be in the area. He had trailed her to her neighborhood and eventually he would run her to ground.

3.

Janet felt a curious emotion when she received Derek's letter returning the cuttings and enclosing the check. Meeting him had left her unmoved, but this did not: she realized that he now understood his past failure and might be acknowledging his inadequacy, though, as Detective Inspector Brooks had said at the time, few men, in such circumstances, would have been able to save Hannah. He had agreed that some would certainly have tried. He and the woman officer who had gone with Hannah to hospital for her examination, and who had made sure that she had the necessary later tests, at the appropriate intervals, for pregnancy and disease, had followed up the case and kept in touch with Hannah and her family for months.

"A fit, trained man—a copper, or a black belt, or a rugby player, someone with quick reflexes and used to action—might have succeeded," Brooks had allowed. "But there were two of them, remember. Sometimes having a go only makes things worse, but sometimes they get scared and quit. It could go either way." And the girl, of course, had not submitted meekly.

"If I'd been there, there would have been three of us," said Janet. "We might have managed."

"Morris might have shot you all," said Brooks.

Life was precious, even a damaged life, one that had gone off course, but Janet still feared that unless Hannah emerged from her chrysalis of isolation, hers would not improve, and nor would Janet's, because every day she felt a load of worry about her daughter pressing down on her. Then, with her usual honesty, she admitted to herself that when things were going well at the shop, she had been not just content but happy; she had had a sense of achievement and personal worth. She must hang on to that. Hannah was young and time would dull her pain and anger.

It cost a lot to travel to Scotland, and was a long drive to Hannah's Highland refuge, but when Derek's check came, Janet decided to visit her.

The cheapest convenient way seemed to be by coach to Glasgow, and from there to catch another bus onwards. She would have to change coaches at Birmingham. Janet altered her shifts so that she could have four consecutive nights off and arranged to travel overnight so that she did not miss the local connection. Hannah, telephoned, was pleased, and said she would meet her off the bus.

Janet had concealed from Hannah the extent of her financial plight, making out that she had closed the shop to beat the recession, not because it had beaten her. As she made the long journey north, she had plenty of time to collect her thoughts, preparing to present a confident front. Derek's check had given her a solid hedge; she would use most of it to pay some of what she owed and keep a little as an emergency fund, something she had lacked. She laid her own problems on one side when the coach crossed into Scotland, ready to receive an impression of her daughter that was not clouded with preconceptions.

Janet had dressed for the journey in a tweed skirt and her strongest shoes; she had taken her warmest coat and two thick sweaters. On the few visits she had made to Scotland in her life, it had always been ten degrees colder than the south of England. The coaches—both of them—were warm and comfortable and she dozed, intermittently. In the local bus she fell soundly asleep for half an hour but then awoke because of the stops they made.

She was stiff when she stepped off the bus, carrying a soft zipped bag; she had brought very little with her. Hannah was waiting beside a shabby pickup with a driver's compartment and an open truck body—useful, Janet realized, for carting birds in cages, wire netting, shovels, all the gear that might be needed in the reserve.

"Hullo, Hannah," Janet said, as they kissed, and Hannah asked about the journey. As she answered, Janet realized that it was Hannah who had made the move towards her first. After her breakdown, she had shunned physical contact with anyone, often even her mother. It was as if her body was encased in invisible armor. Janet rattled on about the trip, describing the comforts of the coach, as Hannah took her bag and led her towards the pickup.

She looked well. Janet cast sidelong glances at her as they drove through thick mist that was almost fog. Hannah drove competently; they met few cars but once a blue Volvo estate came towards them and the driver tooted at Hannah who waved and tooted her horn back.

"That's Charlie MacGregor. He and his wife Meg run a guest house on the loch," said Hannah. "You'll meet them tonight. They've asked us for dinner. You don't mind, do you?"

"No, I'd like that," Janet said, hiding her amazement. Here was Hannah taking part in social life.

"Sorry about the weather," Hannah said. "There should be a lovely view. Hills on either side. Of course, you know that; you've been before."

"Yes." On that difficult visit, the weather had been marvelous, the dark loch reflecting the brilliant sky with its scudding white clouds, the heather-covered hills rolling away into the distant mountains.

"I hope you've brought some jeans, Mum," Hannah said, changing gear as the van ground up a hill. "You'll need them, trudging about up here. I daresay we can borrow a pair of boots. The MacGregors have lots; they keep them for their guests, in several sizes."

"Not jeans, dear, but trousers," Janet said. "My gardening ones."

Hannah had rarely seen her mother other than smartly dressed. Even when she was quite a small girl, Janet, delivering her to school and fetching her in the afternoons, had worn smart skirts and neat jackets, standing out among the other mothers because she was never untidy or ruffled, and when she played tennis—she was very good—her hair would be securely tethered by a band, her pleated skirt in place. At least, now, she was sensibly clad in her thick quilted coat, for though it was only September, the weather so far north could be extremely cold.

There was only one bedroom in Hannah's little cottage, which Janet had not seen before because she was lodging with the warden and his wife on that early visit. Hannah had borrowed a camp bed on which she intended to sleep, giving her mother her own room. Janet protested, but feebly. She admired everything, but secretly found the place bleak and stark, though, with its white painted walls, wicker chairs and gingham curtains at the windows, it had a certain charm. There was a very old cooker which ran off bottled gas.

"We have got electricity," Hannah assured her. "But it can go off in a storm. It's a good idea to have gas too. I've got some camping lamps that run off it, and a battery radio."

Janet saw no television, but there was a stereo system.

"That's good," said Janet.

"I listen to the radio a lot," said Hannah, a little sheepishly. "And recorded books, if I'm sewing. I like them. Dickens and such."

"Well, you were reading English," said Janet, determined to show no surprise at anything, although the sewing was entirely new. "What sewing do you do?"

"I'm making a patchwork quilt. Meg showed me—she's got one her grandmother made and she began one once, but hasn't time now. I offered to finish it for her. She produced all the scraps. I'll show you later, but now I should think you'd like something to eat, then a sleep while I go on my rounds," said Hannah. "I'll fill you a hot bottle."

She's better. She's a different girl, thought Janet, damping down her joy in case it was premature.

After a cup of tea and some ham sandwiches which Hannah had made earlier and wrapped in foil, she allowed herself to be tucked under the duvet in Hannah's white, cell-like room, with a rubber hot water bottle at her feet.

"I'll be back before six," Hannah said.

Left alone, Janet noticed the bars across the windows and the strong security locks on the catch. She had seen three big bolts on the door. No doubt the other windows were strongly protected as well. She was relieved, not worried because Hannah had turned her home into a fortress, for it was completely isolated, out of sight of any other dwelling. In summer, there were campers by the loch and all the year round there were climbers in the hills. Many types of people were attracted to wild, unspoiled areas, and who could tell if one of them was off balance?

There was not a sound to be heard as Janet closed her eyes, not the note of a curlew nor the cry of a gull. She was very tired. In minutes, she was asleep.

After nearly two hours she woke, surfacing with difficulty, wondering where she was. Then she heard movements below and realized that Hannah was back. She lay still for a while, aware that she need do nothing at all except lie there, waiting for Hannah to tell her it was time to get ready; then her normal disciplined habit took over and she got out of bed, put on Hannah's dressing gown which hung on the door—a thick red woollen one which Janet had sent her one Christmas to ward off the Scottish chill—and went downstairs. Hannah was lighting the fire.

"Hi, Mum. You look as if you've slept," said Hannah.

"I have. Sound off," said Janet. "Very idle."

"It'll do you good. I expect you need it," said Hannah. "You probably have too many late nights at The Swan. How do you like it?"

"It's varied," said Janet. "Some of the guests are very nice."

"And some aren't, and come on strong, or smoke big cigars," said Hannah. "It wouldn't suit me, but then this back-to-nature mode of mine wouldn't suit you."

"True," said Janet.

"Wouldn't you like a bath before we go out? I hope you don't mind this plan, but Meg thought you should see that I do have some civilized friends. I wasn't very well held together when you came before, and I hadn't any then, not really, apart from David and Jessie." They were the warden and his wife.

"I'd like to meet Meg. It's kind of her," said Janet. "What about David and Jessie? How are they?"

"He died," said Hannah. "Didn't I tell you?" She knew she had not, for she had not wanted her mother to worry. "He had a heart attack," she added. "Very sudden. Jessie's gone to live with her son in Aberdeen."

"Oh, I'm sorry," said Janet.

"Yes. Well, it was a bad time," said Hannah. "About a year ago."

"So you've a new boss?"

"Yes. Younger, with a wife who's a teacher," said Hannah.

By now the fire in the hearth was blazing up, and Hannah fed it with small coals. "We'll leave it well banked up when we go out, and it'll be great to come back to," she said. "And before you say it's extravagant to light it when we're away out, I'll tell you that there's a back boiler in it and it will mean there's plenty of hot water—it'll boost the immersion."

The bathroom led off the kitchen in a manner that modern planners would doubtless forbid. Janet enjoyed her bath, with pine essence sprinkled in it by Hannah, but was careful with the water, not wanting to strain the supply. Then she dressed in the well-cut woollen skirt she had traveled in, with a cream silk blouse. Her bag, with the second sweater in it, had not had space for anything more elaborate, but she added large pearl earrings and a string of pearls which she wound twice round her neck, and sprayed herself with Magie Noire. She was ready, and sat down by the fire to wait for Hannah.

There was no newspaper, no television to switch on for the news. There were some wildlife magazines and she glanced at one. Hannah's work did not involve noise and bustle and the constant demands made by humans, but the death of the warden must have touched her. She had lived with them for her trial period, until both sides decided the arrangement suited them. Then this cottage had become vacant and she had rented it ever since. She had achieved a total escape, and could probably arrange a lot of her daily program to suit herself, but it must be a solitary life.

But I'm alone, too, thought Janet, who was always glad to shut her front door at the end of the day and know she had no one to consider but herself.

All the same, she wished Hannah could meet some quiet, gentle man who would be a kind lover and overcome her fears. In a safe home, with children, Hannah could be fulfilled.

I want for her what I haven't had myself, Janet thought.

The MacGregors' house was a square granite building with a slate roof and a garden consisting mainly of lawn and shrubs. Some bent bushes testified to the strength of the prevailing winds. It was a cold, raw evening, still light, when Janet and Hannah drove the three miles down the road to the slight hollow in the valley where it crouched with its front facing the loch. A few tall trees made a barrier between it and the hills at the back.

Inside, it was warm, and so was the welcome Janet received. The MacGregors were in their early forties, with twin sons aged thirteen who, it was at once apparent, were fond of Hannah and treated her like an elder sister. One even pulled her neat plait, but gently. Janet wondered if she ever let her hair free to lie on her shoulders, as she had done years ago. She did not feel underdressed; Meg also wore a skirt—hers was pleated all round like a kilt, but it wasn't tartan—and Charlie wore spotless corduroy trousers and a maroon sweater over a fine white polo top. The boys were in jeans and sweaters.

Janet felt shy until Charlie put a heavy cut-glass tumbler half full of whisky in her hand and suggested that a splash of water would insult the fine spirit. Even so, Janet elected to dilute it.

She was not driving, and no Breathalyzing policeman was

likely to spring from behind the heather, if she were. Hannah was drinking whiskey too, but a very small weak one, Janet noticed. Maybe up here you so often got cold that spirits were needed for warmth, she thought, as the first sip of hers sent a grateful glow through her.

Charlie asked about the journey and she explained that because she could be away only four nights, it was too far to drive.

"But you're just with Hannah for two," said Charlie.

"Two on the coach," Janet said.

"I see. Well, you'll not have seen much of the scenery as it's been misty all the day," said Charlie. "But Hannah says you've been up before."

"Yes, but she hadn't got the cottage then, and she didn't know you," said Janet.

"That's true. We met one New Year, first footing," said Charlie, and grinned. He had reddish hair and freckles, and very blue eyes. "Gave her a bit of a fright, I think, stepping up to the door in the dark."

They must have done, thought Janet.

"I got over it. I'm used to their weird Scottish ways now," said Hannah, smiling. She wore a navy skirt and a soft pink sweater, and her cheeks were flushed; Janet had not seen her look so happy for years.

Meg MacGregor introduced the house guests. One couple, in their sixties, were retired teachers, and the other pair, who were not married, were connected with the theater. After a while Janet realized that she recognized the woman, who was about thirty-five; she had seen her in a television soap opera. The man, it transpired, was due, the following week, to start rehearsing for a police series. His part was not large but he was in most installments.

"Regular work," he said, with a satisfied smile.

He was thin and tense, and could not take his eyes off his partner. Janet wondered how long they had been together; she thought he might be a jealous man. That was something that Derek had never been, but then he never had reason to be. People were jealous without cause, however; she knew that; it must be difficult to live with someone so insecure.

Both couples had been out all day, the younger pair walking in spite of the mist and the drizzle which had come on during the afternoon, while the older two had been to visit a castle and a woollen mill. They had done their Christmas shopping at the mill, buying sweaters for the family—two sons, a daughter and their spouses and three grandchildren.

They all sat round an immense table for the meal, and the twins helped Meg serve it while Charlie carved the roast beef and dealt with the wine. Later, Hannah told Janet that there was nowhere closer than Killiemanoch where you could go to eat, so that if you took in guests you had to feed them in the evening. Nearer the bigger villages and in the towns, people did bed and breakfast only.

"It quietens down soon, as the weather closes in," she said, as if the convivial evening at the MacGregors' had been part of a season of constant entertaining. "We often have lovely autumn days, though," she added. "I hope tomorrow you'll get a sight of the loch looking bonny, and the mountain peaks. There's no snow yet."

"I should hope not," said Janet, who had noticed Hannah using several Scots expressions in her speech. It amused and touched her; Hannah was putting down roots up here.

Janet had been rather silent at dinner. She seldom went to the theater, and watched very little television apart from the news and an occasional documentary, and felt unable to talk about their profession with the theatrical pair. The older couple had once been to Norlington and remembered some churches they had visited in the area; the husband was interested in church architecture and the wife had sung with a choral society which often performed in churches and cathedrals. The two boys were interested in Rugby football and the forthcoming season, and a partisan conversation developed about the prospects of England and Scotland in the international matches. Hannah joined in; she seemed to know the names of all the Scottish players.

Hannah was aware that her mother was finding it difficult to adjust to the friendly, informal atmosphere which prevailed in the MacGregors' house, where guests wrote in the visitors' book that it was like a home from home, yet she must be always talking to strangers at The Swan. For the first time, she understood that Janet's brisk manner and attendance to detail covered an inner shyness, and Hannah felt an urge to protect her. After a while, however, and helped by the whisky and the good red wine, Janet began to relax. Where was the real woman, under the veneer of the smart silk blouse, the expensive skirt, the good makeup and the costume jewelry, wondered Hannah: what had she expected from life, and how much had she achieved?

In the soft light from the candles on the table, while outside the sun set behind the mist, the daughter looked at the mother and her mind was full of questions.

A brisk wind sprang up in the night, and the next morning the mist had vanished and the sky was blue, with few clouds to be seen. The hills were tawny brown where heather and bracken had faded into autumn shades. Looking out of Hannah's bedroom window, Janet thought she saw snow on a distant peak. It must have fallen in the night.

When Hannah arrived with coffee and toast on a tray, Janet, surprised, said, "You're spoiling me."

"It's about time," said Hannah. "You're the one who's always doing that." But it was her father who had indulged her, petted her and made her feel that she was special.

Janet was embarrassed.

"It's so beautiful up here—I can see why you like it," she said. She wanted to add, but what's your future? Will you still be here when you're fifty, rising at dawn to go ringing birds or saving nestlings, or whatever it is you do? Two voices quarreled in her head, one saying that this was no life for a young woman, the other envying her daughter the peace that she had, apparently, secured. Why shouldn't she turn into a weatherbeaten woman, striding about the hills, battling with nature, not with man?

"We'll go out later," Hannah said. "I've got a few things I must do and then we'll go for a drive—not too far, as you'll be sitting in the coach again so soon."

When they set off in the rattly old pickup, Hannah said that she had wondered about taking her mother to Edinburgh for the day, but it was a long drive and they would have had to leave early, and the van wouldn't be as comfortable as the bus from Glasgow.

"It's a lovely city," Hannah said. "And the shops are great. Have you ever been there?"

Janet had not, and she was surprised to hear Hannah talking as if she knew the city well.

"I've been there several times," she said. "I met some people who were here on holiday, bird-watching, and they invited me. I've been on the bus, too. It's not difficult. Meg and Charlie drive there now and then, when they're closed, but they can't get away once the season starts."

"They've kept busy?" Janet asked.

"Yes. They've got three doubles—one was free last night but people sometimes turn up unexpectedly. It's getting late now, but it can be lovely in October. They close then—at the end of the month."

"They're very nice. I was glad to meet them," Janet said.

"Yes—well, it's been nice for me, getting to know them," Hannah said. "But everyone knows everyone round here, because there aren't too many of us."

It used to be like that in small towns and villages in England, thought Janet, but things had changed; even in Bicklebury, whose population was about three hundred, people could be strangers. She had not known everyone in the village, even by sight, but Veronica and Roger did; they, however, in the Manor House, felt faintly feudal, with no real justification since they had bought it on the open market at a time when no one wanted large houses with faulty heating systems and roofs which needed costly retiling.

Hannah parked the car by some spindly trees at the side of the loch and took her mother for a walk along sandy paths beside it. The wind was strong, and Janet tied a scarf around her head, thankful that she had brought one. Hannah seemed impervious to the cold as they trudged on, not talking except when Hannah pointed out various birds which she was able to detect with the naked eye, though she had a pair of binoculars around her neck. From time to time she stopped and gave them to her mother, pointing out distant species difficult to discern. Janet, not good at focusing the binoculars or locating the dotlike objects she was meant to marvel at, pretended to have seen them even when she failed. There was no doubt about Hannah's enthusiasm, or her knowledge—not that Janet was qualified to question her ability.

Eventually they stopped for lunch. Hannah had brought sandwiches and packs of fruit juice, which she produced from the capacious pockets of her waxed jacket. She wore stout walking boots and thick socks; Janet was thankful that

120

her borrowed boots, worn with a pair of Hannah's socks, were comfortable, and she was used to being on her feet, though not to striding out in quite this way.

There were dwellings here and there: now and then a gray farmhouse was visible, or a whitewashed cottage, and, amid distant trees, the slate roof of a larger house.

"It's so different from Norlington," said Janet, when they halted at the top of a small rise to look down on the sweeping scene. "It's like being in another country."

"You are in another country," Hannah pointed out. "And if you forget that, any Scot will soon remind you."

Just as Janet was wondering if she would have the strength to retrace her steps, Hannah led her through a clearing and there, below them, was the pickup. They had come full circle. Janet hid her relief. In spite of the scarf, her ears were stinging with the cold, and she was longing for a cup of tea or coffee, but that bliss was to be denied her as Hannah drove home the long way, past one of the castles the MacGregors' guests had visited the day before.

"It's got a fabulous garden," Hannah said. "But it's a bit late now to see it—most things are already dormant for the winter."

Thank goodness she wasn't going to suggest that they should inspect the interior of the castle, Janet thought, although it might be warm inside the building, but heating was not something to take for granted in this part of the country.

When they returned to the cottage, she volunteered to light the fire while Hannah went off to tend some damaged birds. They're her children, Janet thought: less worrying than real ones, possibly, but surely less rewarding?

Maybe not.

She raked out the grate and lit the fire again. Hannah had

said she kept it in all winter, except when it went out by accident. When did she reckon winter started, Janet wondered.

There was a casserole for supper. Hannah had made it before Janet arrived and put it in her small freezer. The pudding was ice cream. The electricity supply was due to the presence further along the road of a large farm where beef cattle were bred; the owner had paid for the installation many years ago, when the cottage had been home for a farm worker. Now, with more machinery, less labor was needed and there were fewer jobs.

"I don't cook a lot," said Hannah. She had produced a bottle of wine. "I have mostly stews and stuff like that, but I do eat plenty. You have to, out all day, or you'd fold up."

"You're happy, aren't you?" Janet dared to say.

"Yes. Does that surprise you? I never thought I'd manage it, afterwards, but it's happened," Hannah said.

"I think you're wonderful," her mother said.

Hannah blushed. How pretty she is, her mother thought, eyes prickling with tears.

"I've been lucky," Hannah answered. "Lots of women have much worse experiences than I did and never recover physically, and they don't have the backup I had. You were wonderful that night, Mum, and afterwards. I'll never forget how good you were—how understanding."

Janet drank some wine. It was clear that Hannah meant them to kill the bottle.

"It was so terrible to see you in that state—to know what had happened to you," she said.

"Dad didn't understand," said Hannah. "Lots of men don't. They think because it doesn't show, it doesn't matter."

"They're learning now," said Janet. "There's been so much about it in the papers and on television—all these dreadful cases."

"There's lots of help now," said Hannah. "I could have had more then, but I didn't think I needed it. Sometimes I think I ought to help other victims, but I'm not ready for that yet. I'm still not reconciled to what happened."

Janet said, carefully, "You may never be, but you may have enough good things in your life to compensate."

"You mean a good sexual relationship, don't you?" Hannah said. "I haven't yet. I've been much too frightened, and I haven't met the man I could risk it with—not after that sorry business with poor Tom. He was awfully good about it."

"Yes," said Janet.

"I'm beginning to think it might be possible, one day," Hannah said. "Not for ages, and only if someone really amazing came along."

"Miracles do happen," Janet said, thinking she was witnessing the result of one. "There are some kind, gentle men around."

"I know, but I think most of them are already married," Hannah said.

"I suppose one shouldn't go by appearances," said Janet, "but I thought that actor looked as if he could be mean. Charles is different, though."

Charles was stocky, sturdy, not aesthetic-looking like the actor, but there was something about him—Janet lacked the personal experience to identify it—which indicated that he felt at ease with women and saw no need to assert himself aggressively. He did not dominate his wife; they complemented one another, like Veronica and Roger. Janet did not feel confident enough to voice this theory to her daughter; indeed, it was a novel perception on her own part.

4.

At last Derek successfully trailed Noreen Carter from The Lunar Moon to a block of flats a short walk from the bus stop where she had alighted. He had pulled his hat low and wound a muffler round his neck covering the lower part of his face while he followed her to the bus on a night when the man in the blue Sierra did not pick her up. Derek sat at the back of the bus, and Noreen stayed near the front; women often did, at night, so that they were near the driver if there was trouble.

When she left the bus, so did Derek, and followed her to her block. He did not enter the lift with her, but ran up the steps as fast as he could, which was not fast enough. However, as he began to get out of breath and slow down, he was able to tell from the light above the lift that it had stopped at the sixth floor.

So Noreen Carter lived on the sixth floor. There were a number of flats on each floor but improvements had been made to this tall block and some of the walkways had been divided into sections. He should be able to identify her flat if he loitered on the landing, and then, if he could time it, he might discover if or when Barry had moved in. Maybe Barry wouldn't do that, but surely he would come to see his mother, or she would visit him? All Derek had to do was keep on following her, and sooner or later, she would lead him to her son, even if it was only to the right prison.

This was exactly what happened the following Sunday.

Derek followed her on the various buses which she took to reach her destination. So Barry was still inside. He had an idea that prisoners were allowed visitors only once a month, but didn't they go into hostels before their release? A book he consulted in the library implied that this arrangement was mainly for those serving long sentences and could be varied to suit particular cases.

Nearly every evening he looked at the newspaper cuttings which he had photocopied. He needed to imprint Barry Carter's features on the retina of his memory. He trailed Noreen again and once more he saw her get into the blue Sierra. This time, he hurried back to his own car and drove after it, guessing it would go to the block of flats to which he had followed her before. He saw the car stop among others outside the block, and a man got out with Noreen. They went into the block together; husband or partner, he decided, and made a note of the car's number.

He had had a letter from Janet thanking him for the check and saying that she would have lent him the whole cuttings album if it was so important to him. *There was no need for subterfuge,* she wrote, reprovingly, then added that she was going to visit Hannah. It was typical of Janet's attention to good manners that she had acknowledged the check at once; she lived by stringent rules; some of them he had mocked during their years together, but others he respected. Janet had been strictly reared by an aunt whose husband was a Methodist minister; her father had been killed during the last months of the war and her mother had died of cancer when Janet was ten. Soon after that her older brother had joined the merchant navy.

He wondered if she would let him know how Hannah was: probably not, he thought. Perhaps he would go and visit her again, or telephone; she would not refuse to answer questions he might ask. Hannah was his daughter, after all; did he have no rights in the matter?

No, he told himself: because she was of age, and children should not be obliged to feel indebted to their parents. This was a new thought for him to have; years ago, he had imagined his old age enlivened by Hannah's devotion, and the affection of the family that she would have, providing him with a stake in posterity. He sighed, thinking once again of the son who had never breathed; he would have been getting on for thirty now, established in a career, a credit to his father—and his mother too, of course; Derek had no fault to find with Janet on that score.

Repining did no good; at the time, it had seemed best not to think about what might have been. There had been one other miscarriage, a much earlier one, before, at last, Hannah had been born and then there was a future.

Janet contemplated telephoning Derek after her return from Scotland. He would be glad to know that Hannah seemed much happier and was looking well, and to hear about her pleasant neighbors, but such news might inspire him to pay her another visit, and that, Janet was certain, would be a bad idea. One day they must meet again; Hannah might eventually find it in herself to forgive him his inadequacies but that must happen in her time and any reconciliation must be something she initiated.

It was odd of him to show this tardy interest in the details of the trial. He had blanked it out successfully afterwards, but at least he had given no press interviews nor stated that he forgave Carter. Now that his own life was so altered, perhaps he was taking stock and facing what he had not been able to accept when it happened. As she had told him, Martin Brooks, who had been the detective inspector in charge of the case and who was now a superintendent, sometimes came into The Swan. Until she started working there, Janet had not seen him since a visit he made some weeks after the trial. With the woman officer who had been a great support to Hannah, he had come to The Elms to see how things were settling down. This was before Hannah's suicide attempt and breakdown. Seeing her behind the bar, Brooks did not recognize Janet at first, and when he did, he showed surprise at finding her in this very different setting. In a quiet moment, she told him that she and Derek had separated, and about Clarice and its failure. He was no longer with the CID, and said he missed actively detecting; there was too much administration in his new position. His marriage, like hers, had come to grief, a casualty of the strains of the job. Sometimes he came in with a thin, pale woman with cropped hair and amber eyes. She was rather striking, but reminded Janet of a cat, vigilant and restless; her gaze roved round the room while she talked to Brooks, and she looked ready to move off, pantherlike, at any second. Janet thought Brooks merited more of her attention.

Shortly after Janet's return from Scotland, he came in again, this time alone. He bought his one drink—he always had a double Scotch, well diluted, and made it last—and stood by the bar, in a corner, waiting until she was free to exchange a few words.

"Can I buy you a drink?" he asked, and she accepted a gin and tonic.

"Thanks," she said. "I'm glad of this tonight, and I'm not driving."

"You always walk to work?"

She nodded.

"It's not far," she said. "If the weather's really awful, I might drive, but I do have a drink or two most nights, and I don't want your lot nabbing me for being over the limit." She tipped her glass at him. "I need it to keep me going," she said.

She'd already had a drink or two this evening, he decided, and changed his mind about suggesting she was safer in her car than on foot, alone, late at night. Better not to sow fear if it did not already exist. Of all people, Janet Jarvis must know how swiftly and at random trouble could erupt. But that night he stayed at The Swan until the bar closed, and then he said that he would drive her home.

When they stopped at her gate, she asked him if he would like some coffee; if she, issuing such an invitation at her age, and to a senior policeman, were not safe from having her suggestion misinterpreted, who was?

She lit the gas fire in the living room and put on the kettle. The last man to have coffee here was Derek, whom she had left with the cuttings album.

She told Brooks about that, while he drank his coffee. She had a cup of herbal tea; coffee at this hour kept her awake.

"I wonder why he was suddenly curious," said Janet.

"Perhaps he realized that Carter will be out soon, and that brought it all back," Brooks answered.

"I think he did," said Janet. "So much for serving seven years," she added bitterly. "They should have thrown away the key."

With full remission, Carter would be out in a matter of weeks, Brooks knew. He kept tabs on the movements of such as Carter. If he was seen in this area, Brooks would want to know, but unless a released man was on parole, there would be no record of his whereabouts. All rapists should be supervised after release, in Brooks's opinion, but it took time and manpower, and that cost money; moreover, it was not in the rules, and if they were amended, do-gooders would insist that such action would be interference with the civil rights of the offender. The rights of past and potential victims were not considered by such thinkers. "How's Hannah?" he asked. "Married yet?"

"No, and I doubt if she ever will be," Janet said. "Besides, it's gone out of fashion."

"What has? Marriage?"

"Yes."

"Not really. More stay together than part, after all."

"But the young ones often don't begin," said Janet. She muttered something which he did not catch, and he asked her what she had said.

"I used the word 'commitment,'" Janet said. "People don't seem to make that, these days. But I think Hannah's committed to what she's doing." She told him about the birds.

"Was she always interested in that sort of thing?"

"No, but Peter—the boyfriend she had at the time—his mother's an ornithologist and Hannah had stayed with them in some remote spot in the Lake District. She said it was peaceful. The mother helped her to get this job—she knew the warden or someone who let Hannah go there and work in return for just her keep at first. Now she's knowledgeable and useful, and is paid a wage, but it's not very much. She works all round the clock—the daylight hours, at least. She seems happy, in a fashion. She's run away from life."

"Hasn't she run from one sort of life to another?" Brooks suggested. "If you lived up there and farmed, or whatever else they do in those parts, or were from a fishing community, you wouldn't think of it as contracting out. I'm glad there's still space enough on this overcrowded planet for people to live like that. Now everything comes out of packets and kids eat on the hoof instead of sitting round tables talking to their family. Soon everyone will be cooped up in monster boxes like battery hens, shopping by computer and patrolled by inspectors who'll make sure they keep in line."

Brooks' rather florid face grew redder still as he made this impassioned speech, to which Janet listened in astonishment. He had always seemed so calm and unemotional.

"I hadn't thought of it like that," she said.

Brooks calmed down a little.

"Sorry," he said. "It's rather my hobby horse. We get involved with youth work—trying to keep them out of trouble, find interests for the bad lads—but it's like trying to turn back the tide. You get a couple of fourteen-year-old kids stealing cars and knocking down pedestrians, and you can't lock them up or try to instil some discipline into them. They get cautioned and do it again and again. If they actually kill someone, they might get put into secure accommodation, so-called, but it's often far from secure and when they get out they do it again. There are schemes to teach them mechanics and let them drive bangers in some areas, and those do a lot of good, but you can't pick up every youngster and get him involved in something that will occupy his time and use his energy. It all costs too much." He sighed. "Sorry," he said. "I'd better go."

She saw him to the door. They would meet some other evening at The Swan.

He's lonely, she realized, watching him get into his Nissan and drive off. You could be surrounded by colleagues all day, be married and busy, and yet feel totally alone, more isolated than Hannah in her solitude. Her companions did not make impossible demands or have unreasonable expectations of her powers; you could not quarrel with a bird, or a vole, or a deer. Perhaps that was why domestic pets were so popular; a dog didn't answer back and gave slavish devotion to whoever fed it.

Though she spent a lot of time alone now, Janet was less lonely than when she had lived with Derek; she no longer felt driven to occupy each spare moment with activity. While she was married to Derek, she had gone out to her evening courses to avoid spending time with him.

And now they were both alone and no longer had to scheme to escape from one another. If he had, at last, begun to understand how he had contributed to their daughter's damage, she could start to pity him.

5.

Derek was sure that sooner or later Noreen Carter would deliver up his quarry. Barry, released from jail, would surely seek her out. He would not admit the possibility that Barry might have nothing to do with her when his sentence ended; where else would he go but to his mother's? At the back of his mind was the possibility that, if all else failed, Sandra Mason might be persuaded to find out where he was living. Using a private detective would leave a line to him when Barry was found dead, but it was a risk he might have to take if patience and observation were unsuccessful.

Meanwhile, he could plan how he would act when the time came. His gun technique was improving and he could use a revolver now, though he would never be a first-class marksman. He applied himself to what he had to learn and left out the social give-and-take which some of the members enjoyed. You could not talk while you were shooting, and that was what he was there to do.

He haunted the block of flats where Noreen Carter lived. The outside walkways were poorly lit and few of what lights there were had bulbs that worked. Derek had seen youths throwing stones and milk bottles at them. He supposed that

Barry had grown up in this place, a high-rise block built to solve housing problems but serving to create them. There was small sense of community here and there must be many instances of isolation.

He traveled to the sixth floor in the lift. It smelled of urine and worse, and there were obscene sentences scrawled on the walls. He already knew that some of the landings had crude graffiti sprayed on with paint. He supposed you got used to it, passing by unheeding; it must be necessary in order to survive. How dreadful to be imprisoned in such a place. No wonder young children were turned out unsupervised, though there was no proper playground for them, just a patch of once-grass between the blocks. No wonder they roamed off and got into trouble. It was easy to understand how young men such as Carter, without jobs, drifted into petty crime, progressing to more serious offenses as they grew older. But to account for it was not to excuse, and there were plenty of families who managed, even under such adverse conditions, to rear law-abiding youngsters and keep things together. Derek felt that society was falling apart, with nothing held sacred or respected. The church failed to condemn evil, and politicians encouraged envy. Wasn't envy a deadly sin, and greed another?

He did not think revenge was on the list, though anger was.

Derek did not know if he felt anger towards Barry; it was not as simple as that. He wanted to even the score, punish the man, prevent him from doing the same thing again, but above all, he wanted to look his daughter in the eye, even if she never knew what he had done.

On the sixth floor there was no clue as to who lived where. There were only numbers on the uniform doors. He walked from the lift along the passage. Perhaps there would be another lift further on and he could descend there. It was like being in a multistory car park, he thought, and felt threatened when he saw some youths in a group at the end of the stretch along which he was walking. They could easily beat him up, rob him, even kill him, if they were so disposed, and he wondered whether if he turned and retraced his steps, they would notice and follow. They seemed to be talking among themselves and might ignore him.

He thought about ringing a doorbell and asking for Mrs. Carter; it would be the wrong flat and he might be told which was the correct one, but in a place like this people probably did not open doors except to someone they knew, and even if he got a response, he did not want Mrs. Carter to learn that a man had been enquiring for her.

Then a door just short of the group of youths opened, and a man came out. He walked towards Derek, who recognized him as the driver of the Sierra which had collected Noreen Carter from The Lunar Moon. Derek walked calmly on, past the man, noting the number on the door through which he had emerged, and he passed the youths. There was space for him; they made no attempt to hassle him; he might as well have been invisible as he steadfastly avoided the eye contact which none of them had sought. When he had gone safely by and traversed another whole wing of the building, meeting only two girls who could have been heading towards the youths, he realized that they might have been doing a deal of some sort: drugs, probably. They had gone quite silent as he drew level; that had been their only acknowledgment of his presence, but they had not been noisy in the first place.

As he left the block, he reflected that it was an indictment of the times that he had expected trouble from them; why should they not be law-abiding lads discussing girls, or motorbikes, or football, or whatever interested them? Perhaps they were.

Later, he checked the address with all the Carters in the
telephone directory but found no N. Carter that tallied. Perhaps she was not on the telephone, or was ex-directory; she
could have had unpleasant calls at the time of her son's trial.

Barry Carter came out of prison on a gray winter's day, his
sentence served with remission earned. During his time inside, his offense of rape had been obscured by his involvement with armed robbery; a man's crime sometimes earned
respect from other inmates, and he was not labeled as a sex
offender needing to be segregated for his own protection.

His only visitor during his imprisonment had been his
mother, who had come to see him regularly, though they
found little to say to one another. He simply shrugged when
told his stepfather had gone, and made no comment about
her work at The Lunar Moon. She, trying to discover if he
had followed any educational or vocational course while
locked up, had drawn blank. Each had parted thankfully at
the end of the allotted period. Even so, unknown to Noreen,
Barry had decided to move back with her as soon as he was
released. His probation officer had found him a hostel room
and even the possibility of a job, but Barry did not intend to
take up either offer. He had finished his sentence and was not
obliged to report anywhere, nor submit to supervision.

He had the small sum of money to which he was entitled
on regaining his freedom, and had been advised about how to
sign on to obtain state aid, but if he lived at home, his
mother would expect no contribution to expenses; Barry had
never paid his way.

To his astonishment, he found that she was no longer on
her own in her council flat. During her visits she had not told
him that she had met a man who drove a mini-cab for a living; separated from his wife, Clive had moved in with her.

After a late night with a fare, he was sleeping when, early one morning, Barry arrived.

His mother was instantly in a frenzy of anxiety. Barry had not told her the date of his release, nor of his plans; she thought he had several more weeks to serve and had been postponing telling him about her new partner. For all she knew, Barry would not come near her when he was freed, and she had told Clive only that she had a son who was living in the north.

Now there was nothing for it.

"I've got a friend living here," she said. "He does nights sometimes and he's sleeping now, so please don't wake him, Barry." She bustled round him nervously. "I'm sure you're hungry," she suggested.

Barry conceded that he might be tempted by a fry-up, and Noreen put the kettle on and fried him some eggs, chips and sausages, keeping back enough for Clive for later. Luckily there was plenty in the fridge; Clive contributed to the food budget but she paid the rent and all the other outgoings.

She felt responsible for Barry's descent into crime. She and his father had split up after several turbulent years during which both she and Barry had been beaten, sworn at and generally tormented and humiliated. She had seen no way to escape and had blamed herself for provoking her husband's anger by her own shortcomings. At length he had left her, going off with someone younger. He made no claim to Barry, and paid nothing towards his support, but Noreen was thankful to see the last of him and struggled on until she acquired a new husband who had three sons older than Barry. They and their father picked on Barry, who was thin and puny in his teens. Noreen could not protect him from their bullying, and she often asked him why he could not be more like other boys, who did well at school and were polite.

Barry took to crime in the beginning to impress his step-brothers with his acquisitions, bringing home the latest in stereos, fashion jackets, and waving money about which he had obtained by selling goods he had stolen.

He was caught, cautioned the first time, later put on probation, and finally sentenced. During his first spell in a young offenders' prison he gained weight, filled out, and took up football, but after his release he began stealing cars. When his mother's shaky second marriage came to grief, she blamed him for the breakup, saying his bad ways had so upset his stepfather that he had turned against her. This was only part of the truth; like her first husband, her second had found someone younger, with a baby. His own sons had now grown up and left home, and he felt needed by the pretty, fragile creature he had met at a club where she had gone for an evening out, leaving her infant with its grandmother.

Noreen felt enormous guilt, however, for the part she thought she had played in Barry's downfall, and for which she must now make amends. She told Barry that Clive was a good man and would be happy to have him living here until he was on his feet again, but that he knew nothing of Barry's past.

"I'll explain that the place where you were working has closed down," she said. "But you mustn't make trouble. Clive's a good man—the best I've ever come across. I don't want things to go wrong."

Clive gambled, hoping to win a fortune on the horses, but he did not drink more than an occasional pint and was never violent; these negative attributes were, in Noreen's eyes, virtues.

Barry's rape conviction had horrified Noreen. Theft was one thing—bad enough, true, but not evil; this was something else. Visiting him in prison, she had asked him why he had done it and he had said that it just came over him that the girl deserved it, looking at him as she did.

"How do you mean, looking at you?" she had asked.

Barry had not got the vocabulary to explain.

"Sort of scornful," he had said.

Noreen had seen his victim in court, a pretty girl, fair-haired and very pale, suffering as she related what Barry had done to her.

She hoped he had not got the habit. Next time he might kill some girl, as well as rape her.

Barry told her that he had got a job, and she felt relief. Perhaps he had learned his lesson and would go straight now. He did not tell her that he had no intention of turning up for work.

Derek, patiently watching the flats, saw Noreen leave. He had managed to park the Citroën nearby, and he stayed in it for a while, wondering how long he could go on haunting the place without being challenged by someone—a resident, or the police—and how many weeks must pass before he struck lucky and saw Barry, when a slouching figure leaving the block caught his eye. He put on his headlights and there, like a startled rabbit, was Barry, brightly illuminated, caught in the beam. Derek knew him at once, despite the small wispy beard he had grown in prison. As Barry turned away, Derek started the car and drove off, elated. He was out. The hunt could begin.

Barry went into the corner shop and bought some tobacco to roll his own smokes. He paid, then moved round the shop to study the rows of sweets and chocolate on display. When the shopkeeper's attention was diverted by another customer, Barry neatly filched a small box of Cadbury's Milk Tray and tucked it inside his bomber jacket. Then he cruised to the magazines and picked one out to read. It was a motoring journal, featuring sports cars.

Another man stood beside him, reading a magazine about domestic pets. He glanced across at Barry, and spoke.

"Interested in cars, are you?" asked Victor Kemp.

"You talking to me?" Barry's tone was truculent.

"Saw what you were reading," said Victor peaceably. "The new Golf's a nice little car. Ever been in one?"

"Not the latest," answered Barry, thawing slightly. "I fancy something a bit more powerful."

"There's nothing wrong with the GTI," said Victor. He riffled the pages of his magazine. "My landlady's daughter's got a hamster. I was looking in this for tips on keeping hamsters happy."

"Oh yeah?" Barry had no interest in hamsters.

"Keep in with the kid if you want to keep in with the mother," said Victor. "That's my motto."

"Oh yeah?" said Barry again.

"Fancy a drink?" asked Victor.

"What, now? They'll be closed," said Barry, glancing at his watch, one he had stolen years ago and which he was wearing when he was arrested. It had gratified him to have it listed as his property when he went to prison and returned to him when he was released. Fitted with a new battery, it still worked.

"You been away or something?" Victor asked. "They can please themselves these days. Open and shut more or less as they like. The Angel's open now."

"Yeah? I have been away, as a matter of fact," said Barry. "Spain."

Victor glanced at his pallid face but made no comment. He had seen the quick snatch of the chocolates; here was someone light-fingered and interested in cars; he might be open to suggestion.

"Let me introduce you to The Angel," he said. "I'm Vic Kemp."

"Barry Carter," said Vic's new friend. "Might as well try it."

Vic Kemp would be paying.

Over their pints, which turned into two, Barry learned that Victor was unemployed at the moment, having been a car salesman, he said, and even a milkman at one time. Barry formed the impression that he was a con man; he had a slick way of talking. He said he was hoping to open his own business as soon as he could find the right place to rent. Radios, stereos and so on always sold, he said, even in a recession, but he needed capital to get started and thought he might begin with secondhand stock.

"There's always a turnover," Barry agreed. Vic's shop could be an outlet for stuff he knocked off. "I might be interested," he added, coolly.

"I come in here most nights, around six," said Victor as they parted.

He walked away, reflecting on the potential of the man he had just left. Barry was no major planner, but he could be led and he was an opportunist; Vic had seen that for himself. He went on down the road, past the police station to the public library, which was a good place for passing the time, warm, and with plenty to occupy the mind. By reading the funeral notices in newspapers, you could surmise when houses would be empty and vulnerable, left by mourners unattended. Those for sale were targets, too; you could pose as a buyer and suss them out, see which were worth a later visit, maybe note a good entry point.

When the library closed, he returned to the house in Herbert Road where he had rented a room in the basement. It was a tall, thin house in a quiet road among other houses which took in lodgers, many of them homeless people being paid for by the social services. What a waste, Victor would think, seeing the mothers wheeling their children in pushchairs with toddlers beside them, going out to pass the time until the next meal eaten from tins in the meager rooms. The house where he lived had no such tenants, and those who occupied it tended to keep themselves to themselves. Victor was no exception, but one day the landlady's daughter's hamster had escaped and he had recaptured it, returning it to a grateful child. This had led to a cup of tea and a slice of excellent fruitcake.

Vic's room had its own entrance from the small yard, and he had a private shower. Most of the other tenants had to share a bathroom on an upper landing. There was a second basement room in which an old woman lived, a Russian countess, the landlady had told him. She was sometimes in the library, dressed in black garments which had originally been expensive, and always wearing a hat. Victor thought she was probably a former actress or high-class tart who, with age, had fallen on hard times. He had once, in answer to a timid yap on his door, changed a light bulb for her.

"I don't like asking for aid," she had said. "But I can no longer stand on steps to attend to such matters."

Victor had needed only to stand on a chair. She had offered him a glass of sherry after his good deed, but he had refused. She was lonely, poor old soul, but one thing could lead to another and he did not want to find himself round there at all hours, either in the role of friend, or to run errands for her.

For his meal tonight, Vic had fish and chips which he had bought on the way home. He followed that with cheese and biscuits. He had simple tastes.

To his mother's relief, Barry was spending very little time at the flat, but she wondered who he was seeing when he was out, and what plans he had, if any. She feared she would not like the true answers to either question.

He was certainly not working. He lay in bed late each morning, and most of the time he kept out of Clive's way.

"I thought you said you'd got a job," said Noreen, after a week.

"It's boring," Barry said. "I'll get something else when I'm ready. I've got contacts."

That was what Noreen was afraid of.

"It's not easy now," she said. "Haven't you heard about unemployment, where you've been?"

"Don't needle me, Mum," said Barry, and though his tone was quiet, he glared at her over the plate of egg, bacon and fried bread which he was eating for his late breakfast.

He was sometimes still in the flat when she left for work, though he was rarely back when she returned. She had had to have a key cut for him and she worried about what he might get up to while she and Clive were out. Or while she was out. Clive's hours varied, and he was sometimes at home during the day. If the two men quarreled, things could get rough. Clive was already suspicious of Barry. He had questioned him about where he had been in the north, and what he had been doing, and Barry had spun a tale of working in a car components factory. At least that had, to some extent, held up, as Barry knew a lot about cars, but so did Clive, and he knew the north, too, for he had been a coach driver for some years, traveling all over the country and even abroad.

"That lad of yours telling the truth about working up north?" he had asked her one night, and Noreen had wanted to know what made him wonder.

"Seems vague about places you'd expect him to know well," said Clive.

"He doesn't like questions. You know what kids are," said Noreen.

But Barry wasn't a kid. He was twenty-six and should be settling down. Clive let it go. Noreen probably didn't want to know the whole truth about her son, and maybe it was better that she shouldn't. With luck, he'd soon move on, and out of their lives.

Barry did not return to The Angel for several days; after giving his mother the stolen chocolates, he'd temporarily forgotten Vic. In prison, most men couldn't wait to get their hands on a woman—and more than their hands—and Barry had joined in the crude talk, but he had fantasies which were not like those of most of the men. Striking fear into a woman was what thrilled him; he could still remember the look on that girl's face as she cringed, at his mercy, on the bed.

He'd do that again to someone, when he got the chance. He'd find some place to break and enter where there was a woman he could terrify.

The word "love" was not in Barry's vocabulary. He saw no purpose in life except to acquire, with the minimum effort, money to buy drink and clothes and a woman to screw, and other things which helped to pass the time, such as a television and radio, and maybe a trip to Spain or somewhere like that, where it was warm and sunny.

One night he picked up a girl on a street corner and went back with her to her room. He had enough money to pay and he made her earn it. Why not? It was her choice.

Later, he went to a club where he had a great deal to drink, and grew rowdy enough to be involved in a brawl which ended with him and some others being thrown into the street.

Barry had enough sense to walk away from the three men with whom he and a fifth had been arguing, but he received a deep cut on his arm.

His mother heard him come home in the small hours and sighed with mixed fear and relief. What had he been doing?

In the morning, he appeared with a towel wound round his arm and she bathed the cut—a deep one. She thought it needed stitching but he said that it would heal. She had to go out to buy a special dressing for it, as it was too large for an ordinary plaster.

He told her that someone had been fooling about the pervious evening and that he had got in the way. It was nearly the truth.

He needed a knife. He would buy one, or steal one, before he did anything else.

6.

Barry bought one the next day with money he took from his mother's purse. It was a flick-knife with a wickedly sharp blade. When he took it home, he flourished it around in his room. Thus armed, he was strong.

Living with his mother wasn't easy, but it was free and she fed him well. She'd kept some of his things in the room he had had before he left home to live with Sandra: posters on the wall, his roller skates, a few other childhood trophies. He'd like to replace them all with modern necessities: a personal television, a music center, magazines. He'd do it soon, as he'd be staying for a while.

At first he made an effort to keep out of Clive's way and cause no trouble.

"We're going to get married once his divorce is through," Noreen told Barry, and it was true that they had discussed the future. Clive had a dream of moving to the country and running his own taxi in a small market town, but he had not told Noreen that there was no divorce in sight. His wife was content to go on living in their former house with Clive paying her mortgage and providing for their children, and neither had raised the subject of a legal dissolution. Clive worked long hours for a mini-cab firm but he also put in overtime moonlighting on his own with private clients he had accumulated. He had drifted into his relationship with Noreen after meeting her at The Lunar Moon, where he had gone for a meal with his sister and her husband, who were over from Canada for a visit. Noreen had served their table. She had been unlucky in her marriages and he was sorry for her; she was a good sort, but not one to set the Thames alight. Living with her was better than being on his own, and more restful than a torrid affair.

Now Barry had turned up and Clive was not deceived by the tale of the job up north—unless the nick he'd been in was there, which could be the case. He must have been inside awhile or he would have appeared before, and that meant he had done something quite serious. But maybe he'd learned his lesson; for the moment, Clive decided to give him the benefit of the doubt.

Not long after his arrival, Barry brought his mother a new portable television set and a hair drier. She did not need to ask if they had been legitimately acquired; neither was brand new though both were in good condition. He was up to his old ways of thieving.

He'd get caught; then he'd be locked up again and she would not be worrying herself sick that he was out cutting up young girls and raping them. After what he had done in Bicklebury, Noreen feared he'd develop a taste for violence. He'd seen his father beating her up, and had been beaten himself; then his stepfather had used Barry almost as a punch-bag; was it any wonder he'd grown up with a chip on his shoulder the size of an oak tree, determined to behave the same way to other, weaker people? She'd hoped he'd learn better ways in prison but it had not worked out like that, and it was in prison that he'd met Morris, who had led him into that last escapade.

Noreen would have been still more worried if she'd seen Barry with Vic Kemp. They'd met at The Angel several times by now, and Vic had spoken to Barry about buzzing some place in the country where there'd be easy pickings because the owner was going on holiday. He'd been in a travel agent's, Vic had said, listening to talk between customer and client and had heard dates mentioned; then he had followed the customer home to learn his address.

"I've done this before," Victor had told him. "Means you can plan without having to pay for information from Gatwick or Luton, off labels."

"You've done that?" Barry asked admiringly.

"I'm not into opportunist hits," said Victor. "That's too chancy. I act on certainties."

His forceful talk excited Barry. This was the sort of thinking behind Morris's organized trips down the motorway and into villages where people did not expect to be burgled and were short on security.

"Sounds good," Barry conceded.

"And folk don't get hurt," said Victor. "I'd rather not get caught and have to react."

"Me neither," Barry said, though it was not true. He touched the comforting shape of the knife in his pocket and thought about showing it to Victor, then decided not to; Vic might not like the message.

"But I'm not good at lifting cars," Victor was now admitting. "And I need wheels to get away, when I do this job."

It might have been Morris talking.

"I'm good at that," said Barry, in a modest tone. He somehow knew that Vic wouldn't be impressed by boasting.

Vic was an odd sort of guy. He had thick brown hair which

ran into his curling beard, and thin pale hands. After another drink he grew confidential and told Barry he had worked several lines for years, raising money by selling slimming pills by post; the checks came but the buyers got no pills. He said he'd never been caught. Barry had known all along that he was a con man.

Not to be outdone, he described how, a few days before, he was walking down a quiet street to where he lived with his mother. He said she had a nice house with a garden front and back.

"She likes me living there—I'm all she's got," he said, and told how, while still some distance away, he saw a young woman run out of a house to fetch her children who were playing along the road. Quick as a flash, Barry had gone into her house, taken the television and the drier, and run off with the woman yelling at him when she saw him go.

"It was as if it was meant," said Barry. "I'd been wanting to get them for my mum. Promised her, I had," he declared. "'Course, I'd got a bag on me, ready," he added, and patted his chest. A rustling sound from the plastic carrier concealed in his pocket could be faintly heard above the noise in the bar. "Best be prepared—you never know your luck. Doesn't do to run down the road with a telly. A real neat little one, it was." He made shaping signs with his hands to indicate the size.

Victor made no comment on the unplanned nature of this snatch.

"Bet your mum was pleased," he said.

"You're right," said Barry. There'd been cash, too: a purse had lain on the table and he had snatched that up. He'd taken the money out and thrown the purse into a litter bin in the street, giving it a rub against his jeans first to wipe off his prints. But the chances of it being handed in to the fuzz if it was found were nil, he reckoned, and in that he was right.

There was nothing else of value in it. The woman had no credit cards.

A week later, in a Toyota which Barry had taken from a station car park, the two of them embarked on their first joint operation.

"This place we're going to—the guy's gone to Tenerife," said Victor as they drove at high speed along the motorway.

Barry accelerated. They were doing ninety.

"Hot there, isn't it?" he said.

"You could say that," agreed Victor. "Slow down, Barry. We don't want to get caught for speeding before we've done anything. Or at all, come to that, in a stolen car."

His tone reminded Barry of Morris, and to show he was his own man, he took no notice for two miles, but then he let their speed drop back and kept below the limit for the last few miles before they turned off and were soon traversing residential streets with cars parked nose to tail on either side. Finally, in the darkness, they drove down a side road into an area where the houses were detached. Street lamps revealed shadowy hedges and high fences; people here guarded their privacy.

"Turn in," said Victor. "Number eighty-two—it's this one," and he indicated a gateway to their left.

Lights burned in a downstairs window, and an upper one.

"They're not away," said Barry.

"Yes, they are," said Victor. "It's to keep the likes of us out that they've got those lights on. We'll ring the bell and see what happens, if you're worried. I'll do that. I'll spin some yarn about does Mr. Wilson live here, if anyone answers. Right?"

"Right," Barry agreed, and watched while Victor walked up the path to the front door and pressed the bell.

Nothing happened, and no security light came on. Barry moved past the entrance, then reversed the car into the narrow drive so that it was ready for an easy getaway, and they could not be seen loading it with whatever loot they snatched from the house.

They broke in round the back where there was a glass door with a key left handily situated for them in the inside lock. Victor smashed the glass, using a stone he found nearby. He was wearing heavy gloves, and he wrapped the stone in a yellow duster. The sound he made seemed loud as the glass shattered, and both men stood still for a few seconds, listening, but nothing happened.

"Well, come on, get on with it," Barry said. "What are you waiting for?"

Vic put his hand through the broken pane and turned the key; then they were inside the house, where Barry seemed to go wild. He tore all over the place and ran upstairs, where he pulled open drawers and tipped their contents on the floor, throwing things around. Victor called up to him to draw the curtains so that his actions were not visible from outside. He concentrated on the downstairs rooms, finding a television and a stereo record player, and, in the kitchen, a microwave oven that looked almost new. There were fifty pounds in cash in a desk drawer and he found checkbooks but no bankers' cards. He worked quietly and neatly.

Barry came downstairs carrying some women's clothes, including a fake fur coat. He tipped them on the floor. He had found some jewelry, too, and had stuffed it into the large pockets of his jacket. He went into the kitchen, still hurrying, so hasty that he knocked a chair over, and a lamp, and returned with a roll of bin liners after emptying all the drawers in his search. He put the women's clothes into bags.

"My mum'll like those," he said. "Not much else, though, is there? No silver."

There was some wine in a rack under the stairs and he snatched a bottle up, cracked its neck across a table end and began to drink it.

"Let's get this stuff into the car, Barry," Victor said. "There'll be time for drinking later."

"I'll bring the rest, then," Barry said, picking up the other bottles and shoving them into a bin bag. He took another swig from the bottle he had opened, cutting his lip slightly on its jagged neck, then, giggling, he poured the rest of a good claret on the pale carpet where it made a spreading stain.

"You're wasting time, Barry," Victor said. "Get on and take that television to the car."

Barry wiped his hand across his mouth. Blood and wine smeared his gloves, but he picked up the television set and carried it from the room. Vic took a quick glance round at the unnecessary chaos; it was that sort of vandalism that got thieves a bad reputation, but he knew better than to mention it to Barry as they drove away.

"I don't think much of your tip-off," Barry said.

"There were checkbooks," Victor answered. "I know someone who'll give a good price for them. Let's get going."

They left the stuff in a lock-up garage Vic had rented as a store for goods for his future business. Barry kept the microwave, the jewelry and the clothing for his mother, and Victor did not argue, simply saying that he'd take them into account when settling up the total profit.

It was a blow to Barry when he found that none of the jewelry was genuine; it was all cheap stuff and not worth more than a fiver for the lot.

After leaving Victor at the lock-up, with some pictures, the television, stereo system and other electrical items they had taken on their raid, and the wine—Vic insisted on keeping that; the countess would enjoy a bottle—Barry took the microwave and the clothing to his mother's flat. She'd like the snug fur coat, which he'd got before the real winter weather. Then he returned for the Toyota, which he'd left outside, ready for a spin around the area. He was elated, on a high after the successful heist, although it had not lived up to his expectations. He'd make sure Vic chose a better place next time, and why not do a series, several in a night? Vic hadn't agreed when he had wanted to cruise round the quiet streets where they had done the burglary, looking for another place to rob. Barry wouldn't listen to him, next time; unless they got a proper haul, he'd pick a second target in the area.

He came out of the building and crossed the road to the spot where he had left the car, and it had gone. Someone had nicked it! Would you believe it? He couldn't. Fancy not being able to leave it for five minutes while he made a simple delivery. He felt choked.

The flat had been in darkness, and quiet. It was very late, but Barry had given no thought as to whether his mother was back from work, or Clive; he had not made much noise, depositing the microwave in the kitchen and the bags with the clothes in the passage. Now he saw Clive's Sierra parked close to where he had left the Toyota. It had an alarm, but Barry knew that the keys were in a mug in the kitchen. He went back upstairs to fetch them.

His spirits rose as he drove off. Serve the bastard right, he thought, muscling it on his mother, getting all her attention.

He did not have to go far. Three miles away, driving down a street where there were shops, some pubs and a disco, he saw a girl alone. He passed her, parked, got out of the car and walked towards her. She was a prostitute and thought she had a customer, entering the car quite willingly. Barry drove her to a straggling park area, and she was still cooperating when they got out of it and went behind some bushes where, after she protested at his methods, he raped her. Then, because she could identify him and he had a conviction for rape, he stabbed her to death, using his new knife.

It didn't do to take a chance.

The next day, Barry slept in late and Clive had gone out by the time he was ready for the large breakfast his mother was waiting to prepare. She had already seen the microwave and was delighted with it, although she knew full well that it was stolen. The coat was nice, too, she told him; she had looked inside the bags he had left on the landing and had hidden them before Clive could see them.

"I got it from a bloke that won't miss it," Barry said.

His eyes were gleaming; there was a look about him which his mother did not like to see.

She did not remonstrate; there wasn't time before she had to leave for work, and the microwave would make things much easier for Clive when he came in late. She left the flat, and Barry went back to bed.

In the evening he met Vic and received five hundred pounds in cash, for Vic had already got rid of the checkbooks. The other items would be stock for the shop, he reminded Barry, passing him an envelope.

Barry had hoped for more, but he accepted Vic's explanation that the checks were less valuable than if there had been cards to match them.

"We'll do a bigger job next time," Vic declared. "That was just a trial run."

Barry had shown himself to be an impulsive partner, given to swift mood changes; Vic would have to bear that fact in mind when planning their next operation. An isolated house in a rural area would be a better target and one that might appeal to Barry more than a suburban hit. He'd plan it carefully so that there were no distractions to tempt Barry into being too exuberant. They parted, with no firm date for their next meeting.

Barry spent a lot of time in the flat in the next days, often sleeping and watching videos. There hadn't been a video at that place he and Vic had done, and he'd gone out and bought one with some of his money—not a new one; it was being sold at a pub by a man who'd knocked it off.

His mother wouldn't know the difference.

In the evenings, Barry went out drinking, and now and then he found a girl who was willing enough, though that was dull. Soon he would terrify some other woman.

7.

Barry had not noticed that a man had followed him when he left his mother's flat, and had watched him buy his knife. Unaware that nemesis was stalking him, he was making the most of being free. His partnership with Vic suited him for the present, because on his own he could only manage small-scale thefts and petty shoplifting. Barry would like to get in with a big-time gang, one planning major raids on banks and wage-delivery vans; then there would be large profits, enough to take him off to South America or somewhere far away from all the fog and rain in England. He'd have a big place to live in, a villa with a swimming pool and someone to wait on him. He dreamed like this at intervals. He could get cars for jobs like that, or drive stolen security vans while others carried out the actual raids, not that Barry would shirk from holding people up with guns; he might try it one day. But though he'd met men serving time for such offenses, who could use an experienced car thief or an expert driver, there had been rumours in prison that Barry had done more than steal, and big-time robbers were not interested in rape. There were plenty of men about who were good with cars;

kids began early these days, lifting them as soon as they were tall enough to drive them.

Planning was Barry's problem. He could take his chance on a snatch, as when he stole the small television and the drier for his mother, but he had not learned how to target a particular house or area, as Morris had done. They had evaded capture until that night in Bicklebury, and Morris had maintained that they would not have been caught then but for the rape; the police would not have put such effort into catching mere thieves whose haul had not been all that great. Taking off his gloves had meant that Barry left a print, and he had tried to sell the girl's pendant independently; both actions were enough to give away his identity. Morris was very bitter about his heavier sentence, when he had not even touched the girl.

Sometimes, in Barry's fantasies, he dreamed of having a perfect woman in his life, someone gorgeous who would clean the minor palace in which they lived, and prepare their meals, then be ready for anything in their enormous bed. But his dreams would darken as he wondered if she would stay true to him: what if she fancied someone else? Sandra had been that sort of girl—not gorgeous, but not bad-looking— and she had turned him out; she had put his few possessions into carrier bags and left them outside her door, changing the locks. He'd meekly gone. He should have punished her for that, not taken no for an answer, hit her until she did as he wanted. That was how his father had treated his mother; how else were women taught their place?

That man Clive, who was living with his mother now, was different. He called her "pet" and often fetched her home from work at night. Barry had heard soft murmurings from their room. It churned him up, made him want to go in there and bash them both to pieces.

Barry knew that Clive didn't like him. Clive would say "Good evening" when they met, very formal and civil, and Barry would grunt something in reply, or not bother. So far, they had not met in the morning as Barry spent most of that in bed. Noreen had shown Clive the microwave and mock fur coat and told him that Barry had bought them for her, but it was obvious from the look on Clive's face that he knew Barry had not got them legally. Next time he had that expression, Barry would wipe it off for him.

Well, he'd used Clive's car now, hadn't he? And he'd do it again, if he wanted to.

Barry had put the Sierra back in its usual place after his night's excursion, and had replaced the key. He got a real kick out of the fact that Clive had no knowledge of what he had done.

He soon forgot the girl he had killed. He'd pushed her body under the bushes and pulled some branches across it. Three days later it hadn't been found.

Vic soon found a new target for them to raid. He had been to the travel agent's on another eavesdropping trip and he had several addresses to inspect. Barry wanted to go with him but Vic insisted that one man, alone, spying round, was less suspicious than two, and that he, Vic, was adept at ringing doorbells and asking innocent questions, pretending he was selling something or doing a survey.

"You've got no wheels," said Barry. "How do you get there?"

"Who says I've no wheels?"

"Well, you want me for nicking the transport," said Barry.

"I've a lady friend," said Victor. "She lets me borrow her car, in return for a favor or two. But I don't want to use that for a job—it could be traced. Besides, it's not fast enough; it's an old Fiesta." He drank some of his beer, getting froth on his luxuriant beard. "I smarten up to see her," he said. "And I do the same when I'm spying out the land. I've got a nice Oxfam suit." He set his glass down. "I fancy a trip to Spain," he said. "A month or two in the sun. How would you like to go back there for Christmas, Barry?"

"Sounds all right," said Barry grudgingly.

"There's a guy I know goes in for pictures," said Vic. "Old masters—that sort of thing. One of these houses I've heard of sounds promising that way. Been written up in a magazine, it seems, and the owner collects art. Might be big money there, if we can get a particular painting that's wanted. That's specialized knowledge, you see."

It sounded a bit deep for Barry.

"People pay good money for paintings?" he asked suspiciously.

"You know that, Barry. Galleries have been raided for special pictures. The buyers can't sell them on, because they're all listed and known, but there are folk who like to gloat over them in private. They pay well."

"Make sure it's worth our while, this time," Barry said, looking fierce. He didn't like being pushed around and it seemed to him that Vic was making all the decisions. Just like Morris.

While Vic was investigating, Barry went on some drinking bouts and played pool. What else was there to do?

The man who watched him saw how he spent his time. It was easy to tail him. Derek knew nothing, however, about the girl Barry had killed, for he had not been watching him then, so late at night.

Her body was found four days after her death, but the police took another week to identify her. There was no doubt about this being a case of murder because she had been stabbed several times. The killer's clothes would have been heavily stained with blood. The postmortem showed that she had had recent intercourse, and she was damaged in the genital area; swabs might provide the DNA profile of her assailant but because she was a prostitute—as it was eventually established—there could be doubt about this for she could have had other clients besides her murderer on the fatal night.

She had lived in a house with two more girls who were on the game, and they had children. When she had been absent for several days they had reported her missing, but her body had been found in an area well away from where she sought business so the connection had not been made at once.

The police rounded up some known sexual offenders whose victims had been attacked in the street, but they did not seek out Barry, whose *modus operandi* had been different and who had not killed. One of the men they took in for questioning was kept in custody for an extended period granted because the police considered him a likely suspect. They took away his clothes and shoes for testing.

Barry, discovering his clothes to be stained, had put them in the washing machine as soon as his mother had gone to work the morning after the crime. He'd turned it on, putting in plenty of powder, and then left it for his mother to empty when she came home and she had been cross because the colors had run on his shirt and there were stains that hadn't come out. She'd asked whatever had he been doing, getting in a mess like that—had he upset tomato sauce over himself? He'd said yes, something like that. She'd suggested that he leave things to her, next time.

"Still, I expect you meant to be helpful," she said, with that silly smile which meant she was trying to get round him.

She'd washed everything again but the stains seemed set fast and she was puzzled.

Barry said it didn't matter. He told her to throw the clothes away; he'd get new ones, and he did. There was someone down at The Angel selling gear he'd knocked off in a raid a few days before, designer jeans and sweatshirts which he'd got stocked in a bedroom at his house. Barry went there and was soon reequipped, much more smartly than before.

Then Vic came up with some news. He had inspected the area around the house where there were notable paintings worth stealing. It was out in the country, an ideal target, isolated from the nearest village, which was so small that it was only a hamlet. He showed Barry magazine pictures which illustrated a feature about it, and pointed out the room described as the saloon in which hung at least a dozen paintings, some of men and women in what to Barry were peculiar clothes, and some landscapes.

"That's the one that's special," Vic said, pointing to the smallest. "It's a Corot—that's the artist's name. We'll get several grand for taking that."

"Straight up?" asked Barry.

"Straight up," said Victor. "How about that, then, Barry? It'd help me get stock for the shop, but first there's our little trip abroad. Morocco might be warmer than Spain just now. What do you think?"

"You can decide," said Barry. Anywhere sunny would suit him.

Wine and women would be available to them, Victor said, as they'd have money in their pockets, but there would be pickings, too, as people on holiday were often careless and left money and checks lying about in hotel and villa rooms.

Barry thought that, with Vic around, he would find it great, but to cope with it alone would be a problem. You booked your holiday and caught your flight, but what happened after that? Barry had never left the country; the furthest he had been was to the Isle of Wight, and that was for a stint in Parkhurst during his recent sentence.

"The owners of the house are off to Madeira," Victor said. "It's a place where people go all year because of its equable climate."

"What does that mean? Equable?" asked Barry.

"Good-tempered," Victor said, his pale lips creasing in a smile within the depths of his beard. "Like me. Not given to sudden changes."

"You been there?"

"No. It's quiet," said Victor. "Not much in the way of casinos and nightlife. That'd be more your scene, Barry, wouldn't it? Tell me, what do you want from life? How do you see your future? Wife and kids? That sort of thing?"

Barry shuffled uneasily. Such talk made him feel embarrassed.

"They don't stick to you, do they? Women?" he said. "Bit of trouble and they're off with someone else. Only good for one thing, really."

"What's that?"

"Oh—you know. Sex, of course," said Barry.

"They've got feelings, same as us," said Victor.

Barry thought fleetingly of his mother. He'd wanted to earn her approval; as a boy, he'd nicked several trinkets from Woolworth's and such places to give her, and scent. He'd thought such presents would win her love, and she'd seemed grateful at the time, but his stepfather had always realized that he had stolen the gifts so that he'd got a leathering for what he'd done. It hadn't stopped him from repeating the pattern, but she hadn't accused him of stealing the things that he had given her since he came out of prison. Nor had Clive. Anyway, he couldn't be beaten now; he was a man, the one who gave out punishment instead of being its recipient.

"You been married?" he asked Vic.

"Once," said Vic. "It didn't work out. But in Spain—and Morocco—there'd be plenty of girls out for a bit of fun," he added. "No strings attached. No wedding bells twinkling in their greedy little eyes."

It sounded so simple when he said it like that. Maybe it would be, thought Barry; maybe all he needed was the chance.

"There'll be jewelry there, too, at that house," Victor was saying. "Good stuff, worth a lot. And a safe, with cash in it."

"Will they leave it there when they're away?"

"Good question. Yes, because they employ someone to mind the house while they're gone, feed the cat and the goldfish, that sort of thing," said Victor.

"Then they'll see us coming," Barry said.

"They won't, because we'll get them away on a pretext," Victor said. "We'll ring up and say their own house has been burgled, and they've got to go home, no time to lose. We'll pretend to be the police."

Barry was taken with this idea and laughed. It was an odd, scratchy sound, seldom heard.

"Well?" Victor demanded. "Aren't you going to ask me how we'll know their names? The house minders, I mean."

"I was just going to," said Barry quickly.

"I'll go round there the day before with a parcel for the owners. One that has to be signed for. Special delivery. The minders—there'll probably be two of them because it's usually retired couples who do this kind of work—will write their name down, so we'll learn what it is. Easy."

"Brilliant," said Barry, looking in admiration at the other man.

"I know," said Vic, who had enjoyed impressing his new partner. "You're on a good team with me, Barry."

"We'll go abroad afterwards? At once?"

"As soon as we've got the money," Victor said. "It'll take a day or two. Not long, because a quick turnaround is the secret in this game. There'll be lots of stuff to take—televisions, radios—as well as the pictures and the jewelry. We'll stash it in the lock-up ready to open the shop when we come back."

He made it sound as easy as catching a train to Wembley. Barry caught his optimism.

"It'd better be soon," he said. "I'm running out of cash."

Victor pulled out a shabby purse and counted out ten twenty-pound notes.

"Have that on account," he said. "I don't want you getting into trouble doing some little snatch on your own."

"I won't," said Barry.

But he couldn't wait. The very next day he lifted some small goods from an electrical shop and had to run when the tagged alarms went off as he left the shop.

The security cameras in the shop picked him up, but not clearly. In due course someone might put a name to his face, but not yet.

Barry did not know that a man was being questioned about the murder he had committed. He did not even know that his victim's body had been found; he had moved on, forgetting the incident which to him had held no more importance than the swatting of a fly. The crime had attracted some notice in the press, but it had to compete with other events where there were dramatic elements in the background which could be exaggerated by sensation-seeking journalists.

He was impatient to get on with the big job Vic had planned. Part of him understood that they must wait until the target house was empty or the scheme would come to nothing, but the other, irrational part could not accept the delay. It was all right when he was with Vic; the older man's talk about what they would do with their spoils kept Barry in thrall, but, on his own, he chafed.

Vic wasn't in The Angel the night after their talk, nor on any of the next three nights. Where had he got to? Barry went round to the lock-up where they'd taken the stuff from that first robbery and, in frustration, broke the lock. He wanted to see how Vic was getting on with building up his stock for the shop.

The place was empty.

He must have sold everything they'd already stolen and not passed on the profits. It was all a con, the line about the shop and about that big house waiting to be robbed. Maybe Vic had already scarpered abroad with the lot. Barry was seething with anger when he left the place, but he didn't know where Vic lived so he couldn't go after him.

That night he got very drunk at The Angel and was in a black, brooding fury when Vic finally appeared.

"What you done with that stuff we got?" he asked. "The telly and stereo? Them electrical things?" He did not say he'd looked for them already.

"Sold it on," said Vic. "You've had your share, Barry, and you kept a few things for your mum, remember? There wasn't enough to start the shop and it was best to turn it over. Cash in the hand, you know."

"You didn't give me enough," said Barry.

Vic didn't remind him that he'd had an extra two hundred only a few nights before.

"Well, wait till we get to Thrupton," he said peaceably. "The folk there go away next week and I'll make my visit with the parcel as soon as the minders have settled in."

Barry wasn't satisfied. He went off in a very disagreeable mood and found himself a car so that he could go for a drive.

Tearing along at speed made him feel good. He wasn't into showing off in front of kids, but he liked to grip the wheel of a fast car and cut up the motorway, flashing his lights at cars he wanted to overtake.

He liked the idea of ram-raiding, which he'd never done. He might get into that when he came back from abroad. You got hold of something big—a digger, if you could—and drove it at a plate glass window, stoving it in, then loaded up a waiting car with as much as you could grab and drove off. But you needed mates for it; it wasn't a one-man job, and Barry had no real mates. He pushed away that thought. With money, he'd get mates; if he flashed it around, fellows would be impressed. Mates would sell goods on, too, like Morris had, and now Vic. He needed to get in with a well-organized gang who'd got all that sorted out, and who could plan things. He had to admit that. But he could knock off the odd radio and stereo and they were easy enough to sell. He could probably coast along on pickings until the raid at Thrupton, wherever that was.

He took Clive's car again one night and drove it north, to Bedfordshire, where he saw a girl walking along a lonely country road. Barry didn't like the country but he'd got bored with the motorway and had turned off to see where a side road led. He didn't like the fields and trees, and the birds that swooped towards you, all that space. But at night you didn't see all that: there was just the tunnel of road lit up in the headlights and you could speed along, frightening the stoats and rabbits.

He nearly hit the girl, silly cow. She was in a dark coat, barely visible, and she pressed herself against the hedge as he raced towards her.

Barry braked hard. What was she doing, out at that hour by herself, if she wasn't looking for trouble?

He gave her plenty, and he enjoyed her terror and her screams which no one heard except him and the wild creatures in the hedgerows, but he didn't stab her. It made too much mess. He thought he had strangled her before he threw her into a ditch at the side of the road, but she wasn't quite dead.

Several hours later, an early motorist driving that way saw her staggering along the road, and he rescued her and took her to hospital.

8.

The mileage on Clive's car had twice increased without his being aware of having clocked up so much. He did not check it every time he went out, unless it was with a fare, but he always knew approximately what it was. He was sure that Barry must be responsible but saw no way to prove it; however, he stopped leaving the keys in the mug on the dresser, and he hid his spare set.

Life in the flat was not as easy now as before Barry came to live there. Noreen was jumpy and quick to snap at the least thing. She had been fine when Clive first met her, grateful for his company and surprised because he was never rough with her, or bad-tempered. She'd not had much decent treatment in the past, he realized, and was touched. But Barry was a complication; he was a real bad penny. After the second time he took the car, Clive decided that he must speak to Noreen about the problem.

He did not tackle her abruptly, in the flat, where Barry might come in and interrupt them, but took her out to a meal on her next night off—she got very few. They went to a pub by the river. Though it was now December, the evening was fine and dry, and the black water of the Thames reflected all the lights on either side; occasionally a boat went by. Clive liked London at night, parts of it.

After they'd eaten, and Noreen had had several glasses of red wine—Clive was careful, because of driving—they walked along the embankment path and he linked her arm through his. That was one of the things she liked about Clive; he seemed really fond of her and took care of her. Noreen had never had this from a man before though she had often hoped for it. But her contentment vanished when Clive mentioned Barry.

"Is he staying much longer?" Clive asked, and she felt a sick sensation inside.

"I don't know," she said, and a primitive desire to protect her wayward son surged through her. "He hasn't said," she added, guardedly.

Clive decided not to ask if Barry was contributing towards his keep because he already knew the answer. Noreen might respond by reminding him that Barry had given her the microwave, the hair drier and the television, and a fur coat, and then Clive would feel obliged to tell her that he suspected they were stolen.

"I'm not sure about having him around, Noreen," he said, and hurried on. "It's awkward for me. I like being with you but Barry isn't keen on me being in the flat."

"Has he said so?" Noreen couldn't believe it.

In fact, the two men did their best to avoid one another, and Barry spent a lot of time in his room, but he was often slumped in front of the television when Clive came home, and, since he had acquired the recorder, watching videos of a kind Clive had no desire to see. This prevented Clive from watching sports, or even the news.

He tried to say some of this to Noreen, who understood at once; indeed, she found Barry's taste in videos unfortunate, but she had her own small television in the kitchen now. She told Clive that he could use it in the bedroom anytime; that might solve one problem.

It was true that Barry had eased them both out of their former routines, and he sprawled on the settee which she had bought only last year, and on which, in their early days together, she and Clive had sometimes made love.

They still made love quite often, when neither was too tired, and it was love, too, which she had never known before.

For an instant she wondered what sort of love Barry made, then shut down her mind because she knew that he did not understand the meaning of the word.

She did not see his gifts to her as tokens of a sort of love.

"I'm sorry," she said. "I know it's not the same now, but what can I do? I can't turn him out. He is my son."

Clive had to say it. He spoke gently.

"It'll be him or me," he said. "Not at once. I'll give it a while longer. But if he isn't out in a month, I'll start looking for a place of my own."

"I'll talk to him," said Noreen.

But she wouldn't. What would happen to Barry if she told him he must leave?

The girl dumped in the ditch in a country road in Bedfordshire after Barry had strangled her almost to death was not fit to answer questions straightaway, but she had noticed the make of the car which her assailant was driving. It was a blue Ford Sierra with a G registration. She seemed sure of that fact, and she thought the number ended in a double three but it might have been three eight, or even eight three; she could not be certain. Still, it was a start for the police. Barry had insisted that she get into the car, though she had said she would prefer to walk, and at first he had driven

along beside her, keeping pace with her. Short of diving into
a field and running away across the countryside, she saw no
alternative but to obey him. He might intend no harm; perhaps he did only mean to give her a lift, as he said. At last she
gave in and entered the car with no force being used.

He had driven a short distance up the road and then
pulled into a gateway, where the assault had taken place. She
had struggled and bitten him, and he had got very angry and
hit her around the face. The rape itself had not taken long;
the whole experience could not have lasted much more than
half an hour, if that, but she thought she would know him
again. After a few days she was well enough to help a police
artist construct an impression of the man.

She was a local girl who had been only two miles from her
home at the time of the attack. Appeals were broadcast asking anyone who had seen a blue Sierra on the road in question, or in the area, to come forward.

The crime had shocked the neighborhood. The girl was
normally collected from discos or parties by one or other of
her parents, and on this occasion she had gone to a party with
a friend whose father had arranged to fetch both girls. He did
not arrive—it turned out that his car would not start—and
the other girl had gone off with a youth she had met at the
party. The victim had not wanted to go with them because
there were two other young men in the car and she thought
they had all had too much to drink. She said she would wait
for the arranged lift with her friend's father, and if he did not
come, she would start walking.

Many questions were asked. Why did the other girl, when
she reached home safely, not tell her father that her friend was
going to walk so that he could alert someone to fetch her?
Why didn't the father, when his car would not start, send a
taxi or ask someone else to fetch both girls? No use now to say

that a generation ago, young girls had safely walked along that road at night, unmolested, and at no risk if they did accept a lift. Times had changed and jungle laws prevailed.

Police enquiries concentrated on the car, but tracing it could be a weary job.

Barry saw a news flash on television about the attack but he brushed it aside. It was a pity that the girl had survived to give an account of what had happened, but it meant he hadn't done a murder; you got life for murder, not that he'd get caught. He forgot the other girl, the one he had killed.

The girl might describe him: he thought of that; but the car wasn't his and if the police traced it, they would find that it was Clive's, and that notion amused Barry. It could cause the man grief. All he did, himself, was to shave off the wispy fair beard he had grown because shaving had become too much trouble, and to have his long hair cut into a short crop.

Vic approved the change in his appearance.

"Much better," he said, when they met again. "Neater. More workmanlike."

"You can talk," said Barry.

Vic stroked his luxuriant beard. His lips were wet from beer he had been drinking.

"When you can grow one like mine, try again," he said, and the implied insult made the blood surge through Barry's veins.

"I'd have you know—" he began, clenching his fist on the table.

"Yes?" asked Victor.

"Women," said Barry, exhaling hard. "I've had plenty," he ended, on a diminuendo note.

"I never said you hadn't," said Victor calmly. "Some of them go for the hirsute. I've found that," and again he stroked his own beard.

"Hirsute?"

"Hairy. Hairs on the chest as well as the face," Vic translated. "Others prefer a smooth man. You can't tell which they like until you try. There's room for all sorts in the world."

"This job," said Barry. "Are we going tomorrow? It'll soon be Christmas."

"Thursday's the day," said Vic firmly. "It'll all be set up by then. We'll be off to the sun before you know it and you can hang up your Christmas stocking abroad. Got your passport?"

Barry remembered that Victor thought he'd been to Spain.

"I've lost it," he said.

"Oh dear. Well, I think that rules Morocco out," said Vic. "But a visitor's one's all right in Europe. You can get it from the post office, but you need to take along your birth certificate and some other form of identification—driving license—anything similar."

"Oh!" This was news to Barry.

"A full passport takes some time to come and costs more," Vic informed him. "Don't you remember that?"

"Of course I do," snapped Barry. He supposed his mother would have his birth certificate somewhere, in a drawer of the dresser, probably. He could ask her. She'd be pleased at the prospect of him leaving, or Clive would; she'd asked him only yesterday if he had any plans for moving on and he'd managed to make quite a scene, accusing her of not wanting to look after him and help him find his feet after all that he'd been through. She'd ended up in tears, and he'd been pleased, though he'd had a funny feeling later. Shame was so alien an emotion to Barry that when he felt it, he did not recognize it.

On the other hand, he thought, instead of asking for it, first he'd try to find it, and then she needn't know that he was going. She might even worry, when suddenly he wasn't there. That was a pleasant thought.

What if he shopped Clive for that business in the country lane? Rang the police up and tipped them off about the blue Sierra? It was a nice idea. Then Clive would go to prison. Serve him right for getting in with Barry's mother when Barry wasn't there. It was well known that the police often got things wrong and locked up the innocent. Why not Clive?

9.

Derek had spent time observing Barry Carter and had formed a picture of the life that he was leading. Most of his watching had been done sitting in his car near the flats, waiting for Barry to come out. This rarely happened until after midday, and often not then. Sometimes Barry would go to shops and stroll around them, up to no good, Derek was sure, but he did not want to be recognized and did not follow him on his shopping sprees. At night, Barry went to pubs or discos, returning home late. Once, Derek saw him steal a car; it was done in seconds, very skillfully. Derek did not go after him; there were some things it was better not to know. He thought that Barry looked like trouble waiting to explode.

He had not solved the problem of the gun. Buying a pistol legitimately would not be possible; he would have to be a member of his club for at least six months and then apply, with four photographs of himself, one of which must be signed by a magistrate or other such worthy citizen who had known him for two years, for a license. Even if he waited for that length of time and went through all the formalities, such a gun, when used, could be traced straight back to him.

A shotgun was easier to obtain; he could say he needed it

to keep down vermin. But you couldn't carry one around while stalking someone. Now he understood why so many criminals used sawn-off shotguns. But villains used revolvers, too. He must find some villains.

He had often seen groups of youths clustered about near the flats or on street corners. Just because they had nothing to do did not mean that they were criminals. He had been careful to avoid their attention and had driven off whenever he saw several approaching. The best way to follow Barry was on foot, and The Angel, which seemed to be his preferred pub, was only a few streets away from Noreen Carter's flat.

Unless he moved out of his mother's place, Barry could be found quite easily.

Derek thought of the youths he had seen when he went into the block, the group of quiet young men who, he had decided, were possibly trading drugs. They had seemed peaceable enough; it was the addicts who became crazed and went on the rampage, like drunken hooligans on an exaggerated scale. It was addicts, too, who stole to feed their habit.

Some of those quiet young men might know how to get weapons.

Derek began to watch the groups of twos and threes. They met and coalesced and re-formed. He saw them on street corners; he recognized a few. One in particular was often around when the children were coming back from school. He stood outside a sweet shop and spoke to various youngsters. Derek wondered what he was up to: was he offering the children drugs?

There were other youths, frequenters of the pubs and clubs Carter patronized. How could you tell whom to approach? They did not wear the sign CRIMINAL etched on their brows, and not every unemployed young man who loitered in the streets was subversive; far from it.

One evening he decided to tackle the young man, little more than a youth, whom he had seen several times outside the sweet shop talking to children. Most of the youngsters passed him by but a few stopped and once Derek thought he saw some sort of exchange, but it was done with great sleight of hand. He would take a chance. There was little to lose; the man would not know who he was and, if up to no good himself, would be unlikely to create a scene.

One late winter afternoon, when the youngsters had dispersed, Derek, who had been watching from inside the shop, followed the man along the road and dropped a large, heavy hand on his shoulder. The man turned quickly, already writhing beneath Derek's grasp, which tightened on his jacket, and Derek saw fear on his face. He thinks I'm a plainclothes cop, thought Derek, who had hoped that the youth would make this mistake.

"Just a minute," Derek said. "You were selling drugs to those kids." It was a statement, not a question.

"I never," said the young man. "They're just friends of mine. I was passing the time." He wriggled, trying to free himself, but Derek now held him firmly by the arm; he was much stronger than the youth. "Here," he said, suspicion now showing on his face, which was pale and spotty. "You're not the law." For if he was, Derek would have said so by now and produced his card. "What's your game?" he asked.

"Just walk along quietly with me," said Derek, "and you'll find out."

He told the youth that he needed to buy a revolver, a reliable one in good condition, with a full round of ammunition.

"You get one for me and I'll say nothing to anyone about the drugs," he said. He pulled a fifty-pound note out of his pocket and showed it to his captive as they reached a lamppost. "You can have this now, on account, and I'll pay you two hundred pounds for the gun."

"Four," said the youth at once, and Derek knew that he had scored.

"Two-fifty," Derek said.

They settled in the end for two seventy-five and arranged to meet in three days' time at a café just round the corner where they could make their exchange. They'd meet at five, when the place was not at its busiest. Derek had already spent time there waiting to follow Carter who sometimes came this way when he was going shopping.

The youth might simply take the fifty pounds and never turn up again, but Derek thought not. Two hundred and seventy-five pounds was a lot of money in anyone's book. It was a chance he had to take.

He had amazed himself. It was not difficult to descend the slippery slope into serious crime.

Weeks ago, he had ended his relationship with Angela.

It had been difficult at first. He told her that he was putting the house on the market and would be moving when it was sold, and sure enough, an agent's board appeared. His job had ceased to exist, he said, and he could no longer afford to pay to have his shirts ironed. At first Angela was upset, but she became philosophical; things had been getting difficult for her because Stephen had noticed that she was always back later on Tuesdays than on any other night. Besides this, Stephen's case for compensation was on the court lists and would soon be heard; they had been advised not to accept an out-of-court offer but to go for a bigger sum. It was a risky choice; in the end they might be granted less than the offer, but Stephen had decided on the gamble. It was doing him good, Angela had declared; he seemed to have more energy of the right kind.

She had said very little to Derek about the wrong sort of energy he displayed; Derek did not really want to know how hard things were for her at home because he had no time to help her. There was no joint future for them; both had always known that; but time bred claims.

"I'm sorry about the money," Derek said. "Will you miss my shirts?"

"I'll find some others," she assured him.

She was tired of ironing. It was hot and sweaty work; she had worn out several irons in the time she had been operating; they burned out from overuse, and it was so repetitive; again and again the same shirts and bed linen came round. The satisfaction she had had at first from seeing the neat piles accumulate had dwindled; besides, Pippa stayed up later now and needed help with homework, which Stephen often would not give though it was something he could easily undertake. Angela viewed the years ahead with deepest gloom; the Stephen she had married had quite gone and she found it hard to love his successor.

She drove past Derek's house from time to time on her continuing errands. Sometimes at night a light was on, and sometimes not. He'd got someone else, perhaps, she thought: someone with whom there was a future. She did not really mind; he was lonely and needed a woman who could offer him more than a fleeting hour on Tuesday evenings.

Derek missed her, but he did not want to involve her in the possible consequences of his action against Barry, for if he were caught and charged, his daily life would be exposed and that would mean discovery for her. Someone would have seen her small blue van outside the house for longer than was necessary to collect the washing; someone would testify to the regularity of these calls. At the very least her marriage, unsteady as it was, would be at risk. His hope was that if Stephen won substantial damages, the quality of help they would then be able to afford would free her to follow an interesting career of her own, though what that would be, he did not know.

In spite of trailing Barry Carter and even, one night, watching him in a very drunken state lurch home from a drinking bout, Derek did not know that Barry had used the blue Sierra owned by Noreen Carter's partner and driven it to Bedfordshire, although he knew about the attack on the young girl. These days, he read every rape case he saw reported in the press, for each victim was someone else's daughter and each victim was, in a sense, Hannah's sister.

Two separate police forces were dealing with the murder in the park and the attack in the country road. The man arrested for the first was eventually released for want of evidence, and another known sex offender, unable to account satisfactorily for his movements on the night when the victim was assumed to have been killed, was taken in for questioning, but in the end he, too, had to be allowed to go for there were no links of fibers from the girl's clothing, and no clear DNA profile of the offender had been obtained from her body. The girl in Bedfordshire, however, was a different case; there, swabs provided a sample which would yield such information, but Barry Carter's DNA definition was not on file because it had never been obtained, though his blood group was known, a common O. He did not live near this second victim; he did not come into the frame of suspects. It might be only when some other girl was attacked by the same man that further clues would be discovered.

A few concerned journalists wrote pieces demanding

longer sentences for convicted rapists than those in force at present, and they demanded supervision for known rapists who had been released, but until the man responsible for this attack was arrested, the message was repeated that severe punishment might deter offenders; later, when this one was caught, if that ever happened, there might be more ammunition for a renewed campaign.

Derek set off for the café where he hoped to collect his gun in a very cautious manner. The young man he was meeting would know he would be carrying a large amount of cash and might intend to waylay and mug him, or could have set up some friends of his to do it for him. He was constantly behaving illicitly, whereas Derek was, thus far, a law-abiding citizen, new to stealth; however, in these weeks of trailing Barry Carter, he had learned to watch and wait and had acquired some guile. He reached the café early and bought a cup of tea at the counter, then, having set it on a table with a paper, which he had bought earlier, went out to the washroom beyond the small, steamy café area. Counting the time, eyeing his watch, he waited until a minute after they had arranged to meet and went back into the café.

The young man was there, sitting alone at a corner table, his back to the wall.

Derek crossed the room, collecting his now tepid tea and his paper, and slid into the facing seat. The money was in an envelope in his jacket pocket and he had worn gloves whenever he touched it; he wore them now. No one was going to catch him; so far, his only illegal act was this purchase of a firearm and he did not intend to take chances.

The man had a polystyrene cup of Coca-Cola in front of him and was sipping it through a straw. He was not much more than a boy, Derek realized, regarding him warily from under his tweed hat. Though he might be an ill-nourished twenty, he could be as little as sixteen; Derek was not used to assessing the age of adolescents. What would he move on to after selling pot and now a gun, assuming he had managed to obtain one? Perhaps he, Derek, had sent him further down the path to serious crime with this deal. Such a thought was not welcome and he would not dwell on it, telling himself that the boy was already damned and might not be selling only marijuana.

Not a word was spoken. Derek felt a hand on his knee beneath the table and he reached out with his own to grasp a heavy package. The youth did not let go, and neither did Derek, while, with his other hand, he extracted the envelope and rested it on the table beside the newspaper.

The boy had to trust him, just as Derek had to take the chance that the package contained the gun. He heard a mutter, "If you've cut me short, you're dead, dad," as the youth released the package, palmed the envelope, and slid from his seat in one smooth movement. Then he was gone.

Derek contemplated staying longer, having a second cup of tea to allay any suspicions the counter-hand might entertain, but decided to get away from this area and back to the apparently law-abiding streets of Petty Linton without delay. He put the package into the large pocket of the anorak he was wearing—his pale raincoat would be too conspicuous in this neighborhood and he had not worn it on his sleuthing trips—and left the café, walking briskly down the road, not looking round at all, his heart thumping hard until he was sitting on a bus which would take him to the spot some way off where he had left his car. He did not look at the gun until he was safely inside his house when, still wearing his gloves, he unwrapped it and examined it. It was a Smith and Wesson .38, exactly like one he had used at the range, and in good condition, and was fully loaded. He had been walking around London with a top-class loaded firearm in his pocket.

Derek carefully unloaded it. His hands were shaking. Now he was ready. Now he had to choose his moment. He must be standing close to Barry Carter; at a distance, hits might not be fatal.

To shoot a man down as he walked along the street was a possible act, though one of chilling intent, but Derek wanted Barry Carter to know why he was being killed; it would be difficult, however, to hold him captive long enough to tell him. Derek did not want to be caught after Barry was dead; though many might side with him, it would reopen the past and cause Hannah renewed distress in that respect, even if she understood why he had done it.

The papers were full of fresh, horrific crimes: few days seemed to pass without reports of savage attacks, shootings for no apparent reason unless it was robbery to feed a drug habit. Haunting the streets, trailing Carter, Derek had seen small children running round with no adult in sight, squalor and filth in the buildings that to them were home, dark corners occupied by dubious clusters of people who could be planning all sorts of evil but who could, equally well, be discussing the latest racing tip or the prospects for a football team. He had seen plenty of neat, clean women and scrubbed children, too, and spotless net curtains at windows. Some families had to struggle against their environment and at school these children would meet the young ruffians, be bullied and mocked for their higher standards and have immense problems to surmount, but they would not all succumb.

When he had made the gun safe he spread the evening paper out on the kitchen table to read. He saw that the girl recently attacked in Bedfordshire was recovering and had been able to give a description of her attacker. A police artist's sketch was printed and Derek saw at once that the face resembled that of Barry Carter, even to the wispy beard. In that instant, fear and shock almost as great as that which he had experienced on the night when The Elms was raided swamped him. He had left it too late; Carter had already found another victim.

He looked at the gun as it lay on the table, a small instrument of death. Need he use it now? He could lift the telephone, dial, and anonymously mention Carter's name: the police would do the rest; indeed, someone else might recognize him and make the call. If Carter had attacked that girl, they would prove it and he would go back to jail. But he would come out again. As the girl was clearly not going to die, he would again get a sentence lasting a few years and be released once more to attack still another girl. He had not been out a month; wouldn't the police suspect him and question him?

While Derek debated the question in leafy, prosperous Petty Linton, Barry Carter also studied the sketch and knew he must create a diversion, one that would last until he was safely in Spain.

He dialed a number and stated that he had seen a blue Sierra in the relevant road at the relevant time, and he gave its exact registration number. The police would pick Clive up and investigate, and they would probably find evidence that the girl had been in his car. That should be enough to get him locked up.

It would be wise to make himself scarce while this happened; he did not want the fuzz coming round and seeing his own face while they looked for the car owner. In a few days' time the danger would be past because he and Vic had their plans. Barry had his visitor's passport, obtained without a hitch. He had not been able to find his birth certificate when he rummaged through the dresser drawers so he had had to ask his mother for it, but she had been glad to supply it when she heard he was planning a holiday abroad, and she did not ask where he was getting the money for his trip.

He held an unblemished driving license and that was enough, with his photographs, to secure him his essential document.

10.

Superintendent Martin Brooks had been to The Swan several times since the night he took Janet home, but never alone. Twice he was with the thin, tense woman she had seen before, and on other occasions his companions were a couple. Janet decided that the man was a colleague and the woman his wife; as she later learned, the wife was an inspector and the husband was in Customs and Excise: similar, but different, Martin said when he explained.

Then, one Sunday morning, he called at her house without warning. He rang the bell at eleven o'clock and she came to the door wearing a loose-knit sweater—an expensive one in soft heathery shades—and a pair of very well-cut black slacks.

"Oh!" she said, in surprise.

"I hope I'm not too early," he said. "I wondered if you had the day free, and if so whether you'd like to have a run out somewhere in the country. We might go over to the Cotswolds where there are some nice pubs for lunch. It's a lovely day, for once, and the forecast's good."

"Oh!" said Janet again. She was astonished at his visit, and even more by his invitation. "Come in," she said. She had intended to clean out some cupboards and perhaps go for a walk, then watch a film she had previously recorded. It was a calm, planned program for a solitary person. "I've got the whole day off," she said, and then smiled. "The Cotswolds would be lovely, but I'll have to change."

"You look fine as you are," he said. "Stay like that, then you'll be warm if it's cold up on the hills." She looked different, relaxed, and, he thought, rather attractive without the glossy front she normally presented. Even at the time of the attack at The Elms she had been immaculately turned out whenever he saw her, and had retained her self-control, though her great distress had been apparent.

"She's as smart as paint," he had commented to Detective Sergeant Susan Fitton, who had been on the case with him and who had spent a lot of time with Hannah. Susan Fitton had said that Janet needed a veneer to get her through life.

"I never go out in trousers," Janet said; she had worn them by Hannah's loch, but that was different.

"You should. You look great," he said.

I'm too fat, Janet thought, but did not say.

"Oh—all right," she said. At least the trousers she had on were well-fitting. Janet never wore what most people would describe as old clothes; even now, when her budget was tight, once things became shabby, they were discarded, and because she had been able to dress at cost from the shop, she had a good stock of garments appropriate for most occasions.

He waited for her in the living room, looking out at the small garden. The lawn was trim, the few shrubs neat; scarcely an autumn leaf lay overlooked on the ground. There were still a few late blooms on the roses but no winter's tasks seemed to have been left undone. He thought Janet probably never put off till tomorrow what could be done today, a motto Martin's own mother had lived by until she died suddenly, while still carrying it out, of a heart attack while planting bulbs one cold October day. It was not always easy to live up to the expectations of such a person; perhaps Derek Jarvis had found it too difficult and that had been one of the causes of their separation. Yet many men sought a wife like that, one who would never be caught on the hop or prove unequal to the social demands of a blossoming career.

Martin could not explain to himself why he had wanted to see Janet again. She wasn't his type, he told himself, but then what was his type? She was alone, like him, and much the same age; she was not a new acquaintance and he was aware of her circumstances and her history. He had driven over meaning only to give her a present he had got for her, and then, on the journey, had thought how pleasant it would be to spend a day at leisure in the country and that he did not want to do this on his own. Perhaps, subconsciously, he had always meant to ask her, if she were free, but he knew that her bar duties might prevent her from accepting.

It need not lead anywhere: better not, in fact. It would be just a day out together and he would give her the present when he brought her back.

She reappeared wearing a polo neck under the multiknit sweater, which was wise, since the day was cold, a rare bright frosty one in a wet winter, and she had put on gold pendant earrings and a large gold locket on a chain. She carried a maroon corduroy hat and a matching padded jacket.

"I got very cold about the head when I stayed with Hannah in Scotland," she said. "I never thought of taking a hat like this." She had not owned one until a week ago.

"It may be windy," Martin said. He felt suddenly eager to give her a happy day.

He was a good driver, as a policeman should be, and he had a few caustic comments to make about other road users they met, but he was not on duty, so unless he witnessed a major breach of safety or an actual accident, he would not be looking out for trouble. It took them just over an hour to get to Burford, where he parked near the church and they walked up the hill to a pub where they ate steak and kidney pie. Martin had a beer and Janet had two glasses of red wine, and he told her about his two sons, one a medical student and the other a forensic scientist. He saw them from time to time, he said. His wife was much happier with her new husband, a teacher, than she had been with him, and their stepfather had been a good influence on his sons.

"And he was there," said Martin. "I wasn't, often enough."

Retirement was in sight for him, and what he would do then he did not know, but he did not mention this to Janet. He supposed he would end up as a security adviser.

After lunch they pottered about the town, looking in shop windows. Janet gazed at the displays in the dress shops and told him what she estimated the markup to be on the clothes so enticingly arranged.

"It was rough, that business of yours going down," he said.

"It was so unnecessary. Do you know, the new tenant is paying less rent than I did, because no one would take it at the higher rate I was being forced to pay?" said Janet.

"You might start up something else one day," he said.

"Yes," she replied, but without conviction, for her capital had gone and she was lucky not to be bankrupt.

The light was already beginning to fade and they returned to the car. Driving home, Martin put on a James Galway tape; listening to it meant there was no need to talk. The car was warm, the wipers swished hypnotically across the windscreen, and Janet had had two glasses of red wine; after a while her eyes closed. She slept.

Martin found that surrender deeply touching. She seemed

so much in control: rather bossy, unemotional; yet now she was defenseless. He drove carefully so that no change of gear or sudden braking would wake her. The world was full of lonely women, he thought: women who coped on their own with life and were often happier than living with an incompatible partner, but others had been abandoned by someone they loved and trusted, pushed into solitude not by death but by betrayal. It took courage to pick up the pieces of a shattered life and build a new existence. Humans were by nature to some extent gregarious and it couldn't be right for so many to live in isolated boxes. Men and women, they went off alone to work and returned to solitary rooms or flats. At work they interacted with others, but without responsibility once the working day or shift was done. Was that the right way to live?

Martin had no wish to assume responsibility for someone else's long-term happiness; in short bursts, however, it might be quite nice to see more of Janet. They scarcely knew one another as people, but they were easy together; it was pleasant to be with an undemanding woman, off duty. He might ask her out again: or would she think he was planning something serious?

She stirred as they left the dual carriageway and slowed down for the approach to Norlington.

"I've been asleep," she said. "Sorry. Poor company."

"That's all right. You must have been tired," he said.

"I don't always sleep very well," said Janet. "I wake up very early, even after a late night at The Swan."

"You worry about Hannah," he said. And other things, he thought: money, and the future.

"Yes, but much less since I saw her at the end of September." She worried, now, about her own security; she had no private pension plan and would be dependent on the state one when she could no longer work.

"When things improve, you may get a job with a better future," Martin said, as though he had read her mind.

"I suppose so," she said, but without conviction.

"You might marry again."

"What? As a solution to my financial problems? I wouldn't do that just to get a meal ticket," said Janet, with asperity.

"You might get fond of some man," he said mildly, as they turned into her road. Some nice old boy, he thought: a widower with money, who would appreciate her competence and good appearance. It did not occur to him that, in previous generations, men like that employed housekeepers in whom they sought just those qualities and whom they paid.

There was no need for her to reply, for they had reached her gate.

"Would you like some coffee?" she invited, hoping he would refuse.

"Why not?" he said, however, and followed her up the path and into the house.

She was not going to ask him to supper, nor offer him a drink, as he was driving. While the kettle boiled, she went upstairs to revive her hair and makeup. When she returned, though still in sweater and trousers, she looked armored, ready to go behind the bar, and unapproachable.

Martin accepted his coffee, then gave her a package.

"I got this for you," he said.

"Oh?" She took the small parcel, a brown paper bag fastened with Sellotape.

"It's not exciting," he warned. "It's practical."

Janet unwrapped it.

"What is it?" she asked.

"It's an alarm. You often walk back on your own at night, I know, and this could be some help," he said. It might not attract support from those who heard it but it could frighten the attacker. "A can of hair spray in your coat pocket's another good idea—the cap off, of course, ready for use. Unfortunately it's against the law to carry any sort of protective weapon."

"It's kind of you," said Janet. "Thank you. I hope I won't need it."

"So do I, but I'd like to think you wouldn't leave it at home," he said.

"I won't," she promised.

He did not want to go. She had lit the gas fire—one that looked just like real coal—and drawn the curtains, and the small room was very comfortable, though not really cozy because nothing was out of place: there was no book in the process of being read, not even a magazine in sight. What did she like doing in her spare time?

"You've got no pets," he said. "No dog or cat."

"No. I'm not very keen on animals," she replied, "and they're a tie, if you go out or away."

"You wouldn't even like a budgerigar?"

"Have you got one?" she challenged, and he shook his head.

"I'd quite like to live in a cottage by the sea and have a dog and a boat," he said, surprising himself as he expressed this ambition.

"Why shouldn't you, when you retire?" she said.

She was thinking that she could soon ring Hannah, who would be home now if she was not at the MacGregors', and she got up to tidy away their cups.

Martin took the hint.

"I must go," he said. "Things to do. People to see." Something might have come up while he was out, though he was off duty until the next morning.

"Thank you so much for the lovely day," said Janet, seeing him to the door.

He suddenly wondered what she looked like first thing in the morning, before she had done her hair and applied her carapace of makeup. He had seen her distressed, unhappy, and very angry, but he had not seen her cry. Had anyone? And had anyone ever seen her ecstatically happy?

He banished any thought he might have had of giving her the most brotherly of kisses.

"See you soon," he said, not suggesting any date.

He'd be back at The Swan, eventually. He wasn't sure if he would take Janet out again. He was not the man to undertake the siege that might free her from her straitjacket of repression, for that was what it was. To attempt the task would demand commitment and some risk, but if someone came along who had the necessary patience, it could be a worthwhile challenge. Leaving, Martin fleetingly wondered if he was turning away from something that could have rich rewards.

After he had gone, Janet washed their cups and put them away. It had been a pleasant day, and she had enjoyed being with a kind and undemanding man. It was good of him to bring her the alarm, but she felt no threat, walking home at night through the quiet town.

By the time she had dialed Hannah's number and was waiting for her to answer, Janet had again forgotten him.

11.

The police were quick to follow up the anonymous telephone call which had supplied the registration number of a blue Sierra seen, stationary, in a Bedfordshire lane on the night when a young girl had been attacked there. They traced the car to Clive, but not to Noreen's flat, for he had not notified the authorities that he was no longer living in Nottingham.

Nottingham was not too far from Bedfordshire; besides, nowadays one of the problems the police had to deal with was the great mobility of the populace; abducted children could be taken miles away from where they lived and thieves could raid areas reached quickly by fast motorways and be swiftly gone again. Sex offenders traveled, too, but often their crimes were committed within a certain radius of their base, and once several incidents occurred within such limits, the search was narrowed down. But no one wanted another Bedford girl to be attacked.

Clive's wife, when two uniformed officers called at the address where she was still living with the children, told them where to find him; they were in touch, she said; he paid maintenance and sometimes came to take the children out for a few hours.

This was an important case. Clive must be taken into custody, and it was possible that soon the victim would be well enough to identify her assailant. After some diplomatic telephone calls to their colleagues in the Met, the local team investigating the crime were able to send two officers down to London to arrest Clive on suspicion. In the middle of the night, he was taken off to a Bedfordshire police cell, and his car was removed for testing by forensic scientists.

It was in vain that Clive protested he had been with Noreen when the girl was attacked. He was at home with her every night, unless he was out with a fare, he said. His log did not show a late fare that night; he must have picked Noreen up at The Lunar Moon after work; he always did that when he could.

"Very touching," said the arresting officer. "But you could have done that and gone out later."

"It's too far," said Clive. "Noreen doesn't finish until gone eleven, and wasn't that girl attacked around midnight?"

"Was she? You tell me," said the detective. "She didn't leave the party until after one, and wasn't found till three o'clock in the morning."

By then she had been suffering from hypothermia, as well as the effects of the attack; left much longer, she might not have survived, and it was lucky that a motorist had been on that quiet road so early.

"There's plenty of blue Sierras about," said Clive. "It must have been another one that was seen up there. I didn't do it."

"If that's so, we'll find out," said the inspector.

They had no other leads, and no one had linked this case with the earlier London murder. Though the law maintains that a person is innocent until proved guilty, circumstantial evidence, for want of other clues, can provide a strong attacking case which is often difficult to refute; meanwhile, the real offender runs off laughing.

When Clive had been taken back to base, the arresting officers, checking, found that he had a record. Ten years before, he had been up on a charge of causing an affray. Clive had pleaded provocation, alleging that he had intervened to break up a fight, but the other combatants had insisted that he had provoked the disturbance. All had got away with fines and being bound over to keep the peace, but this incident did not endear Clive to the arresting officers. They could hold him for thirty-six hours without charging him, and during that time the car might yield some trace of the victim, though if he were the guilty man, Clive would doubtless have given it a very thorough cleaning.

There was concern about the discrepancy between Clive's appearance and that of the alleged attacker; he was older than the girl had said, for one thing. But in the darkness, frightened, hurt, how could she be certain?

Barry was not in the flat when Clive was taken away. He had spent the first part of the evening with Vic, going over the details of what they were intending to do the next night, and Vic had advanced him another fifty pounds on account. He was anxious that Barry should not embark on other scams before they made their joint move, and he urged him not to go shooting his mouth off about their plans.

"I've seen you pissed, Barry," he said. "Not a pretty sight, and you might say too much, if you go drinking. Stick to something safer. Hire some videos and go home."

"I won't breathe a word," said Barry. "I might find myself a bird. Though there's no need to spend money on that. I can get them anyway."

"I'm sure you can," said Victor. "But you should get a good night's sleep. And we need a decent car—something really fast, and with a boot big enough for the pictures if we don't have time to take them from their frames. And not white. Too showy."

"I've marked one down," said Barry. "It's a black BMW. It's always parked near the tube station. The guy commutes. He won't miss it till the evening, and I'll have it stashed away by then. How about putting it in that lock-up you've got?"

"That's a good idea," said Victor. Someone had broken into the lock-up recently, but there was nothing there to take and he had replaced the padlock with a stronger one. There was no need to mention that to Barry. He gave him the key.

"Pity about your shop," said Barry. "I thought you'd be in business by now."

"So did I," said Victor. "But I fancy a trip to the sun much more. When the money's gone, and we come back, we'll get on with it."

Barry might not come back with Vic. Once on his feet in Marbella, it would be the good life for him. Maybe he'd run a bar.

"Where's this geezer live who's after the pictures?" Barry asked.

"We're to meet him at a service area about twenty miles from our target," said Victor. "He'll wait until we come."

"How will he know us? He won't know what sort of wheels we've got?"

"No, but he'll be in a white Ford Transit and he'll have tied a piece of yellow ribbon to the driver's door handle," Victor said. "That's not too conspicuous. We can't tell how many Transits there'll be there at any time, but I know where he'll aim to park it, and we'll do the same. He'll go into the cafeteria, acting normal, and we'll wait for him if he's not in the van when we get there."

"And he'll have the money on him?"

"No money, no pictures," Victor said.

"But we can't hand them over at the service station. We'd be seen."

"No. We'll follow him to some lane," said Victor. "It's safe, Barry. Trust me. Have I let you down yet?"

"Where'd you meet this guy?"

"In a gallery," said Vic. "A picture gallery. He knows his art. Don't worry. The picture won't be missed till the house minders get back from their wild-goose chase. You'll see. I'll make the call to shift them in the morning."

"It went OK with the parcel, then?"

"It certainly did, and I got chatting to them, asked them how they liked the place and they told me where their home is, so it'll be more authentic when I call them. Now, you go and get some sleep."

They parted, and Vic watched Barry slouch off down the street. Would he go home or would he go out and spend the cash Victor had just given him? He had done it for insurance, aware that Barry was easily tempted if he had no money. He was not a reliable partner but Victor thought he had foreseen everything that could go wrong. He went back to his basement room, where he was woken in the small hours by the countess, who thought that there was a rat in hers.

There wasn't, but it took Victor more than an hour to convince her, by the time he had searched under each piece of furniture, then drunk the tea that she insisted on brewing, and listened to tales of her father's life at the court of the last Tsar. He knew that she was simply lonely and couldn't sleep.

After that, he was wide awake himself, and took a long

time to get to sleep again, worrying about Barry and whether he could be trusted over the car.

Still, there was no need to get up early in the morning.

Vic was right to be anxious about Barry, who did not go home at all. He picked up a tart and went back to her room. She was a woman of forty, with wiry dark hair and coarse skin, almost old enough to be his mother; in fact, she looked rather like Noreen, and that was what had made him talk to her. She was businesslike and strong; their encounter was soon over, and Barry had never for one moment of it felt that he was in control.

After Clive had left the flat, Noreen Carter lit the gas fire in the living room and sat by it on her precious Dralon-covered settee, the duvet round her, waiting for him to return, for of course the police would soon discover their mistake and let him go. Time passed, and he did not come back; neither did Barry. She dozed at last, and when she woke she was still alone. Noises that had woken her came from the flats above and round her; she could identify many of her neighbors' actions by the sounds they made.

She put on the radio news and learned that a man was helping police with their enquiries into the Bedfordshire attack. The wording had been just the same when it was Barry who was helping with enquiries five years ago, but that time, he was guilty, and Clive was innocent. The police had not believed that Noreen was telling the truth about being with him all night and, if it came to court, the jury might not believe her, either. But if Clive had not attacked that girl—and he hadn't—someone else had done it, and he was walking around, free, and could attack another girl. Who was the guilty man? What had made them pick on Clive?

She had a bath and made some tea, and tried to eat a slice

of toast, but she could not swallow it. If Clive went to prison for something he didn't do, it would be dreadful, and it would mean the end of the first fragile security she had ever known. Had he found a solicitor? The police were obliged to tell him that he was entitled to one. Noreen knew a lot about a suspect's rights, and those of a convicted prisoner. Attacking that girl was the sort of act that might be Barry's style, she thought, though the girl he had raped had been defenseless, in her bedroom. This second girl had been defenseless, too, walking in a lane, alone at night. But Barry hadn't been there; Barry had no car, and he had learned his lesson. He was going straight; he had told her so.

Since when had Barry told the truth? And what about the presents he brought her and the new clothes he was wearing after getting his others badly stained?

Stained! And with what he had said was tomato sauce but looked to her like blood. All women were familiar with bloodstains, and she was more familiar than most because of all the beatings she had suffered. She tried to remember when she had found those clothes, and, with relief, realized that it was before the attack on the girl abandoned in the road. Barry had told her to throw them away, but she hadn't done so yet. It seemed a waste; she might manage to improve them enough for a down-and-out to find them useful. That had been the day after Barry gave her the mock fur coat which she now wore to work, and the microwave: almost two weeks ago, well before the attack for which Clive had been arrested.

Since Barry's release a girl had been found stabbed beneath bushes in an overgrown park area not too far from The Lunar Moon: the girls at work had talked about it, shuddering, none keen to walk alone at night. Had she got the newspapers which carried the report? Noreen kept old papers because Clive believed in recycling them and every so often took them to a collection point.

Clive always bought a paper because he read the racing news and planned his bets, but Noreen seldom had much time to glance at more than the front page. She found the pile, stacked under the kitchen sink, and began sorting through them, reading the crime reports and glancing at the pictures. She did not hurry: no one needed breakfast, and she did not have to leave for work for several hours.

12.

When Barry went back to the quiet residential street where he had seen the BMW he planned to steal, it was not there. He cursed aloud. He'd seen it on the three preceding days and had been certain this was its regular parking spot. He'd been looking forward to driving it; such a car would give him a buzz, and breaking into it was a challenge. While he was in prison, security devices had been improved, many cars had immobilizers, and BMWs were not among the easiest cars to take, but he'd picked up some interesting tips inside about how to deal with electronic locks. He had a screwdriver in his pocket, and a small hammer, and he had a tennis ball, too; he wanted to try out what he'd been told would undo almost any door.

The street was deserted. This was a quiet, respectable area where probably a lot of people were at work and many of the houses were empty; it was a good opportunity for a bit of thieving, and he was tempted to see what he could pick up. Then he changed his mind. He was here to nick a car and that was what he must do. He sensed that Vic was having second thoughts about their partnership, and without Vic, Barry would have to rely on small scams which would provide only enough for everyday expenses. This time, he was promised a trip to Spain. When they came back—if he came back—he'd think again about his future, maybe join a syndicate supplying stolen cars and shipping them abroad almost before they were missed. There'd be big money in that game.

Meanwhile, there were other cars in the road. He saw a new Vauxhall Calibra, shiny gray; it had only two thousand miles on the clock.

Getting into it was a doddle. There was no need to hot-wire it—that could be dangerous; he'd heard of a guy who'd electrocuted himself doing that, and it had been a BMW he'd been trying to start. Remembering this almost reconciled Barry to the capture of a mere Calibra, and when he drove it away, its swift acceleration and good handling worked the usual magic effect that driving a powerful car had on him: for a short time, Barry was happy.

He drove it around for a while, just to enjoy it, and then, because the tank was only half full, he put it in Vic's lock-up. Let Vic pay for the petrol they would need tonight.

He left the small screwdriver he'd used to start it on the dash, locked up the garage and went home—if you could call it home—to pack up some clothes for his overseas trip: just a few things to tide him over till he bought new ones from one of those boutiques. He had waited until he knew his mother would have left for work. Clive, if the police had not already arrested him, would be either out, or, if he'd had a late fare, sleeping in.

The Sierra was not outside the block; that meant Clive would not be there. Barry wondered if the police had traced him yet. It might take them some time to find him, though their computer was quick enough at picking up a stolen car if you were in one.

The flat was very tidy, much tidier even than normal,

though it was never in a mess, which suited him; he'd learned orderly ways in prison where space was so restricted that you had to keep your few belongings neat. Barry left twenty pounds from the sum Vic had given him the previous day on the table, and put a ketchup bottle on it to hold it down. Then, whistling under his breath, he left the building.

He whiled away the rest of the day in an amusement arcade until it was time to meet Vic. They walked together to the lock-up and Barry asked Vic why he hadn't brought a bag with him for the trip abroad.

"I'll collect it when we've got the cash," Vic said. "We won't get away till tomorrow or even the day after."

"Why not? You told me we'd get paid at once for the pictures—when we hand them over to the guy in the Ford Transit," Barry said.

"We will, but there'll be the jewelry and other things. That'll take a little longer," Victor said. "You are impatient, Barry. And I thought you said we'd have a BMW."

Secretly, Vic was quite pleased to see a different make of car: the sight of Barry at the wheel of a BMW might make any cop suspicious. This was a classy car, but less spectacular.

"Well, it wasn't there today, was it?" said Barry crossly. "Let's get going, then. No point in hanging about."

Belatedly, Barry was feeling uneasy at pointing the finger at Clive over the Bedford business. There were all those tests nowadays; the fuzz would prove he hadn't done it. Still, Barry himself had not been tested in that way so they wouldn't know he was the one they wanted, and they couldn't prove he'd driven Clive's Sierra. By the time Clive had talked his way out of trouble, Barry would be far away in Spain.

Sitting beside him in the stolen car, Vic noticed a sour smell emanating from Barry. He had been aware of it on their earlier raid, but it was stronger now and very unpleasant. It wasn't just an unwashed smell; it was animal, feral. Victor wrinkled his nose in distaste as they joined the stream of traffic driving out of town. The rush hour was long since over and people were returning from their evening's entertainment. They stopped for petrol at a service station where Barry filled the tank and Victor paid, in cash. Then Barry decided he was hungry, so they went into the cafeteria where he ate a large plate of fish and chips and Vic had some ham sandwiches. Barry wanted a beer, but the place was not licensed, so he drank a large Coca-Cola through a straw. Just like a kid, thought Vic, who had a strong black coffee. The meal seemed to take forever, though Barry ate with greedy haste.

Vic was worrying about the car, sitting in the parking lot, stolen, its lock broken, and probably missed by this time. It just needed one sharp policeman to notice it and check the number, and they were undone. Now he wondered how Barry had spent the earlier part of the day. Had he been drinking? The car was fast and Barry would need all his skill to drive it safely. He was a good driver, but Vic had begun to understand that he was reckless and impulsive, given to sudden whims about shortcuts, and overtaking just to show off.

Victor had planned carefully for this evening's operation and knew the route well, and where to park so that the car would not be noticed when they reached their destination.

"They believe you all right? Them folk at the house?" asked Barry. "When you spun them the line?"

"They certainly did," said Vic. "I saw them drive away this afternoon. I didn't want them to go too early or they'd find it was a hoax and be back before we were through."

"Went down in your girlfriend's car, did you?" Barry asked admiringly.

"Well, she's not really my girlfriend," Vic admitted. "She's my landlady. She said I could use it whenever I like. It's not something I've done a lot. You don't want to be under an obligation."

"No—should be the other way round, shouldn't it?" said Barry, and sniggered as they walked back to the car. "Well, I hope you know what you're doing, Vic."

"Oh, I do," said Vic. "And you'll be laughing all over your face when we're through. Señoritas, here we come."

When they were in the country, on the M4, Victor told Barry to keep heading west until they reached junction 14, the turning for Hungerford.

"That's where that guy went crazy, isn't it? Shot all those folk," said Barry. "Began in some wood there."

"That's right," said Victor. "A bad business."

"Made his name, though, didn't it?" said Barry, but he couldn't remember what the man was called.

Vic could, but he wasn't going to tell Barry.

"It wasn't a good way to be remembered," he said. "Too much like Hitler or Stalin. Slaughtering innocent people."

"You ever pulled a shooter on anyone, Vic?" asked Barry, pulling out to overtake a line of cars.

"No," said Vic. "Have you?"

"No. I like a knife," said Barry. "It's quick and clean and silent, a knife is."

"You've not killed anyone, though, have you, Barry?" asked Vic, and now he sounded anxious.

"Uh huh." Barry began to whistle, and at the same time he put his foot down and the car, already traveling fast, shot forward.

"Slow down, Barry. I've told you, we don't want to get stopped before we've done the job. You can have a spin round when we've got the cash, on the way to the airport. You can go ahead, if you like, and I'll get rid of the rest of the stuff and meet you out there. You can leave the car in one of those long-stay parks. It might not be found for days, if you do that."

"Right," said Barry. "Good thinking, Vic." It was, if he had the nerve to walk into the concourse, buy his ticket and head off alone. He slowed down slightly, turning the idea over in his mind.

"Who did you kill?" Vic asked him, after two more miles.

"Oh, just a girl," said Barry, and at that moment they reached the slip road for junction 12. He pulled over to take it, cutting in on a line of cars on the inside lane, causing some of them to brake abruptly.

"What did you do that for? This isn't our turning. We want fourteen," Victor said.

"I've changed my mind," said Barry. "I've been this way before."

"Well—so what? That's not where we're going tonight," said Victor, and then he added, uneasily, "What girl did you kill?"

"Just a tart," said Barry. "It was a few weeks ago now, the one that was found in the park."

Vic tried to hide a shudder, and breathed deeply.

"Why did you kill her?" he asked.

"Don't know, really," Barry answered. "I just thought I would. The other one didn't snuff it—the one near Bedford. I didn't use the knife that time. She would of, if I had."

Vic was silent for some seconds.

"You did that?" he said at last.

"Yeah. She thought too much of herself," said Barry. "Like that one that got me banged up."

"You got banged up for rape?"

"If you want to call it that," said Barry.

"But you said it was robbery. Armed robbery—you said your mate had the gun."

"He did, and he's still inside," said Barry. "I had my knife," he added. "I cut the silly cow's hair. It was all long, like silk." He paused, remembering. "Didn't stab her, more's the pity."

"Well, that's old history now," said Victor, with an effort. "Let's get back on the right road, Barry."

"I'm not sure I like the idea of this job," Barry said. He was driving fast along the country road, the headlights sending silver swaths ahead of them. They had met very few cars since they left the motorway. "I've got some unfinished business," he continued. "We'll do your job after. It won't go away, and you said the place is empty. It'll wait for us." He dipped his lights as a car came towards them and went by. "I know a place that could be better than yours. Bloody great pile, it is. Must be full of paintings, maybe more than the one you was planning to do."

"But your place won't be empty," Victor said, almost pleadingly. "Mine is, and we've got a customer waiting for a particular painting. Come on, Barry. There's a left turn soon. Take it, and we'll be able to get back on course."

But Barry took no notice, driving on, and now he was giggling under his breath, then whistling between his teeth. The car was hurtling down the road and Vic began to wonder if they would arrive unharmed at either destination. He saw his well-made plan starting to disintegrate around him as Barry embarked on a scheme of his own on which he seemed determined.

"It's not much further," Barry said. "There's the signpost to Norlington. We stopped there for fish and chips before we did the job—Morris and me. Then we went on. Bicklebury, it's called, the place. I nearly came this way last week but then I went to Bedford instead. That's when I met the girl. Walking home, she was, from a disco or something."

"A party, the paper said," Victor stated coldly. "What you did was bad, Barry. Didn't you realize that?"

"Offered her a lift, didn't I? She could have paid for it, straight up, couldn't she?"

Victor was silent. Then he said, "What about the other one? The tart?"

Barry shrugged, making the car swerve.

"She was just filth," he said. "All women are."

"You don't mean that," said Victor. "What about your mother? You took her that microwave, remember? And the coat. You must think a lot of her."

"Got a fancy man, hasn't she? Wants me to get out on account of him. Him and me don't get on too well. It's always been like that. Beat me up, the last one did, and my dad, and my mum just let them."

"Did they beat her too?"

"What if they did? She'd earned it," Barry said. "Silly cow."

"But those girls." Vic couldn't leave it alone. "They hadn't done anything to you. They hadn't harmed you. You didn't even know them."

"They were cows," said Barry, and repeated, "All women are."

As he spoke, they entered Norlington, and Barry dropped his speed. In fact he was less sure of the route to Bicklebury than he had made out, but there should be a signpost somewhere. During his years in jail he had often thought of that night, and the car ride to the Manor, the climb over the walls, then the unplanned visit to The Elms.

Maybe that girl, Hannah, her name was, was still there, at the house that they had raided, waiting for a second visit.

Noreen, reading through the papers, had seen the artist's impression of the man wanted in Bedfordshire and knew at once that it was Barry. She sat staring at it, horrified. Clive was accused of committing that crime because his car had been seen near the spot where the girl was found; it did not follow that he had been the driver, and if Barry had taken the Sierra and returned it, Clive might not have noticed. Noreen had seen, however, that he had stopped putting the keys in the mug; instead, he put them in a drawer in their bedroom, and she had mildly wondered why. Now she knew.

He'd tell the police about Barry. Of course he would; he must, to save himself. But he didn't know about Barry's prison sentence or his past; he might suspect that Barry had taken the Sierra, but he wouldn't imagine him capable of such a crime. Or would he? Clive was no angel; he knew what happened in the world, and he'd had all sorts in his cab. He'd not taken to Barry; she knew that, and in the end he'd had to tell her so. Sitting there, the gray sketch of Barry with his wispy beard before her, Noreen wept as she foresaw the wreckage of her fragile existence. Clive would be freed, and Barry would be arrested in his place.

Where was Barry now? He'd not been home all night, and that had rarely happened since his release; indeed, she thought it had been only once, though he was often late— later than she was. She thought about the poor girl left for dead in that country lane; it was apparent, from the newspaper article, that she had almost been killed by her attacker. What had he done to her? Stabbed her? It did not say that she was bleeding but then the papers didn't tell you everything. At least that other girl, the one for whom he'd been put away, had been at home, able to be comforted and helped quite quickly afterwards; she hadn't been near death.

Could Barry have had anything to do with the death of the girl in the park? Noreen got out the stained clothes and inspected them. Marks still showed on the anorak and jeans. If she soaked them in salt and cold water, maybe they'd come out, but after two hot washes they were well set in the fabric. Moving slowly, like an old woman, Noreen folded them neatly and put them in a large plastic bag from Debenhams. They were evidence.

Barry hadn't been kept in prison long enough. After what he'd done, he shouldn't have been let out at all. Men who did that sort of thing weren't cured by being locked up; they were simply prevented from doing it again, and then, when they were free, off they went, most of them, and at the first chance, attacked some other woman. Maybe a few saw doctors and got some sort of therapy, but were those who did get treatment cured? Noreen didn't think so. Barry hadn't had that sort of help; he saw nothing wrong in what he'd done. To him, and to his father, women were there to be used, bullied, beaten, kicked and screwed, targets for their rage.

Maybe, at this very moment, as she sat wondering what to do, Barry was off somewhere hunting down another girl. His weakness was her weakness, his violence her responsibility, because she had not brought him up properly. If someone like Clive had come into his life when he was young, he might be different now. Noreen forgot the good schoolteachers whose paths had crossed Barry's and whose influence, had he been receptive, would have been beneficial; she forgot that individuals make choices. Barry knew that what he did was wrong and yet he went on doing it. It was useless, now, to wish she had managed to escape earlier from Barry's father, to lament the nature of her second husband; the harm was done, and the only way to help Barry was to turn him in— tell the police—and give them the bag of clothes. If he had killed that girl, he'd be sentenced to life, and although, as Noreen knew, it didn't really mean that and he could be out again in maybe nine years' time, he'd be on license so that he could be locked up again if he so much as broke a window, and in the meantime perhaps the law might be changed to protect the public from people like him.

She was still thinking about it when she went to work. Maybe, when she came back, Barry would be at home and she could talk to him, find out the truth and persuade him to give himself up. If he did so, surely that would mean better treatment inside? She saw, ahead, more long years of visiting him in jail, the dingy visitors' rooms, the smell of the prisons, the loss of hope. Clive would leave her. The dream he had of a life in the country, running his own taxi, might not happen now, or if it did, she would not be sharing it. He'd find someone else, someone without her troubled baggage.

When she went to work she was in a daze, and twice muddled orders as her mind churned around with thoughts of her own and her son's ruined lives, and when she went home for her brief break in the afternoon, she was no closer to finding the resolution for what she must do. Clive had not returned: she had hoped that perhaps, by now, the police would have realized their mistake and let him go, and then she could postpone taking any action. Then she saw the twenty-pound note on the kitchen table, underneath the ketchup bottle.

One of them had left it there: Clive, or Barry. She rushed into the bedroom to see if Clive's clothes had gone, but nothing had been touched since the police left. Barry had taken some clothes, however; she saw that a new holdall bag he'd got was missing, and some of those sharp shirts he'd bought. Of course, he'd said that he was going on a holiday.

He'd cut off that skimpy beard a few days ago. Maybe he had seen the paper too. If so, and that was why he'd shaved it off, wasn't it proof of his guilt? And now he'd left the country.

Noreen went back for the evening shift in a state of indecision, and when she came home after The Lunar Moon had closed, the flat was still empty. She sat at the kitchen table waiting for one of them to return, Clive or Barry, but neither appeared.

The twenty-pound note remained on the table. Barry must have left it for her. She couldn't remember him ever giving her money before, and his presents to her had always been things that he had stolen, even as a child.

The twenty pounds was doubtless stolen too. She'd missed money from her bag. He'd thieved from someone else to pay her back.

13.

Vic was arguing with Barry. It wouldn't take them long to get back to their planned route, he said; why risk missing the firm sale they'd got lined up for a chance hit like this?

"We won't be risking it," Barry said. "We'll do it after. My job first, then yours. That's fair." He saw the sign for Bicklebury and turned off; the car purred along, the engine sweet. "We've got all night, and your place is empty. We know that. Stop moaning, Victor. Your geezer in the car park might like what we get here—who can say?" He was driving more carefully now.

"But we haven't had a look round here, Barry. I always go for empty places. You know that. It's too risky, otherwise."

"Well, this place may be empty tonight. It could be our lucky break," said Barry. "We'd sussed it out before, or Morris had, but they was busy when we got here. Cars stacked in rows outside—some party. So we went to the other house up the road. Didn't get a lot there, at all. A few jewels and bits of silver. Nothing great."

"And you were done for that job?"

"Got caught, yeah," said Barry.

"Maybe it was because you did it on the spur of the moment. It wasn't the one you'd planned," said Victor.

"Yeah—well—" Barry wasn't going to admit that. "Have to take your chance, don't you, these days?"

As he spoke they came to the pub at the fork in the road, and Barry realized that they had passed the big place where he and Vic had climbed the wall. For a moment he thought of going on to The Elms, but he'd done all that talk to Vic about the Manor, so they'd better go there first. With screeching brakes, he swung the car round in the road, doing a three-point turn in very little space. Vic expected another car to come winging towards them and crash into them but no set of headlights pierced the surrounding darkness and they retraced their tracks back to the Manor where Barry stopped beside the high wall.

"We had a ladder to climb that," he said. "One of them chain things. Good for getting out of the nick, that would be, if you could get hold of one," and he giggled again.

Vic wondered again if Barry had had a few drinks before coming out tonight. Was he on drugs? He was acting like somebody drunk or high, but maybe he was just fired with the thrill of the job. He seemed to want danger, choosing this house about which his knowledge was several years old. Vic still clung to the hope of getting Barry back on course for their original plan but it might be best to humor him, meanwhile. Perhaps there would be cars stacked in rows tonight.

"We've got no ladder now," he said, but mildly. Antagonizing Barry was not going to help the situation.

"No, so we'll go in the gate," said Barry, and he drove back to the wide gateway, reversing and pulling onto the grass at the side of the drive so that the car was poised for their getaway. Then he doused the lights before turning off the ignition. Victor noticed that he left the screwdriver on the dash.

214

There was no moon and it was very dark as the two men stumbled along the rutted drive, Barry leading, breathing heavily. Once he turned to see if Vic was following, and the other man was aware of the pale globe of his face, dimly visible. Then Barry stopped and pulled on the balaclava mask he carried in his pocket.

Vic was wearing a cap but he had no mask. He had not expected to be seen. He pulled a woollen scarf out of his jacket pocket and tied it round the lower part of his face, over his nose and mouth.

The bulk of the house lay ahead of them, a dense mass with no lights showing. It was difficult for them to find their way in the dark. As they drew nearer, security lights attached to the building came on and both men froze; then they saw a tabby cat walking delicately across the gravel sweep in front of the house. The electronic eye had responded to the cat, not them.

"We'll go round the back," said Barry, pointing. The sudden illumination had given them a chance to spy out the scene, and there were no cars outside the house. It looked as if any occupants were in bed, asleep, as was reasonable at such an hour; Victor had noticed that it was half past one in the morning. Perhaps they would get in and out safely, taking what was obviously saleable, enough to appease Barry. This was the sort of house that was likely to have an alarm, but it might be the type turned on only when the occupants went out, not the beamed variety that sounded when its line was crossed.

Vic followed Barry round to the rear of the house where there were three closed garage doors and no visible car. There was stabling, but no horse's head poked over a door.

Barry had tried the back door and, finding it locked, moved to a sash window. He opened it in seconds with a knife, and very quietly moved aside the secondary double-glazing panel placed across the frame. He sniggered.

"Not had the security guys in, have they?" he said, as he slipped through the space. Vic followed him with an effort, and Barry turned to say, "Not too fit, are you, Vic?"

Vic, scrambling through, barked his shin and cursed beneath his breath. There was no sound of an alarm.

Barry had taken a small torch from his pocket, and he flashed it around. They were in a room that was clearly some sort of office; there was a kneehole desk, cabinets with glass doors protecting leather-bound books, some sporting prints on the walls. A photograph of two blonde schoolgirls stood on the desk and Barry picked it up and stared at it, shining the torch on the smiling faces. Then he spat on it.

"Why did you do that?" Victor asked.

"'Cause they're trash, aren't they?" Barry said. "Maybe they're upstairs."

"Forget them," said Vic shortly. "Hurry up and take what you want, then we can get on to Thrupton."

Barry opened some drawers in the desk and found a checkbook. He put it in his pocket.

"Well, get on," he said. "What are you waiting for? Try the other rooms. Move it, Vic."

He had taken command. Vic left the room and stood in the hall, shining his own pocket torch round. He heard a clock tick in the corner, and the beam lit up a long case clock which was of some value, but Barry wouldn't know that. There was a yellow chrysanthemum in a pot on a round mahogany table in the center of the large, square hall. Vic saw a dog lead hanging on the wall and then he heard a low growl, followed by a bark.

Barry was beside him in an instant.

"Christ, there's a bleeding dog here," he said. "And get the bloody phone, can't you?"

He did not wait for Vic to obey but went up to the telephone which stood on a low chest near the foot of the stairs and cut the line which connected the socket to the main. The dog barked again, louder this time, and Barry, his knife out, slowly opened the door from behind which the sound had come. He held it ajar, and the head of a golden Labrador appeared, to be followed, as the dog yelped, by a gurgling noise as Barry stabbed it in the throat. Then he pushed its collapsing body backwards and opened the door, which led into the kitchen. The dog's heavy carcass lay across the threshold, twitching a little as the animal expired, and Barry kicked it back so that he could pass. A lot of blood was coming from the wound in its neck, which had cut an artery, and Barry, retreating, shut the door again.

"He won't make no more noise," he said. "We'll leave that room." There was blood on his arm.

As he said this, someone spoke from the staircase.

"Who's there?" demanded a female voice, and the light was switched on, revealing a woman in a blue wool dressing gown.

Vic stood still, too shocked to move, but Barry was ready with his bluster.

"You come down, missis, and you'll not get hurt," he said, but the woman did not move.

Barry's knife, stained with the dog's blood, was in his hand as the woman gazed down at them both. Barry shone his torch up at her, trying to dazzle her, and she brushed a hand across her face. Then a second voice spoke.

"What is it? What's happening, Janet? I heard Paddy bark," said Carol Ford, home from university for the Christmas vacation, coming up behind the woman. Carol wore cotton pajamas which looked like a leisure suit, and one arm was in a sling.

"Go back to your room, Carol, and lock yourself in," said Janet Jarvis, who was spending the night at the Manor to keep Carol company while her parents were in London.

Carol took no notice.

"Where's Paddy?" she said. "What's going on? Have you hurt him?" She took a step towards the men but Janet barred her way.

"What's it to you?" said Barry. "Get down here, both of you," and he waved the knife. "Vic, you get the old one. Grab her and find something to tie her up—the light flex—anything. Make her shut up. I'll see to the girl." As he spoke he cut a length of flex off the telephone and moved towards the stairs.

Then Vic acted. To the two women on the stairs it was a terrifying moment when the bigger man, the one wearing the cap and scarf, who had so far remained silent, suddenly produced a gun, but he did not point it at them.

"Drop that knife, Barry Carter," he said, and he was too intent upon Barry to notice the way Janet Jarvis reacted when she heard the name. Not taking his eyes off Barry, he said, "Don't worry, I won't let him hurt you."

"Have you gone mad or something?" Barry said. "You stupid git, you've gone and blown it."

"No. You have, with your stupidity and your violence," Victor snapped. "Drop that knife."

"Not likely," Barry said, and he stepped towards the women.

"If you move again, I'm firing this," said Vic, and as he took a stride in Barry's direction, he pointed the gun at the other man's chest. At the same instant, Barry threw the knife at Vic, who ducked, and it went into the paneling on the wall behind him. Vic went on talking, never taking his eyes off Barry. "Carol, go back to your room and lock yourself in. The phone's cut, so you can't call for help until we've gone, and then the police will be very interested to hear that this is the man who killed a woman in London two weeks ago and assaulted that young girl in Bedfordshire. The other lady can help me tie him up and then I'll take him away."

"Do as he says, Carol," said Janet.

"Oh Janet, are you sure?" Carol, so brave thus far, could not now control the quaver in her voice. "What about Paddy?"

"You can't help Paddy," Victor said. "We weren't coming here tonight, but Barry decided on a change of plan. I'm afraid the dog got in his way." He was holding the gun in two hands, pointing it at Barry, who, now that he was unarmed, had sunk into a crouching posture; he held his gloved hands up to his masked face, and was whimpering.

Janet was walking slowly down the stairs, but Victor did not look at her as she tied her dressing gown sash more securely round her waist. It was an old robe belonging to Veronica, and rather small for her.

"Stand up, Barry, and face the wall," Vic said, as Janet reached floor level.

Very slowly, Barry obeyed, but he began cursing, uttering a string of oaths between gasping wails.

"Put your hands behind you," ordered Victor, and when Barry made no move, he poked him hard in the back with the revolver. "Pick up the phone cord," he told Janet, still not looking at her. "Tie his wrists as tightly as you can."

Janet bent to pick up the cord.

"I'm sorry to have to get you to do this, but I won't put down the gun," said Victor.

"It's a pleasure," Janet answered, tugging the cord, yanking it against Barry's wrists so that it bit into his flesh. The weird, stale smell which she remembered Hannah mentioning came from his body.

"Ouch, that hurts," whined Barry.

"It's meant to," Janet said, giving it another tug, then added, "Carol, do please go to your room."

"Don't you want any help?" asked Carol.

"We could use something to gag him with," said Victor. "A pair of tights."

"There are some on a chair in my room," said Janet. "Get those, Carol. And a handkerchief, if you can find one, to stuff inside his mouth. A tissue will do." She hoped it would choke him.

Carol left to fetch the tights, and Victor said quickly, "Don't let her go into the kitchen, if you can help it. The dog's in there and he bled a lot."

"He's dead," said Janet. It was not a question.

"Barry did it," Victor said. "But he's not mad. He's evil."

By now Barry was shivering with fear, but he was able to go on cursing, raising his voice, calling Victor every obscene name he knew.

"Shut your filthy trap," said Victor, but he did not hit the other man, though one blow across the mouth might have silenced him.

"I've got the tights," said a voice from the stairs.

"Throw them down," said Janet, but Carol brought them, walking down, holding the tights and a wad of tissues in the hand that was free. She gave them to Janet.

"Can you do it?" Victor asked her.

"Watch me," Janet said. "But you'll have to get him to open his mouth so that I can stuff this pad inside."

Barry was by now trussed up, his hands behind his back, and pinned against the wall by the gun held to his chest once more. Vic pulled off his balaclava and took hold of him by his hair, and Janet pinched his nostrils so that automatically Barry's mouth opened wide enough for her to stuff the wad of tissues in it. Then she tied the tights across it, tightly, not caring if they cut his flesh.

"Well done," said Victor, turning to Janet. "Give me half an hour," he told her. "Then you can call the police. Tell them what he did to those two girls. He boasted about it, coming here. Oh, and give them that hood he had on—don't touch it yourself. It may be useful to them."

"Yes," said Janet, and added, "What are you going to do?"

"Better that you shouldn't know," said Victor, and he marched Barry out of the house, the gun still held against the younger man's body.

Janet opened the door for them, and the security lights came on as they emerged.

She watched them leave as she stood in the doorway, sturdy in the too-small dressing gown which gaped above her pale pink nightdress. What a blessing that Veronica and Roger had decided that Carol, with her broken arm—fractured in a hockey match at college—should not be left alone while they spent the night in London after going to one of the dinners Roger, from time to time, attended. Janet had come over after her shift at The Swan and had put her car in one of the empty garages. She had not been asleep long when she heard Paddy bark.

Now she heard muffled sounds as the men moved off down the drive. Vic held the gun in one hand and propelled Barry with the other. Soon they faded from her sight and there was silence until she heard a car start up and, as it drove away, its headlights were briefly visible.

When she went back into the house, Carol was sitting on the bottom stair. She was pale and very shocked, but not in the state that Hannah had been in after Barry Carter's last visit to Bicklebury. This time, tragedy had been averted.

"What about calling the police?" she said.

They must. Janet saw that, though the man called Vic had turned the tables on Carter.

"Yes. We'll have to go into the village," she said. "They've cut this phone. I think you'd better come with me, Carol. I don't want to leave you here alone." There was the dog's body in the kitchen. On her own, Carol would be sure to find it. "We'll take the car."

"They said wait for half an hour," said Carol. "You won't do that, will you?"

"Yes," said Janet. "Longer, even. The man Vic means to do something about Barry Carter. It would be a pity to prevent him." She took a breath. Carol was old enough to hear the truth; she was the same age as Hannah had been when she met Barry Carter. "He—the tied-up one—is the man who attacked Hannah. You were quite young at the time, but he and another man called Morris broke into The Elms to rob it, and Carter raped Hannah. He would have gone for you if the other man—Vic—hadn't stopped him. But I'd have done it if he hadn't," she added, and put her hand in her dressing-gown pocket from which she took a small pair of sharp scissors. "I grabbed them before I came downstairs. We'll get dressed," she said. "We'll feel better with clothes on." Putting some clothes on would take time, giving the man Vic more of a start.

"You don't think they'll be waiting for us up the lane?" asked Carol.

"I'm quite sure they won't," said Janet.

14.

There was a police car outside the Manor when Roger and Veronica returned the next morning.

It had not been possible to tell them what had happened, as Janet had known only that they were staying with friends, fellow diners at the function. Carol could have suggested various possible hosts, but at three or four in the morning, what good would telephoning do, except disturb the sleep of people who might not have the Fords staying with them or, if they had, causing extra distress? Time enough for them to find out when they returned, she thought, and since it seemed that little, if anything, had been taken from the house and no one, except the dog, had been hurt, there was no urgency from the police point of view.

It was nearly an hour after the men had left before the police arrived, and then there was a lot to do: Janet and Carol made complete statements about the night's events and described the men, as far as they could. The fact that one of them, named distinctly by his partner, was Barry Carter, a convicted rapist, made the case of prime importance. If the second man had not prevented him, he might have carried out another attack, and the police—two young constables in a patrol car were quickly reinforced by some more senior officers—soon took in the news that the man with the gun had said Carter was responsible for the assault in Bedfordshire and the murder in the London park.

Both women's accounts tallied: the man with the gun had turned it on Carter as soon as he had threatened Carol.

"But he aimed the gun at you first," the investigating officer stated, ready to write it down.

"No. We saw no gun. He took it from his pocket as soon as Carter started waving his knife around," said Janet.

"He told Carter to drop his knife," Carol added.

They described how the man with the gun had asked for the tights to gag Carter, and Janet related how, at his direction, she had lashed Carter's wrists together.

"Good and tight," she added, with relish. "Carter was the man who raped my daughter," Janet reminded the police. Those at the scene could not be expected to remember this, since they had not been involved in that case. "I didn't know he'd been released," she added. "The other man did nothing wrong."

"Except break and enter, and carry a gun," said the police officer drily.

Janet contemplated asking them to contact Martin Brooks. Could he ease the pressure, come and help? He would hear about this in the morning, but he was no longer in the CID, nor in this division of the force.

"What sort of car were they driving?" the police officer asked, but Janet did not know. She told them she had heard it start up and briefly seen its lights; it had turned towards Norlington.

"Carter had blood on him," she said. "From the dog."

She told them what the man with the gun had revealed: that Carter had killed Paddy. Carol, in the drawing room by now, did not see the officers go into the kitchen, pushing back the door against the dog's weight. They took away the body, and the knife, which was still embedded in the wall, but only after everything had been photographed; killing a dog was, after all, a serious offense.

"Some people treat it more seriously than rape," said the middle-aged sergeant who had arrived in response to the urgent summons from his younger colleagues. He looked at Janet sadly. "Some people think human life is less valuable than animals."

"I know," said Janet. "Some people set no value on human life at all."

"Men like Barry Carter," said the sergeant.

Carol was eventually persuaded to go back to bed for what was left of the night, with a hot drink and a sleeping pill. With the kitchen in its dreadful state, it was difficult even to boil a kettle, but they managed, and two of the officers stayed to help Janet start clearing up the mess. There was no point in leaving it for the Fords to see when they returned, and it would upset Carol. After they left, with the worst mopped up with newspapers, Janet spent the next hours washing off what she could of the remaining bloodstains, but the room would have to be repainted and the curtains replaced.

The police had agreed that nothing would be gained by trying to find the Fords, since they were due back so soon.

"It's a most surprising story," said the sergeant. "A villain with a conscience."

"Yes," agreed Janet.

The reaction did not set in, for her, until she had finished cleaning up as best she could. Then she began to shake and shiver: that was the man who had attacked her daughter, and only the intervention of the second man had saved Carol. But

I'd have done it, Janet thought. Somehow, I'd have stopped that worm from hurting her.

It was easy to think like that, but how could she, physically, have prevented it? Would the nail scissors, stabbed into him in a tender spot, have been enough?

She ran a hot bath and lay in it, soaking. After a while her shivering eased and she even dozed a little in the water, then woke when it turned chilly.

She did not go back to bed but dressed again and lit the fire in the drawing room. Carol, luckily, was still asleep when Janet heard her parents drive up, soon after two police officers had arrived to look for further clues by daylight.

They had found the break-in point the night before: the window in the study. Now they saw tire marks in the drive where the car the robbers used had been parked, but there was very little more for them to discover. Janet and Carol had described the men's appearance—the one thin and sandy-haired, the other in a gray cap, a scarf round his lower face. They knew the identity of one of them; forces throughout the country had been alerted to watch out for Barry Carter.

But no one knew what the man Vic had planned to do with him.

"Probably gave him a talking-to and set him free," said one of the officers. "After all, they were partners. They may have gone on and done some other job."

Janet thought the second man had shot Barry Carter. She did not say so.

"They hadn't planned on coming here," she said. "The other man said Carter had a change of plan."

"If I'd been here, I'd have taken my shotgun to them," Roger said.

"If you could have got to it," said Veronica. "And then you'd have been arrested."

"A man should be able to defend his family," said Roger.

He and Veronica had had a wonderful evening in London, dressed in their best and dining in an ancient hall with paneled walls and beamed roof, among other members of his guild. They had stayed up late, talking and reminiscing with their friends, and must only just have gone to bed when the two men broke into their house. Now, Roger was absorbing the full enormity of what had happened.

"Janet, this was dreadful for you," he said.

Janet was shaking her head vigorously.

"I tied him up. I hurt him," she said, with relish. "I tied him up so tight, I hope his arms drop off from lack of blood." Then she added, "The kitchen was in a dreadful state. Poor Paddy. I didn't want Carol to see it." Or you, she thought. "But it's still in a mess."

"Don't worry about that," said Roger. She was quite a woman, he thought: even now, her hair was neat, her makeup on, though she looked tired beneath the foundation or whatever it was she put on her face. No wonder England triumphed over all her foes, he thought poetically; women like Janet were its backbone. He allowed a passing thought for the Scots and Welsh to cross his mind, as Veronica, who had gone upstairs to see if Carol was awake, appeared.

"Carol's fine. She's getting up," said Veronica. "She says Carter killed a woman in London and attacked that girl near Bedford."

"So the other man said," said Janet.

"But I thought they'd arrested someone for the attack on the girl," said Veronica.

"Perhaps they got the wrong man," said Janet.

"Poor Janet. It's the second time for you," said Veronica.

"No. You forget. I wasn't there, the other time. I came

back afterwards to find Hannah and Derek. I didn't see the men," she said.

"But you met Carter."

"I saw him in court. That's all. His own mother wouldn't have recognized him in that balaclava but the other man yanked it off him. I knew him then, all right."

"The police will get them now," said Roger.

The two officers in the house endorsed this.

"It's just a question of time," said one.

Janet thought about Carter's mother, whom she had seen in court: a thin, sad-looking woman in a smart black coat, pale and dignified. Their eyes had met, anguish in both women's glances. Now she would be facing more disgrace and shame.

Janet was still feeling very shocked, but she did not want the Fords to know that; they had to support Carol, hear her full description of the night's events, for that would be a therapy for her. She had escaped physical injury, but she had had a terrifying experience, and the fate of the dog was distressing for her. Janet, however, could put herself together again alone, and must do so before she went on duty at The Swan.

She drew Veronica aside to explain that, wanting to protect her own good working clothes, all she had with her, she had worn the borrowed dressing gown as an overall while clearing up the kitchen. It had got badly stained, so she had put it in a plastic bag and would take it home to wash.

"Don't be silly, Janet. Throw it away," said Veronica. "I'm sure neither of us could bear to look at it again, much less put it on."

"I'll get off, then," Janet said. "I'm on at the bar at noon."

"You can't go in today," Veronica protested.

"I must," said Janet. "It's for the best."

And she knew it was. Driving home, she longed to talk to Martin Brooks. He had been such a help all those years ago, so understanding about every aspect of the case; he'd be like that again, she thought. She'd ring him, when she reached the house.

But he was away at a conference. She left no message.

Then she thought of Hannah. This would get into the press; it would be on television. Even in her wilderness, Hannah would learn that Carter had been freed and had committed further crimes. She'd better hear it first from Janet.

There was no reply from Hannah's number. Janet left a message on the answerphone asking her to telephone. Then she rang the MacGregors; she could explain to them, she thought, but they were out, too. She left no message on their machine.

By the time she had done all this, it was time to go to work. No one at The Swan had any notion that she had not passed the night peacefully in her bed at home.

Hannah and the MacGregors were not answering their telephones because they were all spending a few days in Edinburgh. The twins' school term had ended, the guest house had closed for the winter, and this was something the family did most years, before Christmas. This time, they had insisted that Hannah should go with them.

Meg had left the invitation until the last minute, to make refusal difficult for Hannah, who had only to arrange her duties with the warden. As she took so little time off, there could be no objection, and things died down anyway at this time of year, with many birds having migrated and the land dormant, wet, or frosted. The MacGregors had been lent a flat by friends who had gone to visit their son in Australia, so there was no expense involved, and Hannah did not need too much persuading; it was some time since she had been to the city, and the nervousness she still felt in crowds would be diminished by the company of her friends. The flat was in New Town, not far from Charlotte Square; very central. There was even a parking space for the MacGregors' Volvo Estate car, in which they all traveled.

The weather was gray and cold, so that the best of the scenery through which they passed was, as so often, veiled in mist. Hannah thought there could be no more lovely country in the world. Sitting in the back of the car with Andrew and Fergus, she played word games and joined in the songs with which they whiled away the journey. The MacGregors knew that Hannah's visits to the city had been few, though she had sometimes gone there with the previous warden and his wife, and they had always encouraged her to go when a chance arose. They suspected that she had suffered some terrible experience in the past; she never mentioned her father, and they thought it must in some way be connected with him. They found it sad that she did not join in many activities popular with other young people, and they had been trying to include her in some of their excursions. Since they opened their guest house three years ago, life in the village of Barriecallan, two miles away, had become livelier because more houses now took in guests, and in the summer there were ceilidhs and various minor festivals. Hannah had been taken to them by Meg and Charles and she had been seen to enjoy herself, though quietly. They were determined to nudge her into the mainstream now and then.

Neither questioned her. Whatever had happened must have been so painful that she would not want to speak about it, and when they met Janet, they realized that she, too, was a member of the walking wounded.

After they reached the flat, Meg sent Hannah and the boys

out together while she unpacked and settled in. She did not want them under her feet, she said, and Hannah was to be in charge of the boys.

In fact, it was they who took charge of her. They discovered that she had seen very few of the notable sights, so they took her to the Castle where Fergus, who was interested in battles, told her a great deal about the wars between the Scots and the English and showed her numerous regimental banners. Andrew was planning to be a doctor, and he was shocked to discover that she knew nothing about Burke and Hare; he treated her to a lecture about the body snatchers and showed her where they had obtained their subjects.

Darkness came early, and the lights of the shops in Princes Street, decked for Christmas, were bright and welcoming after this ghoulish talk. It was much colder now, and the boys were hungry. They expressed the hope that their mother had prepared a large meal for their return, but when they reached the flat there was no tempting smell of food to greet them. In fact, they were all going out to dinner, but Charles and Meg had decided to conceal this from Hannah in case she took fright at the prospect of visiting a restaurant.

"Agoraphobia's her trouble," Charles had stated, but Meg had disagreed.

"It's people," she said, knowing it was men. Hannah had been very ill at ease at first with Charles, keeping her distance, and once, when he had touched her arm as he moved past her, she had flinched away as if she had been hit. Although the boys were now nearly as tall as she was, they had been only shoulder high when she first knew them; their voices had not broken, and she was easy with them. She was comfortable, now, with Charles, who was tall and broad, but not in the least alarming; he was a gentle soul who had aspired to be a concert pianist but was not gifted enough to succeed; instead, he had worked with a music publisher whose business had eventually been absorbed by a larger one. He and Meg had sunk their savings into the guest house and were just beginning to make it pay.

Hannah sent Janet a postcard of Edinburgh Castle, high and somber on its hill; she caught the last post on the day after the break-in at the Manor, and Janet received it the next morning. This explained why there had been no answer when she telephoned, but as Hannah had not given an address, there was no way in which Janet could tell her about last night's events. It would not be long before the press found out what had happened, for, dead or alive, Carter would be found.

But perhaps it might not be reported in the Scottish press or on the television; matters so far south might be of no interest north of the border.

With this consoling thought, Janet struggled on. She did not ring Martin Brooks again, and if someone told him she had rung, he did not call back.

Hannah saw Barry Carter's features on the main television news that night.

The police had taken the rare step of mentioning him by name as a man wanted in connection with the Bedfordshire rape and a London park murder. He was dangerous, and if recognized, should not be tackled; anyone seeing him should notify the police. He might be with a second man, and here the description was vague; he was bigger, had been wearing a gray cap, had a scarf wound round his face, and was armed.

Meg and Charles had turned on the news after their evening in the restaurant. The boys had gone to bed, and Hannah was sitting with their parents, on the point of retiring herself, when there he was, on the screen, the man who had assaulted her when she was nineteen, wrecking her life, and now he had done it again. She caught her breath and made a small sound. Charles, who was muttering about men who did such things needing their balls cut off, did not notice, but Meg did; she saw that Hannah had gone quite white.

The Bedfordshire attack was, Meg thought, not all that far from Norlington, where Hannah's mother lived. It was, in fact, about sixty miles, but she imagined it was closer. She saw Hannah intently watching the short item; it was followed by the sports results.

Hannah was standing up.

"Thank you for a lovely day," she said. "I'm off to bed now, if that's all right. Good night."

Her voice was not quite steady, yet minutes before, she had been happy and cheerful, had teased Andrew about the huge banana split he had consumed, and been teased back by Fergus because she liked eclairs, a weakness hitherto never disclosed.

Meg said nothing to Charles, but later, when she was ready for bed herself, she went along to Hannah's room and tapped gently on the door.

"Are you all right, Hannah?" she asked. "May I come in?"

There was a mumbled response which Meg took to be consent, so she opened the door and entered the room, which was in darkness apart from light cast by street lamps outside. Meg quickly squatted beside the bed: yes, Hannah was crying.

"What is it?" she asked. "What's wrong? Won't you tell me?" Meg was tired, and she longed to be in bed herself. Her thighs began to ache so she moved and perched on the end of the bed. "Come on," she coaxed. "You're not too old for nightmares, Hannah. No one is."

So Hannah told her, and in the midst of her tale began to cry again, desperately, so that the boys, who were in the next room and still awake, heard and had to be intercepted by their father as they rushed out to find out what was happening.

It was a long time before Meg finally left Hannah and joined Charles, who was sitting propped up in bed, his glasses on, reading *The Thirty-Nine Steps,* which he had found on his hosts' bookshelves. He put a marker carefully in the book and closed it.

"Well?" he asked, taking off his glasses. "Sorted her out? What is it? Man trouble?"

"You could say that," said Meg. She shivered slightly; Hannah's story had horrified her.

"Come in and get warm," invited Charles, holding back the covers.

Meg slid in beside him, clinging to him in a most untypical, dependent way.

"You were right about the balls," she said.

Charles had forgotten his earlier remark.

"What?" he said.

"Rapists. They should, at least, never be released," said Meg. "Not that that would have saved Hannah," and she related what she had been told.

"Oh, my God," said Charles. "Well, this explains everything about the girl. Poor kid."

"Yes, and the part that seems to have hurt her most is that her father didn't try to stop it," Meg said. "Not that he'd have succeeded. Hannah was fair enough to say it might have made things even worse. But I think you'd have had a go."

From a previous marriage, Charles had a daughter, now adult, who worked for a wine importer.

"I damn well would," he said.

"Well, at least we now know what her trouble is," said Meg. "Maybe she'll feel better for telling me, or maybe she'll wish she hadn't. We'll just have to see."

"That's why she leaped away from me as if she'd been stung if I so much as brushed against her," Charles said.

"Yes, but she doesn't now. Not that you've got your hands all over the girl, of course, but in our house it can be so crowded that you have to touch people sometimes, to get past them."

"That's true, but I've been very careful not to give offense," said Charles. "I don't want to be accused of harassment. What happens next? Will she be able to hold herself together?"

"I think so. She won't want the boys to suspect anything."

"They heard her sobs. They were on their way to console her when I stopped them," said their father.

"What did you tell them?"

"Well, I didn't know what the trouble was, did I? I said she'd had a nightmare."

"They swallowed that?"

"Seemed to, or decided to," said Charles.

"I said I'd have to tell you, and she understood. She said her mother was marvelous at the time, but no wonder she's—Janet, I mean—so uptight and tense."

"She'll be upset by this development," said Charles.

"She probably saw it on the news herself—or no, she'd be at that bar where she works. She may not know yet," Meg said. "And if she does find out and rings Hannah, no one's there."

"Perhaps Hannah'd better ring her, in the morning," Charles said.

"Good idea. And if she won't, one of us will have to. Poor woman, she has to be considered as well as Hannah. There's that dreadful man on the loose again, wreaking more trouble. Neither of them will have any peace until the police catch him."

The news item had mentioned nothing about the break-in at Bicklebury; there was no reason for the MacGregors to suppose that Janet would know any more about it than they did.

She was at home when Hannah rang her in the morning, and glad to hear her daughter's voice, which sounded calm. Hannah would have to learn the extra details before they were made public, so Janet told her.

"Your identity will still be protected," she said. "And the press don't know I was there. There's no reason why they should." Except, she thought, their own tenacity. "Nothing much happened, after all."

"They killed the dog," said Hannah. "Poor Paddy."

"Carter did," Janet reminded her. The press would like that one, she thought: she could picture the headlines: FREED RAPIST KILLS PET, or something similar. "He'll soon be caught and charged," she said. "Then it will all be *sub judice.*" Only to be resurrected again at trial time, she knew. Unless the second man had killed Carter. She assured Hannah that Carol, though very shocked, and sad about the dog, was quite unharmed.

"Awful for you, Mum," said Hannah. "That—that creep. Did he still smell?"

"Yes. It was disgusting," Janet said.

"I hope the other man killed him," Hannah said. "Then he'd be gone for good."

After they finished their conversation, Hannah promised to telephone when she was back in the cottage. She had sounded reasonably composed, even when revealing that she had told the MacGregors about Carter's assault upon her. Janet was glad she had done so; they seemed so dependable and kind. She had suggested that Hannah could spend a few days with them after they went home if she felt uneasy.

"Just till Carter's been arrested," she said.

"Why should I? I hope he's dead by now," said Hannah brutally. "Anyway, he won't come looking for me up here."

That was true.

"Of course he won't," Janet said. "He wasn't looking for you. He just wanted to get back to some unfinished business."

15.

After a second night in which neither Clive nor Barry came home, Noreen made her decision. While Barry was in Bicklebury, acting out his whim, she made up her mind that in the morning she would tell the police of her suspicions. Not only must Clive, who was innocent, be freed, but Barry, unless he had escaped abroad, must be taken out of circulation, for his own good as well as that of the public, by whom she meant young women.

He hadn't done that murder. Of course he hadn't. They weren't really bloodstains on his clothes; she was mistaken about them, she reassured herself. Anyway, tests made by the police would give the answer. Telling herself all this, at last she went to bed, but she did not fall asleep for a long time, and then she went into an exhausted torpor, not waking up till nearly nine.

She dressed carefully, putting on her good black coat, a fashion model bought at a nearly-new shop ten years ago when life still held some hope; then she set off to catch the bus at the corner, where there was a telephone kiosk. She was not on the telephone at the flat; she had no calls to make. Clive had a mobile phone. She could have used that; he'd left it behind when he was arrested. If she rang, the police would come to her, but she didn't want any more visits from them; there was already plenty for people in the block to talk about, and enough sly looks and mutters after Clive's arrest, with more after his car was removed for testing. But he would soon be free: once she'd told her story, he'd be released. Or would they wait until they'd arrested Barry? She knew there was a limit to how long Clive could be held without being charged, but in a serious investigation, while evidence was sought, the time could be extended and this must already have happened in Clive's case.

Where was Barry now? Abroad?

When she reached the police station, she had to wait for the attention of the desk sergeant who had several other people to deal with. While she sat there, a shabby drunk was brought in, a man who looked as if he ought to be in hospital. Two prostitutes were taken away to be interviewed, and a woman reported a lost dog. At last it was her turn.

The sergeant listened to her attentively, then asked her to wait while he went off to consult someone else, and after that she, too, was led behind the scenes to an interview room where she repeated her story, which was taken very seriously.

She did not avoid a police visit to the flat because they took her back in a police car and removed the stained clothes she had mentioned. There was a pair of shabby trainers, too, in Barry's room, on which there were some dark, suspicious marks, and they took away some of his other clothes. They gave Noreen a receipt for everything.

She did not mention the microwave, the hair drier, or the clothes that Barry had brought her; they had nothing to do with the other business and they were very useful. When she went to work, she put away her good black coat and wore the fur one.

She had to take a taxi to The Lunar Moon; otherwise, she would have been late.

When Clive at last returned to the flat Noreen was at work. His car was still impounded; he had nothing to do.

He was gripped by a fearful sense of injustice. He had been hauled in from his normal, law-abiding existence and accused of something shocking, and he had been deprived, meanwhile, of his livelihood. Presumably the police would eventually return his car, but he must have forfeited the confidence of the firm through whom he worked, and he had let down some regular customers.

There had been an identity parade and he, with several other men, had been lined up to be surveyed by the girl from Bedfordshire. She, pale and haggard, had regarded them all impassively and declared that none was the guilty man. There was no doubt at all in her mind.

Suppose she had been less sure? Suppose he had borne some resemblance to the real assailant? Would scientific tests have exonerated him? Clive liked to think that was so, but people were wrongly convicted all the time, according to the papers. And mud stuck. It would stick to him now, even though the real perpetrator might eventually be found. Maybe he would attack or kill someone else before that happened.

Clive was convinced that Barry had taken his car, but he did not suspect that he was involved in this crime. The young fellow would have just driven it around, used it to get wherever he wanted to go. He was an unpleasant bit of work: even for Noreen's sake, Clive could find in him no redeeming feature; but that did not mean that he was a rapist and a potential murderer. A car like his had been involved. Was every male driver of a blue Sierra suspect? His could not have been the one seen at the spot.

Clive's mind returned to his dream of moving and running a taxi in some country town. He had intended that it should be not too far from his wife so that he could see his children more often. He had no illusions about a reconciliation; all that was over and his wife, he knew, had some man friend who had not moved in with her but who spent a lot of time there, according to the children. But Clive and she could meet and be reasonably civil; some shared parenting, as he had heard it called, would be good for the children and he would feel less out of touch with them, with somewhere to take them to instead of slogging round cinemas, adventure parks and McDonald's.

He had never seen Noreen as part of this rural scene. He was fond of her; they got along well; and he knew she had had a hard time; but she had never lived in the country. He wasn't sure that she would transplant. What sort of work would she be able to find? She might get a job as a waitress, true; one, even, with easier hours than The Lunar Moon; but there was another problem: his children did not like her. They had not seen a lot of her, but on their few meetings Noreen had been awkward with them, too eager to please, and his younger daughter, then six, had said she was ugly. Noreen had been bitterly upset though she had staunchly declared that the child hadn't meant to be unkind, which need not have been true; children could be spiteful. In time, this might have been overcome, but Clive was not anxious to risk more failed meetings.

Now there was the complication of Barry. He might go on getting into trouble, and at best he was work-shy; he would keep running back to his mother.

In any case, this plan was a distant dream because Clive could not, at the moment, easily finance it, and he was living here for much less than a place of his own would cost. A nice win on the horses would put things right, give him his chance, but so far any gains he had were offset by his losses. His wife hadn't been able to stand his gambling; it had contributed to their breakup.

Noreen came home during the afternoon. Clive was watching a football match on television. She looked very pleased to see him.

"They let you go!" she said.

"As you can see," he said. "You look rough. Want a cup of tea?"

"I feel rough." Noreen laughed nervously, brushing a hand across her forehead. Her graying hair was now rinsed a dull blonde, like sand, and he suddenly noticed a resemblance to her son whose hair was the same color. He had the same pale eyes, but in Noreen they were attractive whereas in Barry they were expressionless pebbles. "They believed me, then," she added.

"Believed you? Who?"

"The police. They believed me about Barry. That was why they let you go," she said.

"What about Barry?"

"He—oh—he—" she said, and began to cry.

"He what?"

"He did it. At least, I think he did," she said.

Clive had got up to put the kettle on. Now he paused and looked at her.

"He did what?"

"I found some stained clothes. Barry's clothes. It didn't wash out," said Noreen. "He said it was tomato sauce, but I knew it wasn't. It was blood."

"Blood? On Barry's clothes?" She wasn't making sense.

Noreen nodded.

"And there was the photofit in the paper. When I saw that,

I knew. Deep in my bones, I knew," she said, and now tears were pouring down her face, making runnels in her makeup.

"Are you saying Barry attacked that girl?" Clive demanded. "You mean I was accused of something your boy'd done?" He was standing near her, glowering, and she shrank back, afraid that he was going to hit her. His face was red with anger.

"It's possible," she said. "The police took his clothes away."

"When?"

"Today. I told them today," she said, and in a tempest of tears she explained what had happened. Then she added, "I'd told you he was working up north, but it wasn't true. He'd been in prison. He—he raped a girl. During a burglary, it was, nearly six years ago."

Clive had been transfixed while she said all this, and looking at her thin, weeping form, he felt a wave of pity for her, tinged with amazement.

"You shopped him," he said. "Your own son."

"If he did it, he needs locking up again," she said, dabbing her eyes. Her mascara had run all down her cheeks. "He'll not stop now. There'll be others. That picture in the paper was just like him. The girl had described him. It wasn't at all like you." She had not mentioned the other case, the murdered girl, and Clive did not ask about the stains.

"That's why I got off," said Clive heavily. He went to the sink and filled the kettle. While it was boiling he came back to face her. "You didn't save me," he said. "It was the law that did, for once. For once they got it right. But what if I'd confessed meanwhile, because I couldn't take it? Blokes do."

"They couldn't have proved it. Not if Barry did it," Noreen insisted. She blew her nose and wiped her face with a tissue. She had to return to work that evening and would look a fright if she kept on crying. "I did right to turn him in," she said.

"Convince yourself," said Clive. "You don't have to convince me."

The police were looking for Barry in the area around his mother's flat. Local shops and pubs were visited and Noreen's neighbors were questioned about when they had last seen him. He was nowhere to be found, but the police discovered that he had been seen in the company of an older man and that he had been flashing money around. Someone said that he had boasted that he was expecting a lot of money and was going abroad. The police began to look for the second man, Victor Kemp, who was possibly his companion on the raid at Bicklebury.

They had been seen together only in a few local places, mainly The Angel, but no one interviewed knew where Vic lived. They would discover his base in time; someone would come forward.

Thirty-six hours after the break-in at the Manor, a telephone call to Scotland Yard suggested that a car parked on a cliff top in Cornwall might interest the police. The vaguest of hints were given as to the location; a large stretch of the land was owned by the National Trust and to search it all would take time. There was no reason to link the call with the hunt for Barry Carter; the car might contain terrorist bombs or be connected with drug smuggling, or simply be abandoned. A police helicopter flew over the area and, eventually, the gray car was seen on a lonely headland, with jagged black cliffs below, and the white spume of the waves as they crashed against the rocks.

A police car was directed to the spot, and in the boot of the Calibra, discovered to be stolen, was Barry Carter, still alive but almost out of his wits with fear, and shivering with cold. He was taken to hospital suffering from hypothermia and dehydration, and there, as he began to recover, he gave his name but admitted nothing else. However, Roger Ford's checkbook was found in his jacket pocket, and his clothes were stained with blood which could be tested to see if it came, as had been alleged, from the stabbed dog.

After some hours, he was adjudged well enough to be discharged and removed for questioning, and then, ready to save himself if he could, he admitted going to Bicklebury with intent to steal, but said the plan was Vic's.

"Then he went mad," said Barry. "Vic did. Pulled this gun and tied me up and frog-marched me to the car." He did not mention the women, nor Janet's part in tying him up.

"I was afraid for my life," he whined, and affected to tremble still at the memory.

Whether his shakes were genuine or not, they earned him no sympathy from the interviewing officers. Various police divisions were concerned, now, with his fate, as he had committed crimes in London and Bedfordshire as well as the break-in in Berkshire.

He said Vic had driven for hours and hours, and the last part of the journey had been over rough ground. Vic had not stopped for petrol; the tank had been filled less than forty miles from Bicklebury and had held enough for the distance, though it was almost empty when the car was found. After it stopped, Barry had heard the door close and then there was silence. Vic had said not a word to Barry, nor let any air into his prison.

"I might have suffocated," Barry said.

"Oh dear," said one of the officers.

Barry was beginning to get his act together. Soon he would deny all responsibility for anything that had happened that night, justifying his actions and saying he had been led astray by Vic. But everything was being done according to the book. He had been charged with breaking and entering Bicklebury Manor with intent to steal; the other more serious charges could follow. For them, there was as yet no confirmation apart from hearsay evidence provided by Janet Jarvis, and more than that would be needed, but once scientific tests had been done, proof would follow. DNA profiling could confirm his part in the Bedfordshire attack, and the girl could be asked to identify him. Meanwhile, the interview was taped; he was granted respite and food at the required intervals; no tiny administrative slip which might let him off the hook was made.

It had been dreadful in the car, he said. There he was, alone in the boot, trying to struggle out of his bonds. He showed the officers marks on his arms from the flex so well secured by Janet. Victor had bound his legs when he was folded into the boot. He was cold, and he was hungry, and then there was the noise. A gale had sprung up and the parked car had rocked to and fro in the wind, and the sound of the sea had petrified him. In fact he hadn't known what it was; the soughing and crashing of the waves on the rocks under the cliffs was terrifying.

Although he was anxious to off-load the blame on to Vic, and did not yet know that he was wanted for the two other serious crimes, including murder, Barry did not mention the first robbery he had done with Vic. That might cost his mother her microwave and fur coat.

16.

Martin Brooks came into The Swan after Barry's arrest. It was early evening, and he was with Susan Fitton.

Janet was behind the bar, and he ordered a Scotch for himself and a bitter lemon for Susan, who did not drink alcohol; it was her way of coping with the beery sessions enjoyed by so many of her male colleagues, and she had earned their respect, not their derision, which was an achievement.

"I hear you rang me," Martin said, as Janet handed over their drinks. "You weren't in when I rang back this afternoon."

"Oh—well, never mind," said Janet. She had gone over to the Manor again today, to see how Carol was. "I expect you can guess what it was about."

"Yes. Well, I've got news for you. Carter's been found."

"Has he?" Janet's strongly marked eyebrows shot up in two high arcs. "Where?"

"In a stolen car, abandoned on a cliff in Cornwall," said Brooks.

"Alive?"

"Bit the worse for being shut up for a good few hours but

otherwise all right," said Brooks. "Chose the Manor this time, I hear, not a repeat visit to The Elms."

"Yes," said Janet. "I was there."

"Were you?" Brooks had not heard that part of the story.

"I was staying in the house with Carol, who's got a broken arm, because her parents had gone away for the night," said Janet. "Carol's the Fords' daughter," she explained.

"Oh God, you're unlucky," said Brooks. "That's terrible."

"Thank goodness I was there," said Janet. "She's only nineteen—just like Hannah was. It would have been much worse if she'd been alone."

"A repeat performance," Brooks said.

"The other man didn't let it happen like that," said Janet. "He saved her."

"I haven't seen the reports," Brooks said. "It's not on my patch, but there was an alert out for Carter and his pal."

"Have they got him?" Janet polished a glass. "The other man?"

"Not yet. I expect Carter will soon supply his name and address," said Brooks.

"I suppose so," said Janet. "What will happen to Carter this time? He's killed a woman since he got out of prison. The other man said so. And he attacked that girl near Bedford."

"If the murder can be proved, he'll get life," said Brooks.

"And be out again in eight or nine years," said Janet bitterly.

"Not necessarily. He won't get parole if it can be successfully alleged that he represents a danger to the public, and a judge might decide he should not be released for twenty or thirty years. Sentencing is getting tougher."

"So I should hope," said Janet. "A few years is no deterrent to a young man like Carter."

"I agree," said Brooks.

"And the other man, if they catch him—he'll get a stiffer sentence, of course, like Morris did last time, though he hurt no one." Janet had forgotten Derek's scratched and bruised face.

"Not in this case," said Brooks. "This time, if it's as alleged, Carter has committed a murder."

"The other man didn't do much except break in, armed," said Susan Fitton, who was informed about the incident. "He'd go down for that, but not for long, unless he's wanted for other offenses." She sipped her bitter lemon, which contained ice and a sliver of zest. "Most people would applaud him, I should think, for saving you and Carol."

"Well, Morris got a heavy sentence last time," said Janet. "This man—Vic—might, too."

"Yes. Morris was violent," Brooks pointed out. "He had a gun. So did this man."

"He didn't rape Hannah," Janet said. "I hope they don't catch the other man."

"Plenty of people will share that opinion, once the story gets out," said Susan. "But he was armed. He's a villain."

"What did he do after he left Carter? I suppose he drove the car down to Cornwall and just went away?" said Janet. "I thought he was going to shoot him."

"I think leaving him to sweat it out in the boot of a car on a Cornish cliff, where he might starve or suffocate to death, was a good punishment," said Brooks. "He knew that if Carter survived, we'd get him in the end, and he kept his own hands relatively clean. Carter wasn't worth taking a murder rap for. Maybe he thought that, too."

"Maybe he did," said Janet.

Brooks was wondering who had told Scotland Yard about the abandoned car.

* * *

Vic Kemp had become a folk hero in the press in the few hours before Carter was returned to Norlington and charged with the break-in at Bicklebury. After that, the details could not be reported for fear of prejudicing the trial.

A friend of Carol Ford's had come to see her and discovered what had happened. She was easily trapped into making some disclosures, and then a reporter waylaid Janet, who was asked about the earlier attack.

Janet had done a deal. In return for revealing something about events at the Manor, the link with Carter's other visit to the village would be played down, and everything possible would be done to protect Hannah. Janet did not entirely trust the journalist; she knew that some reporters were unscrupulous and ignored the effects of what they printed on victims and relatives in their anxiety to get a story, but if she did not appear to cooperate, someone else would tell the media everything, and get it wrong.

"After all," she pointed out, "rape victims are not supposed to be identified."

In theory this was true, but photographs of their houses or their parents could give clues, and neighbors often knew what had happened. Some assailants lived in the same area and after their release, or if on remand, could be encountered daily by their victims. Hannah would not be totally safe from media attention until Carter had been locked up again, securely, or was dead.

She could not describe Vic, except to say that he was bulkier than Carter and probably older. His face was hidden and he had worn a cap and a black leather jacket over jeans and trainers.

"As he brought a gun, he must have been prepared to use it," said the reporter.

"Yes, he did, to good effect," said Janet. "He saved us with it."

"You wouldn't have been too sorry to hear that Carter was dead," the reporter suggested.

"I wouldn't have shed a tear," said Janet, who would not permit a photograph or her name to appear in the paper; that could start a trail leading straight to Hannah.

"You've not forgiven him."

"No."

"Some people do forgive their assailants," the reporter pointed out.

"Then they're saintly souls, and I'm not," said Janet. "He—and men like him who attack children and old people who just get in their way—are wicked and evil. They destroy others just to satisfy some whim or lust for power or money, or a need to terrify. They deserve no mercy."

"What if they reform and become model citizens? Some do."

"Very few," said Janet. "But men like Carter are freed because they've served their time and haven't been reformed at all. Perhaps it's impossible to cure them. But if they knew that they'd be in prison for life for this sort of thing, it might discourage some of them."

They went on to discuss the death sentence, about which Janet was uncertain, fearing miscarriages of justice, and the reporter went to town with all this material while he could.

It would be only a matter of time before Victor Kemp joined his partner under lock and key.

After leaving the Manor with Barry, Victor had had no firm plan. He had stowed his prisoner in the boot of the Calibra, tying his legs up tightly, then driven off at speed, moderating it as soon as he neared Norlington. It would be unfortunate if he were stopped for the same offense that he had cautioned Barry against committing on their outward trip.

It had all gone wrong. Due to Barry's reckless whim, Vic's careful scheme had been thwarted and now he must decide what to do next. The man's sudden switch to violent conduct, and his boasts about the two women he had attacked, had horrified Vic and he was surprised at his own inability to pull the trigger on him as he threatened Carol. Such a man—if he could be called a man—needed taking out to stop him harming other women, but a quick clean shot was too good for him. He needed to be made to suffer, and, locked up in the car, knowing Vic had got a gun, he would be terrified.

Gradually, driving westwards through the damp, cold night, Vic decided what to do. He still meant to shoot Barry, but not yet.

He knew that much of the Cornish coast was wild and lonely, in between the clutches of small towns and spreading caravan camps. If he could find such a place, he could leave the car there, shooting Barry where he lay, leaving him to be found when someone passing saw the car.

He did not change his mind about killing Barry until he parked the car. He had found a track leading past a farm, and after going through several gates, which he had to open and then close after him, he reached the headland where he turned off the engine.

Gun in pocket, he stepped onto the wet grass. The sea was roaring, and the wind caught at his hair. He had taken off his hat and it was in his pocket, holding down the gun.

Suddenly, shooting Barry seemed a worthless act. The man might suffocate in the boot. Vic wondered how long he could survive, shut in there. Perhaps he was already dead, from fear if nothing else, but a little air must leak in from outside, Vic thought. Barry could last a few days without food or water. When he was found, he would be linked with his various crimes because the people at the Manor knew about them, so the law in its slow and tortuous way would exact some retribution, and Barry Carter would be locked up for a good long spell.

Not opening the boot to look at his prisoner, Vic left the car where it was and walked back along the track. Now his main concern was his own escape, for as soon as Carter was found, dead or alive, the hunt for him would begin in earnest in this area.

He must return to civilization undetected.

Vic had a long walk before he reached the main road. Now the remoteness of his dumping ground seemed less attractive as he trudged along, physically tired already. Dawn was breaking. He climbed over the farm gates, so as not to risk opening them and making any sound, as farmers stirred at this time of day and he did not want to be seen.

He walked four miles along the road until he reached the next village where he saw a bus for Plymouth. He boarded it.

People on it might remember him, if asked. He sat at the back, head down, bearded face concealed, but though exhausted, Vic did not sleep. Others on the bus, going to work, were tired too; he was a stranger, and they saw him, but were not concerned today, though they would recall him later, when a description of him would be circulated. But neither Janet nor Carol had seen more than his eyes and figure; likenesses would be made from details supplied by those who knew him in The Angel.

In Plymouth, when the shops were open, he made some purchases, and in a public toilet he clipped off his whiskers, leaving a neat beard closely trimmed around his jaw. He shaved his cheeks. Then he cut his hair, hacking it short around his ears. The result was jagged and untidy; he would have to have a proper haircut somewhere, but not here.

He had bought a nondescript fawn raincoat, and he put it on, bundling his leather jacket into the carrier which had contained the raincoat. He changed his scuffed trainers for black lace-ups, and his jeans for dark flannels. On his head he wore a checked tweed hat.

He packed his old clothes in a small suitcase bought for the purpose. Dumping them in this area would be most unwise. Now, looking like a representative or a clerk, he went to the station and caught a train to London.

He still had the gun. It was in a pocket of his raincoat.

17.

Barry Carter had been remanded in custody for a week. He was safely locked up in prison and could do no further damage for the present. Now the police set about obtaining the evidence which would enable the Crown Prosecution Service to go forward with his trial. Months of work lay ahead but in the end there would be enough to convict him.

His Bedfordshire victim courageously agreed to attend another identity parade, and there she picked him out with certainty, even though he no longer had a beard and the police had managed to find several other young men looking not unlike him.

Evidence for the London murder would be more difficult to collect, and unless he could be convicted of that offense, he would not receive a life sentence. The knife with which he had stabbed the dog at Bicklebury, found embedded in the paneled wall and still stained with Paddy's blood, was sent for testing. It might match the wounds on the woman's body, but that would prove only that it was similar to the murder weapon; her blood would not be on it now. The clothes which Barry's mother had surrendered to the police would be examined; after their washing, they were unlikely to be very useful but fibers from them might match fibers on the woman's clothing. In the end, Carter might be persuaded to confess, but unsubstantiated confessions were nowadays, and rightly, subject to query.

No convincing traces were found in Clive's car. The Bedford victim had not been in it long, and Clive had cleaned it very thoroughly several times since Barry took it; a blurred fingerprint on a doorframe could have been hers, but it was not clear enough to be acceptable as evidence.

The search for Vic continued. Carter had mentioned the lock-up Vic had rented, where he had stored goods he had stolen on earlier robberies with which Barry said he had not been involved. It was empty, though tire marks on the dusty floor showed that the Calibra, or a car with similar new tires, had been parked there. When this was pointed out to Barry, he said Vic had stolen the car and put it there. There were prints on the doors which could have belonged to any number of people. Boys skateboarded outside the row of lock-ups, and youths met there. Sometimes smaller boys played football in the space. Questioned, two youngsters said they had noticed the man, and described him, but they had seen him only once, and that was several weeks ago. No one knew where he lived, and inquiries in the area around the lock-up and, two miles away in the neighborhood of The Angel, brought no results.

Then someone came up with an address. A man answering to Victor Kemp's description had been renting a basement flat in Herbert Road. The daughter of the landlady, seeing the sketch of Victor on a poster, recognized him. He'd rescued her hamster when it ran down the garden, and he'd mended its cage. She saw no harm in mentioning this when two police officers came to the house inquiring about him, saying that they could not find him. Poor Vic was lost, it seemed; he needed, like her hamster, to be found.

The police gained admittance to his flat. They could easily get a search warrant if the landlady had denied them access, so she let them in. The place was deserted. There were no clothes there, not even a piece of soap or a toothbrush.

"He's done a flit, then," said Detective Inspector Burton, who had come himself to inspect the place. Kemp had to be the man they wanted.

The old woman in the other basement flat said she could tell them nothing. He had been a quiet neighbor, kind and helpful, and she cited examples of small tasks that he had done for her. He kept himself to himself and often she didn't see him for days at a time, though sometimes she saw his light at night, and it was good to know that he was there. She had never seen him bring anyone else to the flat; he was always alone, and he had no car. The last time she saw him, he had said something about going on holiday to Spain. That was a country she had never visited, she said, and began to talk about her native Russia.

Burton interrupted her to thank her for her help.

"We'll be round again to see if he's come back," he said.

"I hope he's not in any trouble," said the countess.

"We do want to talk to him," said Burton, evasively. Vic seemed popular at home.

The police sketch for the poster had been done with the help of the landlord of The Angel. Kemp had probably got away to Spain. Carter had had a visitor's passport on him when he was arrested, but he had so far not said much about vacation plans. As the night's robbery had gone wrong, he was not likely to mention how a trip overseas was to be financed.

Examination of the stolen Calibra offered plenty of evidence of Barry's presence in the boot. There were scratches from his kicks and struggles. Nothing concrete which could point to Vic was found, apart from sole marks from his trainers on the rubber mat by the driver's seat. Vic's trainers, by this time, like the other clothes he had worn, had been cut up and burned, and the ashes collected to be dumped. He had covered his tracks.

On remand in a prison cell, Barry was bitter. Innocent until proved guilty, why should he be locked up while Vic was sunning himself on the Costa Brava? If Barry could drop Vic in it, he would, but he had scant information to offer the police. To admit to their earlier joint raid would be to convict himself of another crime; he mentioned that they had intended to go to some large house where there were pictures for whom Vic had a buyer, but he could not provide an address except to say that Vic had shown him magazine features abut the place, and that it was not too far from the Hungerford turn-off from the M4. He'd mentioned Thrupton.

"Why did you go to Bicklebury, then?" was the reasonable query from the police, and Barry made out that Vic had changed his mind.

Another version of this decision existed: the one given by Vic at the time, and reported by both Janet and Carol; that was the story the police preferred to believe, and Barry had been to Bicklebury before.

The police thought that Vic would return from Spain when his cash had gone, but since no successful raid had been carried out by the pair, what was he using for money?

He was into other scams, said Barry, ever ready to be helpful; he had given Barry sums of money from time to time. Barry resented his exclusion from whatever sidelines Vic had pursued; they were partners.

The police decided that Vic was a petty thief who had got out of his league when he teamed up with Carter, and the tip-off about where to find Carter had probably come from him. All the same, he had a gun. Perhaps he had carried out building society and bank raids, using that. They began combing through security films to see if any men wanted for those sort of incidents answered the meager description they had of him. If this was his usual line, he might try it again and be caught, after which he could be charged with anything else he might have done in the past, if there was evidence to prove his involvement. Possession of a gun, without a license, was a serious offense, and that would do for a start if he reappeared, as the police thought he probably would in time. It had to be assumed that a man with a gun was prepared to fire it if circumstances provoked him.

Noreen was told that Barry had been arrested. She did not understand, at first, that her information was not what had led to this, but his solicitor—the one who had acted for him before—told her what had allegedly happened and how his partner in crime had turned on him because, again allegedly, he had threatened two women in Bicklebury.

"Oh, my God! That place again," Noreen exclaimed. "What did he want to go back there for?"

"Who knows?" said the solicitor, whose duty it would be to do all he could to obtain Barry's acquittal for this new crime and the others of which he would soon be accused, but who knew the man ought to be locked up for life.

"The girl wasn't there, was she? The one he went for before? He didn't do it to her again?" asked Noreen.

"No. There was a different girl involved. It was another house in the same village, but the first girl's mother was there, keeping this girl company, it seems," said the solicitor.

"Oh my God," said Noreen again. "Oh, I'm sorry. I did try with Barry, when he was younger," she wailed.

"I'm sure you did, but he's a big boy now and must answer for his own actions," said the solicitor.

"I suppose you've got to try to get him off, but I wish you wouldn't," said Noreen.

"I won't succeed, any more than I did last time," said the solicitor. "But I can make sure he's properly treated and has his rights."

"What about the rights of those young girls?" Noreen said. "Their whole lives are wrecked, and one's dead."

"Yes—well, we're not sure if that was Barry. He did attack the Bedford girl, I'm afraid; I think there will be proof of that," said the solicitor. "But evidence for the murder will be more difficult to find."

"Maybe he'll confess. Ask for it to be taken into account," Noreen said.

"Maybe," said the solicitor, sounding doubtful.

He bade her farewell. He had other pressing work waiting for him.

It had been nice of him to come and see her, Noreen thought: well outside his duty. She closed the door behind him and turned back into the flat. There was her microwave, a present from Barry, and the coat he had given her hung in the cupboard. As far as he was able to love anyone, he loved her, but he was all warped and twisted inside.

So am I, Noreen thought: so am I.

Clive had gone. She couldn't blame him, now that he knew what Barry had done and how nearly he had been charged with her son's crimes. Barry must have tipped off the police about the Sierra. No one else knew that it was the car involved in the Bedfordshire rape. Clive could have been charged with that, if the girl hadn't been so sure he was not the right man. It was true that the DNA test would have eliminated him eventually, but he might have been held on remand for weeks while results were obtained; Noreen did not know how long such a test took but it wasn't an overnight job. She had tried to tell him how sorry she was, but he had cut her short. It wasn't her fault, he said; he didn't blame her at all; but it was just too much, and if his wife heard about it, she wouldn't want him to see the children.

He had decided to cut and run. He had rented a cheap room which would do until something better turned up. That meant another woman, one with a flat or a house, Noreen thought, doing Clive an injustice because he had decided to see if he could get a driving job in the Nottingham area.

Noreen was too wrung out emotionally even to weep, after he left. She had turned in her own son, for his own good and for the safety of other women, and now her lover had gone. She had nothing left.

Except The Lunar Moon, and it was time to get ready for work.

PART FOUR

Afterwards

1.

Derek heard on his car radio that Barry Carter had been arrested. No details were given, except that he was wanted in connection with a recent attack on a young woman, and that he had been apprehended during an investigation into another matter.

So the police had got him. That was good news, as long as they put him away properly this time. Derek remembered the young girl in Bedfordshire who had helped the police produce such a good likeness of him. He patted his gun, obtained with so much guile. He had not, after all his planning, had to commit murder, though he would have regarded it as execution.

He reached home and drove into the drive, where he got out of the car to open the garage. He had just put the Citroën away and gone into the house when the doorbell rang.

Who could this be? Not a last-minute buyer for his house, surely? Due to the depressed state of the market, he had decided to let it, unfurnished, for six months, which would bring him in an income to meet the mortgage.

He went to the door and opened it. There, on the step,

stood Angela, her small blue van parked beyond her where, each Tuesday, it used to rest for an hour or more.

"Angela!" He was very surprised. He had not seen her for three months. "Come in."

"I've been past several times," she said. "But it looked as if you were away." She did not tell him that she had rung the bell on two of the occasions. Another time, late at night, when Stephen, after a sudden acute illness, had been taken to hospital, she had wanted comforting and had passed by, only to see a strange car in the drive. She had thought it must belong to some other woman and had driven on to the friends who had taken Pippa to spend the night with them.

"I haven't been home much," he said, standing back to let her in. They stood apart, silent, looking at each other, both embarrassed but for different reasons.

Angela was staring at him hard, and she smiled, head on one side, eyebrows raised.

"My, how thou art translated," she said, and laughed.

Derek did not recognize the quotation, and he blinked.

"Your beard," she said. "It looks very distinguished."

A neat brown beard adorned Derek's chin.

"It's going," he said. "If you'd come tomorrow, it would have been gone."

"And your hair! You've dyed it!" she exclaimed. "What's been going on?"

"I've been doing some amateur dramatics," said Derek. "It was easiest to grow my own beard, and gray hair didn't suit."

"I'm surprised your beard didn't come through gray," she remarked. "They usually do."

If she looked at him closely, she would see that the fresh growth, close to his face, was gray.

"I'll be back to normal tomorrow," he said.

"What was the play?"

"Oh—" Derek suddenly remembered a sign he had seen on a hoarding. "It was *Treasure Island*," he said. "I was Long John Silver."

"What—peg leg and all?"

"Yes—and parrot," he said, and hoped she would ask him no more. "It was a success," he added. "Christmas revelry and all that."

"Where were you doing this?" she asked him. "Not locally?"

"No—not here. Near where I used to live," said Derek. "What about you, Angela? How are things? Would you like a drink while you tell me?"

"Well, Stephen's been ill," she said. "He caught an infection from somewhere. He's been quite bad—in hospital. But he's better now and we've decided to settle out of court. We're going to accept an offer the insurers made last week. They upped it, because of Stephen's illness, and our lawyers have said we can't be certain of getting more if we press them. We're going down to my parents tomorrow and we'll look about for a bungalow not too far from them, somewhere where there's a good school for Pippa."

"I see," said Derek.

He did not move towards her, or try to kiss her.

"I'd like that drink," she said. "Could I have a brandy?"

"Right." He led the way into the sitting room, where she saw cardboard boxes full of books and papers. The shelves were bare.

"You've sold the house?" she asked.

"No, but I'm letting it. I need the income," he said. "Maybe things will improve in the spring and the buyers will appear."

"Like the swallows," she said.

"Yes."

"A job might appear, too," she suggested.

"It might."

"I suppose rehearsals kept you busy."

"Yes. It was surprising how much time it took," Derek said. "There were props to buy, too—lines to learn—all that."

"Funny, I never thought of you as keen on theatricals," Angela said.

"Well, I never did, either," Derek said. "But somehow or other, I couldn't avoid it."

She didn't stay long. It seemed rather sad that they felt no great urge to embrace.

"I learned a lot from you," Derek told her, as she got up to go.

"Did you?"

"Yes."

He could not tell her, now, what it was: he was too ashamed to acknowledge that he had grievously failed Janet as a lover and that, indeed, he had raped her in the way Angela had described as date rape. He had damaged her as badly as Carter had damaged Hannah.

When she had gone, he went up to the bathroom and shaved off his beard. Then he washed his hair several times to rinse out the dye and the last traces of Victor Kemp. He would get a better haircut in the morning, but not locally, where he might have been seen in his bearded persona, though he had tried to leave the house and return while it was dark. He had used this house as a way of keeping Vic Kemp off the streets except when he was tailing Carter or, later, learning to fraternize with him.

Carter was capricious and volatile. Derek had soon discovered that, trying out his scheme with his new beard in the paper shop. His plan had been different at first; he had meant to trail Carter, learn his habits and shoot him down in the street, once he had acquired a gun. When he found how easy it was to talk to the man, gull him into accepting a drink, then string him along with the promise of future thefts, he had gradually devised the notion of doing the first raid here, in his own house. In that way, it would be a safe escapade because no one would surprise them, nor would it be reported, and he could later restore his own property, which he had done, apart from the microwave and the clothes. He had bought, from a charity shop, some women's clothes, cheap jewelry and cosmetics to make it look as if a couple lived in the house. He hoped Noreen Carter was enjoying the proceeds of that adventure; poor woman, she had little enough to console her.

On the streets, in his jeans and leather jacket, with his hair encouraged to grow, and his dyed beard, he had been a different person in outlook as well as in appearance. He had seen poverty and petty crime; he had understood Noreen Carter's despair. Then the man she lived with had been picked up for the rape of the girl in Bedfordshire. Derek had not realized that at the time, but he had pieced it together since; Barry had used the man's car. Carol had called him a creep. Well, he was worse than that.

Acquiring the gun had been the big problem. If the youth whom Derek suspected of pushing drugs had not been able to get one, he hadn't known where to try next but he might have asked Barry. Barry would have known how to obtain arms and with his increasing confidence, Derek might have managed to spill him some story which would indicate a change of heart on his part about going armed on a raid, and then he would have had to get the weapon from Barry. He'd have done it: the new model Derek knew that he would have managed it somehow, if only because Barry was such an inadequate person. Why, he had laid down his knife at The Elms all those years ago, and Morris had put down the gun. He should have tried to snatch one of them.

Derek had financed his campaign by using his redundancy pay, but he had anticipated being caught and so he had wanted Janet to benefit. Because of him, her life had been wrecked. He could still remember how she had struggled against him when, after an evening out together, he had advanced beyond mere petting and would not listen to her protests. He had had a good deal to drink at the dance he had taken her to, and she had invited him up to the flat she shared with two other girls for some coffee. As he persisted, she had fallen from the sofa where they were sitting when he began to kiss her, and when she was on the floor, beneath him, it had not been difficult to overpower her.

"You'll like it," he'd told her, forcing himself into her body. Like Hannah, she had bled.

But unlike Hannah, she had become pregnant, and in those days when abortion was difficult, they had married. As they had already been out together several times, it was only what Janet's aunt expected, and Derek's parents thought Janet a most suitable girl.

Then, at five months, her son was stillborn, and they were tied together by their past. Hannah was not born for another four years and they both adored her, which was enough to keep them together until she was attacked.

Now, he had begun to understand just what he had done to his wife. He was not much better than Carter.

His plan had been to drive to Savernake Forest and there, in a remote glade, get Barry out of the car and shoot him, leaving him in the undergrowth. He would drive away and dump the car in Southampton, then catch a train to London and pick up the Citroën which he had left in a quiet street in

Rickmansworth. He had already obliterated all traces of Vic Kemp in London; once back in his house, his beard would come off, his hair would be washed and he would cut it as well as he could. Vic's clothes would be burned and the ashes removed. He would resume his life as Derek, moving, however, to a new district not only for financial reasons. A new start would be wise.

There had been no house at Thrupton, a place which did not exist and which Barry could have checked for himself on a road map, but by the time Vic had spun this particular fable, he knew Barry would swallow everything he was told. Spending so much time with him had been eerie, but he had learned to act his part, and when he suspected that Barry had already attacked another girl, his resolve had strengthened. He had not foreseen the sudden whim to go back to Bicklebury; Barry's mood swings, and the way he so quickly switched to violence, had been horrifying. When Janet and Carol appeared, Derek was shocked, but seeing Barry run true to form had been enough to make him react instinctively. Janet had stayed calm; afterwards, reflecting, Derek knew that she had always been calm except on the night when he assaulted her, using his sheer physical strength to exert his will.

After the baby was born dead, she had cried, but in private. They had not shared their grief then, nor after Hannah's ordeal.

He longed to ring Janet up, to find out how Carol was— and Janet herself. Why should he assume that she was able to cope with the aftermath of a terrifying experience?

Now he wondered if he would have been able to carry out his original plan, had Barry not made it impossible by his impetuous drive to Bicklebury. Driving off from the Manor, he had still meant to kill Barry.

Somehow, seeing Janet had contributed to his altered attitude. Killing Barry was too good for him, and though it would remove him from circulation for ever, there were other men who were just as dangerous, and who, after serving a sentence, were freed to claim more victims. It was the law that needed changing.

In the morning, he burned the clothes he had used as Vic, and he took the ashes in bags to the river where, in a lonely spot where no one was looking, he tipped them into the water and watched them swirl away downstream. Then he dumped the bags in different litter bins. He had burned the carriers from the Plymouth shops where he had bought his new garments, and he thought that he ought to get rid of those, too, because the police were clever about tracing where things had come from; if they suspected him they could try testing his clothes. They were good, new clothes, so he took them to a refuge he had seen while he roamed the streets of London.

He had decided to go on a cruise for Christmas, blowing some of his remaining funds, and, returning from London, he went to an agent and fixed up a last-minute booking. He would leave in two days. That would give him time to move his major possessions into the flat he had rented in Reading, paying three months in advance. His future, as far as he could see it, was now arranged. Much depended on police actions and the ability—or luck—they might have in getting on his trail, but going away would remove him from the scene and if Barry said they had planned to go to Spain, the police might think Vic had succeeded. He chose a cruise which avoided all Spanish ports, and would do his best to enjoy himself while on board; he had done so before, when he and Janet and Hannah had gone away. He would live in the present, join in the shipboard activities which, as an unattached male, would offer him scope of all kinds, and face the future on his return. If all was well, and no one suspected him of being Victor Kemp, he would get a job—any job—and make a new life. He had widened his experience during the past few months and felt better able to confront challenge and the unexpected than he had done before. He would tell Janet he was going away and give her his new address. His guilt about her would never be assuaged, he was sure, but he could not make it up to her now, nor could Hannah ever be told that he had made an attempt to avenge her. But she would learn of Carter's rearrest; perhaps she knew about it already.

He was very tired. Though he had slept quite well after Angela's surprise visit, he still had arrears to make up and he was, he supposed, suffering from the strain of the preceding weeks. The removal men were due the next morning to take his possessions to Reading. He had planned everything down to the last detail, expecting by now to have killed Barry Carter and be making a legitimate escape.

All that could be done had been done. He slept soundly and woke early, and was prepared for the removal men when they arrived. While they were carrying out the furniture that had been in his study at The Elms, a small car drove up and parked near their van. Janet got out and walked up the path.

Derek was on the step, watching the sofa depart.

"Janet!" He was astonished to see her.

"You're moving." She, too, was surprised.

"Yes. I was going to tell you. The letter's written, ready to post," he said. He explained about the flat in Reading.

"I didn't ring before coming over. I hope you don't mind me just turning up like this," she said. She sounded nervous.

"Of course not. Come in—though there's not a lot of

comfort left in the house. But there's still a kettle and some instant coffee. Would you like a cup?"

"I'd love it," she said, following him inside. Objects familiar to her from their life together were stacked around, ready to be removed. "Why Reading?" she asked.

"Fairly central. Good trains," he said.

"You're not working?"

"Not at the moment. I'm going away for a bit—for a short holiday," he said. "I'll be looking for a new job in the new year."

"That's a good idea," she said. "The holiday, I mean. Are you going somewhere nice?"

"Oh yes," he said, not elaborating. The less she knew the better. Then, for a wild moment, he thought of inviting her to join him, but it would only have embarrassed her. There was no going back.

He made the coffee, took mugs out to the men as well, and led her into the sitting room, which was empty except for some packing cases full of books and papers.

"The men have finished in here," he said. "I'm taking these in the car. We can perch on them."

Janet lowered herself awkwardly on to a carton.

"There's been some trouble in Bicklebury," she said carefully, sipping her coffee, holding the mug in both hands. She was wearing trousers, which for her was very unusual, and she had on a sweater knitted in a variety of soft colors, with a padded jacket on top. She was casually dressed, he realized, amazed.

"I saw something about it in the paper," he said.

There had been mention of a break-in at the Manor and the death of the dog had been reported.

"The papers have been quite good," said Janet. "I don't think they'll dig up the past—or not yet. I've told Hannah what happened. She'd seen that Carter was wanted by the police."

"How has she taken it?"

"She was very shocked at first," said Janet. "She was in Edinburgh with those—" She remembered that Derek did not know the MacGregors and amended what she was going to say. "Some nice people who run a guest house near her," she said. "She told Meg MacGregor—her friend—about what had happened before, and now that Carter has been arrested, she's quite calm."

"That's good," said Derek. He swirled the dregs of coffee in his mug, peering into it intently.

"She was anxious about Carol. She was afraid she might be very upset."

"And was she?"

"Of course, but the danger retreated so quickly that she had barely time to be frightened. The death of the dog upset her more."

"I suppose so. She loved that dog, didn't she? They'd had him for years."

"Yes." Janet sipped some more coffee. "I spoke to Hannah again yesterday, before I went to work. She's coming down for Christmas. I'm going to be busy at The Swan for some of the holiday period, but she'll go to the Fords while I'm there. She's thinking of going back to college. She's not going to give up her wildlife job, but she wants to get properly qualified so that she can become a warden herself, or take up other work of the same kind. I'm not quite sure what's involved, but it will be possible," Janet said. "She'll be eligible for a grant, as a mature student. She's got to find out all about it, and of course she can't begin until the new academic year."

"She's decided all that so quickly?"

"Meg MacGregor thinks she'd had it in mind for some time, but wasn't sure she could cope with being among other students and new pressures. She may change her mind when she finds out what's involved, or decide to do something else, but she's going to go forward now."

"That's very good news," said Derek.

"Yes. She thought she might go and see that girl—the one Carter attacked—or offer to. She thought it might help the girl. I don't know. It might be better left, but it's really up to the two girls themselves."

"I suppose it is," said Derek, then added, "Were you very frightened?"

"Not as soon as I realized that the man called Vic was going to deal with Carter," said Janet smoothly. "It was obvious he had made some other plan which Carter frustrated."

"So it seems," said Derek. "Perhaps he meant to shoot him somewhere else."

Janet did not ask why he should have that intention.

"Perhaps," she said. "I'm not curious. He put right something that went wrong a long time ago." She looked at him then. "Much longer ago than what happened to Hannah, as well as that dreadful night."

"I didn't know," said Derek, in a low voice. "I didn't understand. Forgive me, Janet."

Both of them thought of the night in the flat when, after a single violent act, she had become pregnant.

"It's not important now," she said.

They should not have married. It wasn't the answer, and today it wouldn't have happened.

"I let Hannah down, too," he said. "I didn't realize how much it mattered."

"It's all right," Janet said. "Don't tell me any more, Derek. It's better if I don't know too much. You'll be safer then."

She'd recognized him. In spite of the cap, pulled low, and the scarf, she had known who he was all the time.

Janet saw that he needed some explanation.

"I think that the man called Vic knew I would recognize Barry Carter's name, when he used it. He meant me to know there was nothing to fear, even though Carter had committed two more serious crimes, including murder, since leaving prison. The man called Vic told us about them and I told the police. They believed me." She gathered up her bag. "I'll go now," she said. "Thanks for the coffee. Have a good holiday."

He thought of saying he'd send her a postcard, but decided not to make any such promise. The letter he'd written her was on the mantelpiece, ready to post, but he did not give it to her. Time enough for her to read it tomorrow. In it, he explained that he had left everything that remained to him to her; it was not a lot, but there was still some insurance. He walked with her to the car.

"It's a pity Hannah can't know the truth," she said. "Whatever that is."

"Much better not," he said.

One day she might, when he was dead. Then she would not think so badly of him.

As he drove to his new flat, he thought about what he had learned during the hours he had spent watching Barry, and in his company. It had often been difficult to resist attacking him as he sat in a pub, lounging back, pleased with himself, with no sense of right or wrong, no remorse for what he had done. This time, if he were convicted of murder, he would not be free for years. Derek hoped the police would be able to build up a strong case against him.

When the removal men had unpacked everything from their van and had gone, Derek wiped the gun free of prints, wrapped it in a towel, and hid it under a floorboard. He put the ammunition in a box under some nails and screws. He knew how to use the weapon now and it might come in useful one day, for there would be other rapes and other rapists at large in the future. He had acquired more skills, too; he could steal a car and break into a building. He would never again be the tool of another man's violence.